Masters
OF THE
Night

bound *by his* blood

JENNIFER AUGUST

Dear Reader,

I've long been fascinated by creatures of supernatural origins. I love the idea of living side by side with a secret society, beings who have different abilities and ideologies than we do but who, are at heart, just as human as us.

I hope you enjoy Bound by His Blood and my take — and breaks — on vampire traditions. If you have any comments, thoughts, or questions, I'd love to hear them.

You can email me at
jenniferaugust@jenniferaugust.com
or snail mail me at:
1501 South Loop 288
Suite 104/PMB 197
Denton, TX 76205

I'm also on Facebook: **jenniferaugust08**
and
Twitter: **@jennifer_august**

You can visit my website at **www.jenniferaugust.com** to see what's going on with me.

Happy reading,
Jennifer

PROLOGUE

Boston, 1888

"Come on, Logan. It'll be a grand night. It's your eighteenth birthday. Time to become a man."

Logan McCallister gave Joseph Kilkairn a sour look. The Scotsman was bound and determined to drag him to a brothel. McCallister wanted to go. He really did. Fear held him back.

If Father finds out where I've gone...

His straight-laced father would have an apoplectic fit if he knew his first-born son, the one he'd been meticulously grooming to join the family shipping business, had left their stately Beacon Hill house to pay for sex. Boston Brahmins did *not* engage in salacious activities, nor did they cross class lines.

The fire in the hearth crackled and popped. Wood groaned as it shifted into ash. The big house in which he lived with his father, younger brother, and sister was as empty and personable as an ancient tomb. None of his family had stayed to celebrate his birthday with even a special meal much less gifts or well wishes.

Not that I expected anything different.

His father ran a strict household. Frivolities like presents, celebrations, and affections were frowned upon.

Logan set his jaw as a spurt of rebellion tempted him.

One night out of a lifetime of duty won't matter.

McCallister shifted the perfect knot of his cravat, brushed away non-existent lint from his custom-tailored jacket and nodded his head. "All right. I'm in."

Joseph chortled and thumped him on the back. "You're going to love it," he said. His dark blue eyes gleamed. "I was there last week, myself. Had a gorgeous dove named Claudine take care of me. Gor, she was something else."

Excitement thrummed in McCallister's veins, easily beating away any lingering fear. Following Joseph from the house, McCallister leaped into the waiting coach with a light step born of eagerness. As they bounced and jostled over the cobblestone road leading from Beacon Hill, the gaslights flanking each side of the street streaked past like falling stars.

They arrived at Desdemona's Palace a quarter hour later. McCallister climbed from the coach and stared at the elegant house in front of him. A full moon washed over the two-story building and graceful wrought-iron railings. Soft golden light flickered in nearly all the windows. A curtain moved on the upper right and he saw the perfect form of a woman outlined against the light. A taller male figure joined her and they disappeared from sight.

McCallister rubbed his hands together, suddenly eager to find and bed a woman with large breasts and a lusty appetite.

Joseph sprinted up the stairs and pulled the discreet gold chain near the door.

"Ready for the most incredible night of your life, McCallister?"

He grinned at his friend. "Absolutely."

The door opened and a tall man with shoulders wider than the entry looked down at them. Recognition flickered in his black eyes when he looked at Joseph. He stepped back and waved them inside.

"Madam Desdemona will be with you shortly."

He disappeared down the hall and McCallister looked around, trying to calm his racing heart.

A flight of stairs to their right led to the upper floor where he assumed the actual bedding took place. The entry in which they stood flared into a long and mostly dark corridor with a closed door at the end.

Sounds from around the house buffeted him. Throaty laughter and deep moans floated from above while from what seemed below, indeed under his feet, he swore someone sobbed.

He frowned. "Do you hear that?"

"Yeah," Joseph said. He rubbed his hands together. "Sounds just like Claudine when she was riding my cock last week."

The far door opened and McCallister straightened, all thought of the peculiar sound dispelled.

Desdemona was beautiful. Tall, raven-haired with a voluptuous and lush body revealed by the satin gown she wore.

A sheer robe hung over the gown and trailed down her curvaceous form as she glided toward them. Beneath the robe, her full breasts and wide hips pressed against the white satin. McCallister swallowed hard. Her nipples puckered visibly through her dress.

"Good evening, gentlemen." Her throaty contralto wrapped around his cock and held fast. He prayed he didn't disgrace himself.

"Madam Desdemona. You look ravishing as always." Joseph bent over her hand.

McCallister thought his friend overdid it a bit with the bowed head and near subservient posture but then she was an incredibly beautiful woman. Her eyes were a shade of blue he'd never seen before. They looked as though they were lit from the inside by flashes of lightning. Her mouth was full, lush and ruby red.

"Who have you brought me, Joseph?"

She didn't take her gaze from McCallister and he forced himself not to squirm.

Joseph made the introductions. "I was hoping you would personally see to his entertainment, Madam Desdemona."

Her small smile revealed a set of perfect, white teeth. McCallister found himself captivated by them. He wanted to feel them on his body – nipping, tugging, scraping. He licked his lips.

"I'm sorry, but I don't do that anymore. I'll be happy to set you up with one of our other girls, though."

Joseph leaned forward. "But Madam, it's his eighteenth birthday today." He tossed a wink over his shoulder at McCallister. "And he's a virgin."

"Damn it, Kilkairn," he snapped, embarrassment engulfing him like a ravenous beast.

The look on the madam's face changed dramatically. Her brows lifted and the lightning flashed in such quick succession McCallister had to look away. His head spun as the air leeched from his lungs, and his knees shook like the eagerness of a new colt.

The madam stepped closer and curled her long fingers around his forearm while nestling her breast against him. "Is this true, Mr. McCallister?"

He didn't want to admit to it, wanted to lie and claim he'd bedded dozens of chits. But he couldn't. Her blue gaze demanded only the truth.

"Yes," he said with a rasp. "I'm a virgin."

Her smile was like a gift and she squeezed his arm before letting go. "Joseph, I will send Claudine to you. Mr. McCallister, come with me."

Joseph hooted and pounded him on the back. "See you soon, you lucky bastard."

McCallister followed Desdemona down the hallway, his gaze glued to the sway of her ass and hips. His hard cock bounced with each step and anticipation made his balls tighten painfully.

She opened the door, stepped through then beckoned to him. "Shut the door, Mr. McCallister and let me take you."

McCallister carefully did as commanded, sucked down a deep breath and turned to face the beautiful whore.

† † †

The whimpering woke him. Soft, pathetic sounds of despair bounced inside his head. McCallister frowned and struggled to open his eyes. They were gritty and painful.

Cold, damp cement pressed along his back.

He forced himself to keep his eyes open. The room was mostly dark but for a single beam of sunlight streaming from a narrow slit in the wall across from him. It took long seconds for his eyes to adjust to the shadows.

Something cold surrounded his throat. His arms were thrust over his head and manacled to the hard wall. Fear exploded in him.

Where am I?

He yanked at his chains and choked as the collar bit into his throat. The stench of piss and putrid water rose from the ground, gagging him. He continued to pull until sweat poured down his temples. His neck, chest and arms burned from the effort.

"It's no use," a weary voice said.

McCallister squinted into the darkness. Three men were chained to the far wall in similar fashion. One man with golden eyes that burned like candles stared back at him. The room was too dim for any other impression but fear again shuddered through him.

"What happened?" he asked.

"Don't know."

A sudden cacophony of noise, voices and movement assaulted McCallister. He groaned against the painful intensity. Just when he thought he would die from the sheer volume, it disappeared.

He fell back to the wall and sucked down a deep rasp of air, shaking and shivering like a newborn colt.

"Where are we?" he croaked.

"In that whore's Desdemona's basement," the golden eyed man spat.

"Who are you?" He didn't know why he asked except talking seemed to help keep his burgeoning fear at bay.

"Leopold Caine. You?"

"Logan McCallister." He squinted into the shadows at the other two men. "Them?"

"James Robinson and Edward Fontaine."

Each man made small noises that could have been grunts of hello or pain, he couldn't tell which. Exhausted by the conversation, McCallister slumped back to the wall. "Now what?" he whispered.

The golden eyes flashed harshly in the dim light. "Now we wait."

The creak of wood and rusty iron sounded in the shadows. McCallister managed to turn his head enough to see a door open.

A familiar voluptuous figure was outlined in the doorway.

"Good. You're finally awake."

CHAPTER ONE

"McCallister! Get your ass in here." Chief Holland's voice shook the walls of the old brownstone that housed the Boston Supernatural Homicide Division. It rang out over the clacking of heavy-handed cop hands on computer keyboards and the constant static of radio chatter.

Logan McCallister cupped his hand over his phone and yelled back, "In a minute. Phone." He returned his attention to the warbled voice on the other end of his cell. "I'm trusting you on this, Domingo. This Dust is bad shit. It needs to come off the street before any more humans are hurt."

"I swear, man, I'm not lying. Got word two wanna-be *jefes* are moving a bunch of it tonight."

"Names?" McCallister asked coolly.

Domingo coughed and his voice lowered even more. "You know I can't do that. I'll be dead. I say their names, they know."

McCallister gritted his teeth "That's bullshit and I've told you that a hundred times. Vampires can't get a hold of you just because you know their name. Besides, I thought you said you didn't know if they were human or vamps."

"Yeah, yeah. You also said garlic and holy water is crap, too."

McCallister rubbed the back of his neck. "Do you know how many Italian vampires there are? Every single one I know adores tons of garlic in their pasta. Come on, Domingo, help me out here."

"Tonight. Six, near the abandoned hospital on Dorchester, close to Adams."

"McCallister!" Chief Holland's voice roared through the squad room.

The line went dead.

McCallister growled and slammed the phone on his desk. He heard an ominous crack. "Damn it," he muttered and picked up the phone to study the screen. Fortunately, it appeared intact. The same couldn't be said for the back.

A large, heavy hand plopped onto his shoulder and McCallister swung around, fangs dropping with a quick, defensive *snick* as he batted the arm away.

Chief Holland glared, his own lethal teeth appearing. "You going deaf?"

McCallister retracted his fangs and rubbed the back of his neck. "Sorry, Chief. I was on the phone with my informant."

The rotund homicide boss jerked up one bushy gray eyebrow. "My office. Now."

The chief executed a precise military about-face on the toe of his highly polished shoe and marched toward his glassed-in office at the back of the squad room.

"What'd you do now, McCallister?" someone called out as he passed through the gauntlet of desks.

"Get another speeding ticket from the Other Side?"

"Forget to fill out your reports again?"

"I bet he got busted looking at porn on his laptop."

McCallister ignored them until he reached the chief's office. As he walked in, he shot them the finger. His response was met with loud laughter.

"Shut the door," Holland said.

He stood behind his desk, hands folded behind him, ample stomach pushing against the starched blue of his dress shirt. His expression was as grim as the daily news. "The Brigade leaders are on my ass night and day, McCallister. They want answers yesterday on this Dust situation. They're threatening to send in a Guardian to *help* us out."

Irritation immediately swamped him. McCallister crossed his arms as he leaned against the closed door. "No way."

Holland's expression turned black. "I wasn't trotting that out for your approval. You'll work where you're assigned and if that means partnering up with a Guardian, then you'll do it. Understood?"

McCallister ground his back teeth together but gave a short nod.

The chief's shoulders relaxed slightly. "Listen, I don't want a damn Guardian in here anymore than you do. I don't trust the sons of bitches." Holland stuffed a well-chewed straw in his mouth and worked it over like baseball card gum. "Too much power for our own good."

McCallister wasn't going to argue with his chief — mostly because the man was dead on. Guardians — those vampires who acted as the Brigade's law enforcement — had more rights than just about any other vamp on the planet. Except Brigade members, of course. The leaders of all vampire society were much like congressmen and senators — the laws they passed often did not extend to themselves. "Then we gotta solve this case pronto." He shifted, feeling the chill of the frosted glass seeping through his green polo. "I have a lead. Slim, but still a lead."

The chief's eyes narrowed to tiny slits. "Your informant?"

"Yeah." McCallister shoved his hands in his pockets, rocking back on his heels. "He swears there's a drop going down tonight." He checked his watch. "In about an hour or so."

The phone on the scarred, cramped desk shrilled. Holland stabbed the ignore button, moved the straw to the other side of his mouth and nodded, eyes grim. "We need to catch these bastards, McCallister. We can't keep covering up these human deaths."

"Doing my best, sir."

"Do it better," Holland muttered. "We had six more die overnight."

McCallister's eyes widened. "Six more? Damn."

"That makes a total of thirty-three in two months. There are rumbles of panic starting in the human communities. I've heard whispers of everything from Ebola to anthrax in the water." Holland picked up a folder from his desk and handed it over.

McCallister flipped it open and winced at the picture staring back at him. A young man, or what once had been a young man, lay crumpled on the concrete, his body contorted in the shape of an S. His fingers were drawn into sharp, wide-spread claws while the skin on his face sunk inward, giving him the look of an ancient mummy.

"Our guy inside the ME's office says they're still stumped. They can't isolate what's in their bodies that's causing them to die."

McCallister looked up. "What about our labs?"

Holland shook his head. "Stymied. The best guess they have is some sort of mutated vampire DNA but they're not sure. Hell, maybe it is possible it's just some sort of virulent form of crack. We're not getting a large enough tissue sample to do adequate testing." The straw flailed up and down between the chief's lips. "For once makes me wish we had some sort of open dialogue with the Other Side."

McCallister snorted. "Yeah, that's not happening. Like old Ben Franklin said 'Three people can keep a secret if two of them are dead.' As soon as we revealed ourselves we'd be rounded up and exterminated like cockroaches."

"You don't give them enough credit."

"Humans are just food sources, nothing more."

A small smile flipped the straw up again. "You keep telling yourself that."

McCallister ignored the remark and leafed through the report and pictures of all the victims. They mirrored each other in pose, facial expression and clawed-hands. Unfortunately, most of them had been under-class citizens. Hookers, drug abusers, homeless people who wouldn't necessarily be missed right away.

He sighed and handed the folder back. "How much time do we have to resolve this before the Brigade demands a Guardian?"

Holland grimaced. "The Brigade High Councilor said a week or fifty victims, whichever comes first."

McCallister's temper rose but he tamped it back. It wasn't his place to criticize the Brigade's leadership, at least not right now and not in front of the chief. It seemed to him waiting for seventeen more victims was a damn waste of humanity.

He strode for the door. "I'll find them, Chief. Before the week is up."

Humans might not know vampires walked among them, but McCallister was going to do everything in his power to protect them, whether they knew it or not.

† † †

"Surveillance is boring as hell," Leopold Caine muttered. "How do you cops do it regularly?"

McCallister grunted. "I didn't promise you a good time. This is nothing, anyway. We've only been here an hour."

Leopold shifted in the car, his broad shoulders blocking out the fading evening sun as he turned. "Yeah and the only thing that's rolled through is that tacky-assed purple Caddy."

McCallister scanned the deserted streets again. The back of his neck prickled and a soft wind whipped through his open window. He frowned as a sweet scent tickled his nose before dissipating. "You smell that?"

"Smell what?"

The wind brought the aroma again and McCallister's entire body tightened. His heart picked up speed until it thumped in harsh beats against his ribs. He rubbed the center of his chest. "That."

Leopold's golden eyes narrowed and he ran a hand over his leonine hair. "I don't smell anything except the stench of gutter rot and piss." His expression hardened. "Reminds me of that hellhole at Desdemona's the night we were turned."

McCallister ignored the reference to their shared past. "No, it's not that. It's different." He looked down all the avenues he could see but nothing moved. He hesitated.

Leopold's expression sharpened. "What is it, McCallister?"

"Ah, nothing. Forget it." He arched his back until he heard a satisfying pop. "You picking anything up?"

"We'll get back to your phantom smell but no, I haven't picked anything up." He frowned. "I'm not sure why you asked me out here, anyway. You're a supernatural cop. What do you need with a Hunter?"

"Hey, most of the idiots I arrest are not as sophisticated as the vamps you hunt. I need your crazy ability to hear and sense vampires." He bent forward over the steering wheel and stared down the rapidly darkening corridor of Dorchester Street. The abandoned hospital towered over the concrete road like the rusted side of a mountain. Jagged, broken windows on the top floors looked like rotted teeth and graffiti colored nearly the entire bottom section of the old brick building. The streetlights had stopped working long ago and the more the shadows lengthened, the more tense McCallister grew. "We've got about fifteen minutes before the sun sets for good."

"Not scared of the dark, are you?" Leopold asked with a grin.

"Bite my ass," he muttered back. "I thought you'd be helpful but I see I was mistaken."

"McCallister, you don't even know who you're chasing. I can tell you whoever is in that car is almost certainly not of vampire blood."

He snapped his gaze back to Leopold's golden one. "Humans?"

His friend hesitated. "Probably."

Probably. "I don't like those odds. Can't you just do your woo-woo shit and figure it out?"

Leopold's fist slammed into his shoulder and McCallister grunted. The wind whipped suddenly, rocking the car back and forth before settling down.

He froze. "Okay, seriously, you don't smell that? It's like an ocean of flowery shit."

"Fertilizer?"

"Wise ass," McCallister said. "No, like tons of different kinds of flowers. Roses, lavender, hydrangea. Stuff like that."

He stared out at the darkening street, tension threading his neck.

"Uh, McCallister, maybe you've been on this case too long," Leopold said. "I think it's starting to affect your brain."

McCallister didn't respond. He knew what he smelled but he didn't know *why*. It was the oddest damn thing, too. Such a sweet and pure aroma was completely out of place in the dankness of Dorchester Street. This particular strip was unused save for the seedy flesh business, cut-rate liquor stores that did drug business in the back, and convenient places for hookers to take a john for a quickie. Demolition was scheduled for the old brick buildings standing grim sentry above them but nothing had been torn down yet. As darkness descended, a few more people edged into the streets.

He recognized the down-trodden look of most of them. He'd seen his fair share of poor and homeless people over the last hundred and forty years. No matter the times, misery is always present.

His gaze shifted to the Caddy which still hadn't moved. Unease bit him again. "What are they waiting on?" he muttered.

"I don't know," Leopold replied. "But I don't think it's anything good."

Movement came from the corner of the hospital and McCallister sat up in his seat.

"Well, well, well, take a look at her," Leopold murmured. "That is one fine bit of goods."

The words made every nerve ending in McCallister's body go on red alert and a haze of anger swelled. His fangs throbbed in time with the building rage. He tried to shake himself free of the odd sensation.

He studied the platinum blond woman strolling up Dorchester Street. "Why is she glowing?"

Leopold leaned forward. "What are you talking about? She looks like any other hooker on the street."

Again, McCallister was hit with a rush of anger. He curled his hands into fists. "No, she doesn't."

She had a willowy body. Long and lean with muscle in all the right places, highlighted perfectly in her too-damn-short leather miniskirt and peek-a-boo red top. Her tits looked good in her matching red bra, too. Full and round and buoyant. Despite the attire and ridiculously tall red heels, McCallister didn't get the "for rent" vibe off her.

She stilled in mid-stride and her head whipped in the direction of their parked car. He'd pulled into a dark alley and killed the engine, so he knew she couldn't have seen or heard them. But her gaze hit him directly in the solar plexus.

The air in his car hung heavy with a sensual, evocative tone that worked its way through his entire body. His fangs twitched, grew sharper.

"Shit," Leopold muttered. He slunk low against his seat. "Get down before she sees you."

"Too late," he replied. He couldn't take his eyes from her. She was young, too damn young to be a hooker.

She looked fresh, too. Even stacked with layers of make-up, her face appeared smooth and clear. The woman continued to stare in their direction but her pace picked up again, aimed directly at the Caddy.

"Don't do it," McCallister whispered.

"Maybe she's what they were waiting for," Leopold said. He sat back up and peered out the windshield.

McCallister pulled his gaze from the woman to look at his friend. "Your woo-dar getting anything?"

"No," Leopold snapped. "Kinda hard to pathfind when I don't even know *what* I'm hunting. I need something to sense."

"Like what? A piece of clothing? A scent."

The fist to his bicep was much harder this time. "I'm not a freaking dog, McCallister. I'm a vampire hunter." Leopold's eyes glowed bright and furious in the darkened car interior. "Give me a name, a specific location, a memory, an object, anything and I can start to narrow down the search. It's not instantaneous. If it were, there'd be a hell of a lot of renegade vamps locked in the Brigade's cellars."

"Sorry," McCallister muttered. He looked down the street at the Caddy again. Suddenly, his usually excellent night vision narrowed to only her. A soft white and pink nimbus outlined her entire body. The glow was very, very faint.

"What the hell?" he whispered.

"What's wrong?" Leopold asked.

The hooker was leaning down now, propping one elbow on the doorframe and looking into the open window.

A shiver raced over McCallister's spine.

Something is not right with this situation.

Just as the door to the Caddy opened and she bent to enter, he shifted from solid into mist and reappeared behind her, shield in hand, flashing it at both the hooker and the johns.

"Boston PD," he barked.

The girl screamed and jumped backward, one hand pressed to her impressive chest, the other held out to ward him off.

A quick swipe of his teeth assured him his fangs were hidden.

A dark curse rumbled from the car before it sped off, tires smoking behind as it left.

"I wasn't doing anything, officer," she said, eyes batting so wildly, one false lash fluttered off and landed on her cheek like a mutated spider.

He smothered a chuckle. "'Course not, sweetheart, and I'm Huck Finn out for a raft ride."

She glared at him and he was taken aback by the stunning beauty of her eyes. A shade of blue so light, they looked almost like the brightest part of daylight.

Leopold appeared in the shadows behind her and McCallister shook his head. The other vamp nodded, rolled his eyes, then vanished into mist.

"What?" the girl asked and turned to look behind her. "What are you staring at?"

McCallister shook himself out of his stupor and pulled his cuffs. "Sorry, ma'am, solicitation for prostitution is a crime in Boston." He tipped his head. "I gather from your accent you hail from Texas?"

She looked startled and took a step backward, gaze darting nervously around. "Can I see your badge again, please?"

"Why?"

"'Cause I'm gonna call in and check you out. Make sure you're legit."

"You do realize you're resisting arrest, don't you?"

She glared at him as she rummaged in her tiny red purse and pulled out a cell phone. "Good luck making that stick. Badge."

He rolled his eyes. How in the hell did the Vice guys on the Other Side do this every day?

Clean, French-manicured fingers snapped in his face. "Anyone home?"

McCallister growled, hand lifting to grab her wrist, then stopped before he touched her. If Chief Holland found out he'd flashed his badge at a human, even for a second, he'd be in even deeper shit.

"Fancy nails for a hooker," he said as his hand fell back to his side. He raked her with a long glance. "Expensive clothes, too."

Her pulse quickened and he felt it all the way through his body, from his head to his cock.

He could be in real trouble here.

She took two more mincing steps backward on her stilettos, look clearly distrustful. "I saw enough to know you're Homicide, Detective," she said, voice accusatory. "You have no business arresting me."

He moved closer, standing pecs to tits before she could blink. One good deep breath on either of their parts and they'd touch.

He noticed she held her breath.

He did laugh out loud then. "As a cop, I'm sworn to uphold the law, no matter which division, ma'am."

She swallowed hard and moved away. It took everything McCallister had not to follow, but he didn't want to spook her too much.

Not yet.

"Look, I gotta be honest with you, you can't arrest me," she said.

He lifted a brow.

"Seriously," she said. "I wasn't doing anything wrong. I was asking for a ride." Her pointed chin lifted and she glared at him, eyes triumphant. "And you can't prove otherwise."

Again the wind changed and this time brought an ominous feel with it. The shadows around them darkened and he spun.

Nothing.

No one.

Yet, he was certain someone watched them. Someone with a malevolent agenda.

He turned back to find her striding down the street, toward a group of hookers who now congregated on the corner.

In fact, it seemed like Dorchester Street and surrounding roads was suddenly becoming a lot more populated.

He should just chuck the whole thing and leave. She was right, he wasn't Vice, it wasn't his collar. What did it matter?

But it did matter. *She* mattered.

McCallister swallowed a curse and stalked toward the group who scattered as soon as he got within five feet.

Just like normal hookers did. They could smell a cop, regardless of division, and make a run for it.

Not this little spitfire though.

The closer he got, the stronger the scent of flowers became again and the more she glowed. McCallister froze between one step and the next as a sudden realization swept over him.

Impossible. It doesn't exist. It's legend.

He shook his head to wipe any stupid ideas from it and set his jaw in a grim line as he stalked toward her.

She whirled on him, hands propped on her hips and that damn perma-frown creasing her forehead. "Look, Neanderthal Man, I already told you, I was looking for a ride. Until you can come up with something to the contrary, this is harassment and I'll report your badge number."

His patience snapped and he curled his fingers around her taut upper arm. As soon as skin touched skin, time slowed, then froze. All around them, people moved and bustled along the darkened and dirty strip. Drug deals were made, hookers jumped into cars and some punk-ass kid tried to rob a dude stumbling out of an alley, but McCallister was powerless to move.

In that moment, he saw into the blonde's mind. Saw the fear and anxiety. Caught a glimpse of the face from the dim interior of the Caddy. Felt the apprehension she suppressed and the resolve she exhibited.

Her emotions ran deeper, her thoughts wilder. He saw a glimpse of a large man with a porcine face and lust in his eyes. Heard the strident voice of the hooker telling the man to go to hell then watched as she slapped him so hard his jowls shook for long seconds in the aftermath. The vision shifted to a small, neat house filled with knick-knacks, throw rugs and lace doilies on the arms of a large couch. A middle-aged man stood with his arm around a slightly younger woman. They looked worried, resigned, and afraid. The hooker, now with a mane of honey-blond hair instead of short platinum, hugged them. The scene morphed into a paper-strewn office and another man with a head full of fuzzy white hair, sweat rings under his armpits and wary glee in his gaze. Next came an empty house that vibrated with determination and elation, the flash of a laptop, a rush of excitement for a new assignment and the worry over investigating, finding the drug's source. All of it crammed into his brain in a nano-second.

McCallister hissed as his fangs dropped of their own volition. Her skin seared his palm and he released her.

She gasped and stumbled backward then looked up at him, eyes going wide.

"What the hell?" she whispered and crossed herself.

Then his little spitfire did the only thing she could. She ran.

McCallister watched her flee.

Go after her.

Let her go.

Damn it, go. Now.

She reached the end of the block and darted around the corner.

"Well, hell," McCallister said and shifted into mist. She was not going to be happy when he caught up with her, but then, his mood wasn't exactly rainbows and unicorns right now, either.

Taking a gamble, he re-appeared at the shadowy end of the block she'd darted down. Luck was with him, for once. She ran right into him.

"Oomph," she said as she bounced off his chest and went down in a legs-wide sprawl.

McCallister's blood immediately heated up, his nostrils filled with her flowery aroma. Lustful need hit him hard and fast. He felt powerless to resist the draw she presented and that freaked him out. The last time he'd succumbed to a woman with such strong emotion, he'd ended up a vampire.

McCallister fought through the sexual temptation and reached a hand to her.

"Up you go."

She ignored him, pushed herself upright then swatted at the torn butt of her leather skirt. "Great," she muttered. "This skirt was still thirty bucks at the thrift store."

"I'll replace it."

She snorted. "What, you arrest me, then clothe me? That's fucked up, man."

He frowned at her vulgarity. "Don't curse," he said.

"Up yours, pig. What kind of flimflam is this anyway, bub? What's with the abracadabra and fake chompers? You some kind of goth cop? Get a kick out of scaring innocent citizens with that get up?"

McCallister's anger rose swiftly and he crowded her into the hard brick wall behind her. He braced his arms around her and leaned close. "Listen up, sweetheart, I'm a cop, you're a hooker, ergo, I take you in."

She shoved at his chest and McCallister braced himself for another psychedelic occurrence of the memory game, but nothing happened.

He breathed a little easier.

Until the shadows sharpened and her profile outlined to pink-tinged white once more. Even the brilliance of her blue gaze grew sharper. Her voice dimmed and seemed to be coming through a speaker doused in honey.

McCallister turned his head and spied the purple Caddy doing a slow crawl along the road. As he watched, four bright bursts emanated from the rolled-down window.

Bullets.

He wrapped the hooker in his arms and dropped to the ground as the ammo struck the bricks, spraying them with bits of red dust and shrapnel.

Her scream reverberated in his ears. McCallister winced even as he looked up at the car.

Once more the Caddy roared off, its deep engine rumbling through the night.

He pulled back and stared down at the girl, whose eyes were now as big as baseballs.

"What just happened?"

"Someone tried to kill you."

"What? No, they didn't!" She glared at him. "Probably some other mug you ticked off."

He rose, reaching out to her again. This time she placed her trembling hand in his.

McCallister sighed, shrugged out of his beat up sports coat and draped it over her shoulders. "I get the feeling you know why."

Guilt covered her face in shades of pale panic and red awareness. "No. That bean-shooter's lead was meant for you. Not me." She bit her lip, stared at the bullet-riddled wall, and gulped. "They weren't after me."

"Liar," he said gently. "Hold on."

"What?" she asked, looking up at him.

But McCallister didn't give her any time to think. He wrapped himself all the way around her, staved off the rush of memories and feelings she poured into him, and misted.

He'd never shifted from once place to another with a passenger and he grew tired and disoriented with frightening speed.

Doggedly, he tightened his mental grip around her and focused on his house. Within seconds, he managed to find the living room and re-appear just in time to collapse onto the sofa.

The girl lay sprawled atop him, still somewhat dazed and incoherent.

He groaned and dropped his head back to the sofa cushion, hoping for time to regain his equilibrium.

Unfortunately, her delectable body pressed along his in all the right places which made his cock spring to attention. McCallister constricted his arms around her, pressing her full tits closer to his chest. He shifted his legs apart and caught her pelvis against his.

He smothered a groan.

She sighed and nuzzled his throat.

Did she feel his erection? Feel the carnal tension pervading his body?

Apparently not, because she muttered something soft, moved again, and curled her fingers onto his chest.

He gave serious thought to tugging her sheer red top off and unhooking her bra to free her tits. He really, really wanted to feast on them.

His damned inbred gentlemanly manners prevented it, however. Sometimes, being born in the eighteen hundreds with all that damn formality was a pain in the ass.

McCallister nudged the girl.

She stirred, stretched, and pressed down on his hard cock.

He gripped her hips and pulled her into him.

Her light blue eyes snapped open.

"Hi," he said.

Her fingers curled savagely into his chest and her knee came up, knocking his erection to hell.

He grunted as she shoved off him.

"What do you think you're doing?" she yelped, halfway across the room. Her wild eyes locked on the door and she bolted for it. The white and pink aura now raged red and black.

McCallister rubbed his sore dick and sat up. Couldn't blame her. Good instincts. Nice fighting abilities.

He shook the thoughts away.

"Who are you?" he asked.

She pulled and tugged on the door, fighting the impenetrable lock his good friend Sullivan Alexander installed.

"You're not getting out unless I allow it," he murmured and moved behind her, though he kept a respectable distance. One blow to the balls was enough to last a lifetime.

Or six.

"Easy there, Sapphire." He held up his palms, hoping she'd accept the peaceful sign. "I'm trying to figure out what's going on, just like you are."

She slumped, head pressed to the door, then turned to face him. Her eyes were wild and scared, but held a rush of determined fervor. "I think the question is who are you? Or, more accurately, *what* the hell are you?"

McCallister hesitated. He thought about lying through his fangs but decided she'd probably call him on it instantly. *How is she going to react to what I am?*

"What do you think?" he hedged.

She snorted and crossed her arms but uncertainty covered her face. She shook her head. "No. Not possible. I don't believe in fairies, ghosts, or vampires."

McCallister shrugged. "Well, I'm not a fairy or a ghost."

Her gaze widened then she flicked him with a taut stare that grew more incredulous by the moment. "You— The street—Then we— And you're a— Holy shit."

She trembled and fell against the door, one shaking hand holding her neck. She licked her lips and he groaned.

"Try finishing a sentence, Sapphire."

She looked like she was in shock and maybe even about to faint.

"You need to sit down," he said and reached out toward her.

She cowered against the door. "Don't touch me!"

His hand curled and dropped back to his side. "I'm not going to hurt you."

"Uh-huh."

Irritation nicked at him like fleas on a dog. He gritted his teeth. "It's true—I am a vampire."

She whimpered.

He sighed. Loudly. "But it's also true I won't hurt you. That's not how it works."

Her eyes went a little wild. "How it works? Like, you have rules? Oh my God, does that mean there are more of you?"

McCallister knew he was quickly losing control. That never happened to him. Well, not since he'd escaped Desdemona's.

He quickly shut down that line of thought and focused on the scared woman in front of him. The woman who called to him on such a primitive level that it scared the shit out of him. If he had half a brain, he'd take her back to Dorchester Street, drop her off and vanish without a backward glance.

Too damn bad the very thought made his entire body rebel.

He moved a few steps into the living room and sat back on the couch. "Come sit down," he said softly. "And I'll explain what I can. You have my word as a cop that I will not hurt you."

Repeating the words seemed to ease her mind a tiny bit because she peeled herself from the wall and took a couple of steps closer.

"You're not messing with me, are you? Those," she waved her hand in his direction, "things could be goth props, right?"

"They're real," he assured her. "Come sit down."

She finally inched her way to the recliner that sat to the right of the couch and perched on it like a bird ready to take flight.

She took a deep breath and more of the tension flowed from her. He could smell her fear, could hear the rapid beat of her heart but he also saw the growing curiosity in her eyes.

"Are you going to bite my neck and turn me into a vampire?"

He cursed the very existence of movies, idiotic lore and legend.

"No," he said and tried to cover his exasperation. Apparently he didn't do a good job.

"Don't get snippy with me," she snapped and more color appeared in her cheeks.

Good, she's getting back to normal. I think.

He didn't know her, had never laid eyes on her before today, but something about her seemed as familiar and necessary to him as blood and breath.

"Look, most of what you know from popular entertainment is crap."

She lifted a golden brow. "Crap, huh?"

"Think about it. Drive a stake through a vampire's heart and it'll kill him? Well, yeah, but it'd kill anyone."

A smile twitched her beautiful lips. "Never thought of that."

"And sleeping in a coffin? Forget it. Those things are too small. I prefer my king-sized bed." He left out the part about the dirt of his grave. *Start small, graduate to the bigger, freakier things later.*

Her breath hitched and her pulse picked up as she flicked a glance over him.

Some of the tension gripping his shoulders released.

"What else?" she asked. Her blue eyes glowed with interest now, all fear seemed gone.

He wracked his brain for some of the more innocuous things. "I happen to love garlic. I use it all the time."

She laughed. "Yeah, I always wondered about that one. I mean, why garlic? Why not onion, too? They're part of the same family."

McCallister heaved a sigh of relief. Maybe now he could steer the conversation back to her. He needed to find out everything about her. The thirst for the information thrummed in his blood like a hard and fast drum beat. He tipped his head. "Your turn. You don't act or really look like a hooker."

Her gaze skittered away and he knew he was right.

"Spill it, sweetheart."

She sighed, slumped into the chair and raked her fingers over her platinum blond hair which came off in her hand.

Long, tangled honey-shot golden hair cascaded around her elfin face.

She met his gaze squarely. "I'm Sheridan Aames. I'm a reporter for the Boston Metro."

CHAPTER TWO

Sheridan studied the handsome vampire. *Vampire.* That was still a little difficult to take in. *Okay, a lot difficult. Improbable. Impossible.*

If not for the very unsettling way he'd winked them from the alley and onto his couch, she would doubt his claim. She didn't remember much of the journey but the leftover jiggly feeling still rang strongly in her body and mind. Not to mention his fangs and super-human—super-vampire?—speed. Add it all together and she should be uneasy, not intrigued. But Sheridan found herself unable to look away from him. No denying he was damned gorgeous, but something else caught and held her.

Mesmerism, perhaps. Is he waiting for the right moment to strike?

Although...he claimed the vampire lore she'd grown up with was crap and he made some good points. She'd sometimes wondered about the whole vampire/garlic connection herself. His confirmation just sealed the deal for her. Plus, she didn't feel in any kind of danger.

Being a reporter, she was used to that uneasy sensation. In fact, before McCallister appeared in the middle of the street and nearly gave her a heart attack, she'd been getting a distinctly disquieting feeling about the guys in the Caddy.

But maybe that disquiet had been him *all along.*

A burst of energy flitted through her. Sitting still suddenly put her on edge. She rose and paced from the recliner to the door and back again.

She could feel his green eyes on her every step. "You didn't really explain anything, you know."

His jaw pulsed. "What do you want to know?"

Everything.

"I'm a reporter," she said. "I like to think I'm pretty savvy. Where did you come from? How do you stay so hidden? And by you, I mean the vampiric race."

When he smiled, his entire face transformed from hard and unyielding to mischievous. Her heart fluttered at the scamp look. She always had been a sucker for a bad boy and if she were reading McCallister correctly, then he was a *really* bad boy. That breath-stealing sex appeal was exactly why she stuck with bland-as-bread-soup guys who usually talked non-stop about their favorite video game.

"I could tell you of our origins but it might freak you out."

She shook her head. "Oh, no, now I'm even more intrigued. Besides, I haven't flipped yet, have I?"

"As a matter of fact, you haven't. You're not going to back down until you get your answer, are you?"

"Nope." She winked. "A lot of my colleagues call me Bulldog."

"Figures. All right, Cliff Notes version. After the Crusades, during the time of the Templar persecution, horrific torture and experimentation was carried out on those men sworn to God. Because of these acts, through a perversion of holy and unholy, vampires were created."

A great chill, as if she'd been impaled by a giant shard of ice, encased her. "Are you saying your race is the remnants of the Knights Templar? The Holy Protectors? The Pope's private army?"

He shrugged. "So legend says, with one exception."

She leaned against the wall. "Unbelievable." She cast through the memory banks of her high school and college years, searching for every piece of knowledge she'd ever gleaned on the Templars. She was coming up mostly empty.

"Who performed these experiments?"

"Priests, bishops, men who had the Pope's ear and his blessings. They were given free rein over the Templars. Men who'd faithfully served were now tormented. Pushed beyond their physical capabilities." He swallowed hard. The stories of Beginnings continued to haunt him. "Turned them into vampires."

His tone spoke of great sorrow wrapped in great horror. She wanted to ask more questions, demand answers he clearly did not wish to give. "Wait a minute. What's the exception?"

"A Viking." His voice grew even more distant.

"A Viking? But how did that happen?"

"A discussion for another time."

The stop sign was loud and clear. She closed her eyes. *What have I gotten into the middle of?*

"Sheridan?"

He stood halfway across the room between door and couch. *How did he move so silently?*

She looked at his feet to make sure he was standing on the ground and not hovering. His black running shoes were firmly on the carpet. She lifted her head and found herself ensnared by his brilliant green gaze. Sensual danger pulsed in those mysterious eyes, in the clench of his jaw. Hell, even his sandalwood scent tempted her to drown in him.

He easily topped six feet by a good three inches and carried a frame of solid muscle. Hell, he'd squished her with that strapping strength when he tackled her to the ground.

Not that she minded really. He appeared physically perfect and wasn't half bad to look at.

She swallowed another burst of awareness. Okay, he was damn good to look at. *Almost too good.*

Thrilling in a way. His hair, a sort of wavy brown that looked as inviting as any dark chocolate bar she'd ever savored, was kind of long and shaggy, the edges just brushing past the collar of his knit shirt.

"Is this where you mesmerize me and convince me to be your slave, McCallister?" she whispered.

He gave her a disgusted look and stalked forward, his mane of brown hair rippled with the motion. His powerful arms bracketed her head. She was enveloped by his heat and smell. Mixed into the sandalwood was leather and spice. Rum, perhaps.

She liked it.

Sheridan licked her lips and he groaned, his compelling green gaze dropping to her mouth.

"That's dangerous," he whispered.

"What is?"

"Darting your tongue out like that. Swiping it along your lips."

Her nipples puckered at his soft, evocative words. "Why?"

The cop eased closer, leaned in and nuzzled the side of her neck. His breath wafted warmly over her throat and she shivered. Again, not in fear, but in growing awareness and stirring need.

"You know why."

There was a soft *snick* and she trembled again, fairly certain he'd just let his fangs out.

A roil of emotion blindsided her, started in the middle of her thighs and traveled upward. She should be terrified. Horrified. Not...turned on.

No, this wasn't fear she was feeling. It was hardcore sexual attraction and she was honest enough to admit it. Who *wouldn't* be attracted to this man?

McCallister was the epitome of dark, sexy and mysterious.

He pulled back and met her gaze.

"I'm going to kiss you, Sheridan Aames."

"Are you asking permission?" she whispered.

He shook his head and one lone lock curled over his forehead, dipping down toward his incredible, startling green eyes. They shone eerily from the inside as if they were backlit by some mysterious source. "I don't ask permission, something you'll soon learn."

Sheridan's breasts throbbed. She wrenched her eyes from his gaze and looked down, gasping and covering herself when she saw just how peaked her nipples were. Even through the padded bra, they jutted out like stiff pencil erasers.

The air around her thickened and her breathing grew labored. His scent assailed her with tempting demand as though he was invading her very pores. Flutters rose in her stomach and she dropped her hand.

"Look at me."

Compelled once more by something unknown, she lifted her gaze. "Are you using your vampire powers against me?" she asked.

The right corner of his mouth kicked up. "No need to, you want me without them."

Damn. "So, you admit you have them?"

This time, the vampire closed the distance between them entirely, fitting their bodies together, shoulders to knees and every valley in between. Heat exploded from each point of contact and she couldn't separate herself from the feel of him.

His erection nestled in her belly and the contact shot straight to her pussy before careening wildly to every other erogenous zone she had.

He lowered his head and brushed a soft kiss along her lips, traveled the fullness of her bottom lip to each corner of her mouth and back again.

His touch was light and tender.

She whimpered, hands fluttering up to clutch his waist. He pulled back.

"More?"

I should say no. "Yes, please."

His grin was electrifying as he swooped in again, his arms coming down to crush her to his chest. He melded their mouths. God, his lips were impossibly soft.

Sweet, too, with that exotic hint of spicy rum.

"Open your mouth for me, little one, I want to taste you, too."

Sheridan did as he commanded and groaned as his tongue glided slickly inside. The air stilled around them, the only sounds the tiny moans she made and the satisfied whispers emanating from him.

She tightened her grip and suddenly she was airborne. "What are you doing?" she gasped.

"Kiss me," he said and sat on the couch, settling her across his lap.

The position thrust his hard cock perfectly between her thighs. Instantly, her pussy flooded.

His nostrils flared and the green light in his eyes flashed brilliantly before he took her mouth again.

She felt devoured, pushed to the edge, left hanging on for dear life. A swirl of confusing emotions ripped along her brain, but Sheridan pushed them all away, concentrating only on the intense sexual rush his kiss evoked.

She could not get enough of his mouth, his touch, his taste. Squirming on his lap, she half-turned and cupped his face, slanting hers so she could delve deeper into the kiss.

He growled and without losing contact, flipped her to the couch, his long body covering hers in an instant.

He pressed the fullness of his erection to her pelvis and plucked at the luscious mounds of her breasts.

She tore her mouth away and looked down between their bodies. His cock strained from the tent of his black slacks. Her pussy throbbed and ached. Just this touch had her on the verge of orgasm.

She looked up at him, eyes going wide at the feral intensity on his face. His eyes were shadowed by dark brows and fangs peeked from between his lips.

McCallister stilled, breath coming in hard, ragged gasps. "Scared?"

"No," she said truthfully. She wasn't intimidated by him in the least. There was something about him that spoke to her core and fear wasn't anywhere in the equation.

"You should be," he whispered.

"Why?" Sheridan lifted her hips, undulating softly. She wanted him. Desperately. Urgently. The carnal need filled her body and mind with a roaring demand she could not quell.

His hand clamped over her abdomen, stilling her instantly. "You're playing a dangerous game, Sheridan. Are you sure you want to continue? If I take you, it will be on my terms. And you *will* be mine."

Now *that* freaked her out. She was an independent woman. Relationships, one night stands—not that she'd ever had any—and jobs were done on her terms. *No one* else's.

She sucked in a deep, considering breath then pushed at his chest. He gave way immediately, going from prone to standing with no effort.

She struggled to pull down her torn leather skirt and re-arrange the mess he'd made of her sheer top. It, too, was probably ruined. She tucked her still-tingling boobs back into the red bra. All the while, she tried to ignore the flare of disappointment coursing through her veins. It was damned difficult. Her body yearned for him like a two-year old whined for candy.

"I knew there was a reason I didn't engage in one-night stands," she muttered.

"Sheridan."

She ignored him, looked around the room for her purse and spied it sticking out from beneath the couch. She bent and picked it up, brushing off non-existent dust. For a guy, his place was remarkably clean.

"Sheridan." His tone was demanding but she still didn't look at him.

She was too damn busy trying to calm both her heart and her libido.

"What did you mean by your terms?" The question popped out and she cursed her wayward tongue immediately.

The silence was long and torturous. She refused to give in to curiosity and look at him. She asked a question, he could answer it. Or not.

She fidgeted with the purse. Looked toward the door. Scuffed the pristine hardwood floor.

Silence.

"Damn it," she grumbled and whirled around. "Ack!"

He was standing two inches away from her. *How did he move with such freaking silence?*

"Don't do that," she snapped. "Don't you know you can scare someone to death? Inconsiderate—"

His finger pressed against her lips and she went quiet. Once again that weird pull connected her to him. A shadow danced through her mind, flashes of carriages, candles, a two-story building which morphed into a panorama of Victorian row houses — Boston, she realized — and a sense of shock.

This last feeling made her buck. His shock. His despair. His agony. The emotions threatened to send her to her knees, but some inner strength kept her upright.

He lifted his finger and tipped his head. The emotional barrage immediately receded. "You have naturally strong defenses, Sheridan. That's very intriguing."

"Defenses? Do you always talk in circles, McCallister?"

He smiled. "When it suits me."

She rolled her eyes.

His expression grew serious and he returned to the sofa. "Come here and sit with me."

Before she thought about it, she was easing down two cushions away.

"That'll do for now. To answer your question about terms, I'd like to know what you know about BDSM."

Sheridan's jaw dropped. "As in whips and chains?"

His shoulders tensed as his face went a little gray and queasy, but he quickly recovered. The expression happened so fast she would have missed it if she'd not been so focused on his handsome face.

"I don't like chains but I have a special affinity for whips. Floggers. Crops. Leather straps." McCallister smiled. Her heart did that annoying flip flop again. "But it's much more than that. More along the lines of submission."

Sheridan squeezed her tiny purse. "Geez, I figured we were going to talk about vampires and such. Not normal things like BDSM."

"Answer the question," he commanded.

Sheridan glared at him again. "You're very high-handed."

He lifted a brow. His intense green stare compelled her to speak. She plucked at one of the holes in her fishnet stockings, debating what to say. She'd never tried anything kinky like that before. "I don't like pain, so, uh thanks but no thanks."

Before she could blink, he was sitting next to her, his hand tangled in her hair, tugging her head back.

She gasped and the pulse in her throat beat wildly against her flesh and rang in her ears.

"It's not about pain, either." McCallister drew the blunt end of one finger over her lips, down her neck and settled upon the mad flutter. "It's about pleasure. Letting go. Submitting. Giving up all control to the one who can sear your body with delight."

Heat built beneath his small caress, radiating down to her breasts. As before, her body responded effortlessly to his touch.

"I don't want to give up control," she said and her voice sounded breathless and unconvincing to her own ears.

"Yes, you do," he replied, as smug and arrogant as before. "And I can prove it."

"Ha. Not without some woo-woo, I bet."

He shook his head and let go of her hair. "I don't know what kind of fictional crap you think you know about vampires, but we *cannot* impel people to do things they don't want to do. I can't gain any kind of mind control over you and make you cluck a chicken."

Boy, was he testy. "All right, copper, settle down there." She dragged a hand through her hair, fluffing the tresses he'd messed up, hoping she didn't look as bedraggled as she felt. In her idiotic mind, though, she was thinking furiously about what he said. *Submission. Pleasure. Letting go.* Her body perked up once more, all eager and willing despite her rational side screaming itself silly. "You can prove it, huh? How?"

His smile was dangerous, made all the more feral by the points of his fangs. She shivered as an image of him raking her breasts with those fangs flashed into her brain. She really wanted to know what that felt like.

"Easy enough," he said smoothly and held out his hand. "Come with me."

Sheridan stared at his hand like he held an offering of writhing snakes. With a slow, hesitant motion, she placed her palm in his. "All right, McCallister," she whispered. Prove it."

He tugged her to him and he kissed her again with a light, sweeping stroke that was so gentle and tender, it brought tears to her eyes.

This is coercion?

I'll take it.

As before, even his simplest touch roused her desires. Lust built between her toes and surged upward, invading every part of her body.

Oh, yes, she wanted him. She hungered for him in ways she'd never experienced before.

He pulled away and pressed his big palm to the small of her back and urged her forward. "Come with me."

They passed into a long hallway fitted with beautiful brass and copper sconces and several doors.

Several pieces of art hung on the wall, but she didn't get a chance to peruse them all. One, however, screamed for attention. "Is that a real Monet?" she asked in disbelief.

He gave the painting a glance then nodded. "A gift from my friend Sullivan. Here."

He stopped in front of a door, twisted the handle and ushered her in. "I invite you into my bedroom, Sheridan."

The words flowed over her with smooth enticement, urging her inward. She crossed the threshold and stopped just inside the doorway.

His bedroom was neat, almost utilitarian in its sparseness. A huge king bed, encased in gleaming black head- and foot-boards, dominated one side of the room. Four rounded and jutting legs stood out at each corner. Stark white linens covered the bed, and matching black nightstands guarded each side.

A black dresser nestled against the far wall. A long wooden box with a golden lock was the only ornament atop the furniture.

Nothing else. No TV, no computer.

Just a room.

With a bed.

A very large bed.

She swallowed a bout of rising excitement. This was a challenge and while she freely admitted she was attracted to him *and* horny as hell, she wasn't about to cave to his so-called control demands. She would play his game. And win.

"It's very nice, McCallister."

He chuckled and flicked on the iron bedside light before shutting off the overhead. Immediately the room deepened with shadows, though she could still see him clearly.

McCallister stood at the edge of the bed and slowly lifted the bottom edge of his green knit polo shirt.

When his abs came into view, she swayed on her feet. Forget six or eight, this guy was packing an entire brewery. Muscles rippled with motion as he pulled the shirt higher, over his pecs and finally off his head. He tossed the shirt to the floor, crossed his arms, and spread his feet a bit apart.

Sheridan could not control the sheer wave of lust beating at her sub-conscious. He was gorgeous, no other word fit.

The vampire had wide, broad shoulders any football player would envy. Strong and sculpted and perfectly in line with his equally muscular chest and sleek, ripped torso. Her mouth watered in anticipation.

McCallister smiled at her before drawing her attention to his pants. With a quick flick of the wrist, he unbuttoned his slacks, then drew the zipper down with a slow rasp. He spread his fingers inside the flap and peeled the fabric slowly away. Curly brown hair peeked out.

He wasn't wearing any underwear.

Sheridan took a few steps closer.

The pants fell to the floor, and he kicked them out of the way. His thighs bunched and contracted with the movement.

Sheridan stared at his cut calves for a long moment before pulling her gaze upward to his crotch.

"Oh, God," she half-whimpered.

He was breathtaking.

McCallister stood arrogantly, legs spread, hands on hips and long, thick, stiff dick proudly protruding. If he got any harder, one touch would snap his erection in two.

With great effort, she dragged her gaze up his body to meet his searing, green eyes.

"Watch me," he said. "I don't want you to do anything else, just watch."

CHAPTER THREE

McCallister saw the lust and attraction on Sheridan's face and quashed a knowing grin. He cupped the base of his shaft and her nostrils flared.

Her need swirled around her in tiny motes of pink and white lights.

When he stroked slowly upward, her entire body quivered and she took another few steps closer.

McCallister started a slow up-and-down movement on his cock, sliding his palm over the head and back down. Clear drops of pre-cum formed on the tip and he used his thumb to gloss the shiny liquid over himself. Her rapt stare excited him as much as the stroking.

"Like my cock?" he asked softly.

She nodded.

"Want to touch me?"

Lust blazed in her eyes and she gave another, slower nod.

"Take your shirt off."

The soft order threw her for only a second before she lifted trembling fingers to the buttons. Within seconds, the scrap of sheer material drifted to land at her feet.

His erection swelled in his hand and he hissed lightly. Damn, she looked good. Ripe. Eager.

Her tits quivered in the boundaries of her red push-up bra and goose bumps rose on the mounds.

More pre-cum slickened his grasp and he spread it along his entire shaft, all the while watching her reaction. Feeling her rapidly rising lust.

She shuddered.

"Come closer. Right in front of me."

She did, stopping only a few inches away.

McCallister sped up the motion of his hand and she swayed toward him. "You have a beautiful mouth, Sheridan. Perfect for kissing. Perfect for sucking cock."

She licked her lips.

"You like that? The thought of wrapping your beautiful red mouth over my hard dick?"

"Yes." A bare whisper of sound, but filled with desire.

"I want that, too. Want to see you swallow my entire length."

Sheridan's moan was an aphrodisiac and he gritted his teeth, reminding himself this was a lesson.

"I see you do, too. On your knees, Sheridan, and clasp your hands together behind your back."

Her hesitation was so brief it was practically non-existent as she obeyed again, sinking slowly to her knees in front of him. Her warm breath washed over him and his cock jerked.

"Oh, damn," she whispered.

"Keep your hands behind you. Do not let them come forward. For any reason. If you do, I will remove my cock. Do you understand?"

"Yes."

"Good." McCallister stepped closer. "Open your mouth."

When her ruby red lips parted, he slipped the head of his dick into her moist warmth. They both gasped.

The backs of his knees trembled and he reached down to clasp her shoulder. *Just to touch her, not to steady myself.*

He didn't believe his own words.

Her hot mouth throbbed around his cock and drove him nearly insane.

"Take as much of me as you can."

Her throat worked as she swallowed, her teeth just grazing the sides of his dick. The small darts only served to elevate his need. McCallister's eyes slitted as he looked down at her, kneeling in front of him, mouth stretched by his dick.

He spasmed in her mouth and her eyes went wide, her shoulders jerked in his grip.

"Don't move your hands," he barked.

She stilled.

"Take me deeper. I know you can. Use that fantastic mouth, Sheridan. Use it like the whore you pretended to be."

A low moan vibrated the sensitive, cut underside of his dick and he fought back his own shudder. Calling her a whore had been a risky move but her response was telling. A little humiliation with her submission seemed to be in order.

Slowly she sucked him deeper and deeper, gagged a couple of times and swallowed before moving forward again.

When she stilled at last, she held a full three-quarters of his entire length in her mouth. She looked up at him, eyes wide and afire.

Slowly, McCallister pumped his hips, pushing in and out of her mouth. He snarled his hands in her hair, forcing her to follow his rhythm. He paced himself. He wanted to fuck this little beauty, not spill his seed in her mouth, talented as it was.

She'll make a beautiful Consort.

McCallister had known from the moment she'd turned around from the

Caddy he was going to join with her. Knew she would be a woman he'd enjoy having at his feet, bound to his bed, taking his cock and begging for more.

Once more he pulsed between her delectable lips. "You look so good, there, Sheridan. Kneeling at my feet, my dick stuffing your mouth." He drew back until just the tip parted her lips then slowly drove back inside. "Good girl," he murmured. "Keeping your hands behind you so obediently."

The suction around his dick increased and her heart jumped several notches. The sweet scent of flowers churned around him and McCallister forced himself to concentrate.

Not possible. Sine Qua Non didn't exist. There are no soul mates.

He continued the same slow pace, all the while forcing back his orgasm, and watched her closely. When her eyelids drooped and her hips started writhing, he knew it was time to step up the lesson.

Good thing, too, because she'd had him at the brink several times.

Once more, McCallister withdrew just to the head before he tugged his erection from her mouth with an audible pop.

Her eyes went wide. "What? What are you doing?" She looked hungrily at his still-hard cock and he stroked himself, squeezing out more pre-cum when he reached the head.

"Stand up, Sheridan."

She rose.

"Take off your skirt and those fishnets."

A hitch in her breathing, a flare of emotion in her brilliant blue eyes.

Would she do it?

Though her fingers trembled, she reached around and unzipped the tattered black leather skirt. She peeled the stockings from her waist and shed both garments. Now she stood before him in only a pair of serviceable, black, boy-short panties and the rocking red bra.

"Take your panties off."

Her shoulders twitched and she shook her head.

He smiled gently. "I can work around them but I can't guarantee they won't end up ripped like your skirt."

She gave him a slow smile in return. "Good point." Her fingers tucked into the black waistband. Her tummy sucked in as she breathed. He saw the tremor in her hands as she pushed the panties down.

His mouth went dry and his dick went even harder as she revealed her sweet pussy to him. She kept her hair trimmed but not over done in some crazy shape as he'd seen before. The golden brown patch was just a shade darker than her head.

Her lower lips pouted downward with a fullness that made him even more eager to sink into her. He desperately wanted to feel her hot pussy clenched around him as he fucked her.

"Turn around, bend over the bed and put your hands on the mattress."

"Why?"

"Please?"

Her mouth pursed in an adorable way and he wanted to kiss her again. But right now, he was slowly exerting control. No time for tenderness or she might get the idea he was not serious about this.

"Turn. Around."

Sheridan regarded him closely, brow raised and eyes snapping. She probably knew what he was doing, but would go along with it to prove he had no control over her.

A win-win situation for him.

Slowly, she pivoted and traced the path to the bed. On a raised pedestal, the top of the mattress came to navel-height on her.

McCallister followed her but kept a small distance between them as he eyed the full roundness of her ass. The honey-cream flesh made his palms itch to smack it then kiss away the sting.

His control was nearly blown when she scooted her legs just past shoulder-width apart and bent over the bed.

Her musky aroma tinged with that damn hint of floral tease walloped him like a jackhammer.

Further proof she wanted him.

He stepped between her spread legs and enveloped her body with his. Her soft sigh and shudder pleased him. He slid his hands over her shoulders, down her arms, and to the mattress where her fingers were spread and slightly curled into the comforter.

He tangled their fingers together and squeezed lightly. She trembled.

McCallister exerted a bit more pressure against her back with his chest. "You have beautiful skin, Sheridan. As soft as cashmere and as smooth as melted chocolate. I bet you taste as sweet, too." He nuzzled the hollow of her neck and shoulder.

"McCallister."

Just his name on her breath aroused him.

He dipped his knees then came back up, his hard cock now nestled along the slickness of her pussy.

"Oh God," she whimpered.

He began a slow grind, his own breath wrenching from the sensual contact. Her fingers tightened on his and a tremor built up then dispersed through her frame.

More enticing hints of her scent swelled and hovered between them. His dick was soon coated in her juices and the slow slide was damn near killing him.

"Sheridan?"

"Hmm?"

He bared his fangs and lightly scraped the skin of her nape. She shuddered and moaned.

"I like that," she said.

"From how wet your pussy is, it seems you like my cock, too."

Her back stiffened and pushed against him but he didn't move away. After a long moment, she relaxed again.

"Are you always so cocksure?"

"I'm sure you like my cock. That's good enough for me."

She giggled at that. Sheridan looked back at him, the corner of her mouth tipped up in a seductive curl. "Are you waiting for an invitation?"

Though her words were light, he heard the seriousness flowing beneath them.

He nipped at her shoulder again. "Yes, I am. You can tell how much I want you, Sheridan." He pumped his hips between her slick outer lips a few more times. "But I want you to tell me what you want."

She bit her lip and looked down, but not before he saw a rosy blush on her cheeks. "I can't," she whispered.

"Why not?"

"Good girls don't, you know."

He untangled their fingers and cupped her tits, pulling her up from the bed and into his chest. "Good girls always make the best bad girls. It's in your genes." He pistoned lightly. "All you have to do is ask and I will fill your sweet pussy with my cock, Sheridan. Just ask me for it."

She covered his hands on her tits and pressed inward, squashing her flesh. He noted how turned on that made her and filed the knowledge away for future use.

"Ask me, Sheridan."

He knew the instant she gave in, even before the words tumbled from her lips.

"Fuck me, McCallister."

The air around them flared bright and pink. His vision grew dim, leaving him able to see only the beautiful woman in front of him.

Bending Sheridan to the bed again, he cupped her ass cheeks and spread her pussy lips wide then fitted the head of his cock to her dripping slit and eased his length inward.

The room dimmed even further, highlighting only Sheridan. She filled him, her thoughts and desires pounding at him from every direction.

He clenched his teeth and battled the temptation to go even further into her mind.

She gasped and writhed in his touch. "What is that?"

McCallister pulled out to the tip and steadied her hips. "What is what?"

"The noise. It sounds like rushing wind. Damn it, you're torturing me. Fuck me, McCallister, fuck me."

He dismissed the noise and focused instead on sinking back into her warm, grasping pussy. He ground his pelvis against her butt, buried all the way in.

"Oh, damn," she whispered.

"How do you like to be fucked, Sheridan? Soft? Slow, with tenderness?" He imitated the words and she squirmed on him. "Or do you want it rough and fast?" He increased the pace of his thrusts and she groaned, fingers curling into the blanket.

"Ah, rough and fast," he murmured. Still fucking her, he gathered her hair into a ponytail and placed his other palm to the small of her back, forcing her head up and her body down.

She whimpered but didn't protest. He looked down between their bodies, watched his cock slam in and out of her, slick and shiny with her juices.

Unable to resist a taste, he pulled out, dipped his finger into her pussy then brought the digit to his lips. One long suck and it was his turn to shudder.

Sweet. Like manna.

He fitted himself back to her opening and again fucked her. She bounced and writhed, spewing all sorts of demands his way. Her pussy clenched tightly on his dick and he responded by swelling impossibly large.

"Fuck," she yelled, hips whipping even harder. "I'm going to come, McCallister."

Instantly, he stopped and pulled out.

She waited, breath escaping in harsh beats then turned to look at him. "Why did you stop?"

He moved a step away. "Because I didn't give you permission to come."

She snapped straight up and glared at him. "What the hell do you mean?"

He winked and stroked his dick. "I want to be in your pussy, Sheridan. I love how your muscles clamp around me, trying to keep me in. But I don't want you to come unless I say you can. Can you do that for me?"

"Hell, no," she retorted and pushed away from the bed. Rage and frustration chased across her face. Her intense blue gaze focused on his still hard dick and she seemed to falter for a moment. McCallister waited tensely.

"I'm out of here. God, and they call women cock teases." She stormed across the room, scooping up her clothes as she went. "You'd better get this damn door unlocked or I'm calling the fire department," she yelled.

He sighed and raked a hand through his hair. He'd not counted on such resistance. He should have, though. Her willpower and strength of mind was incredible.

When he re-entered the living room, she was dressed in the skirt and shirt, but her fishnets were nowhere to be seen.

"Just so you know—" she stabbed a finger in his direction, "—I'm going home, getting out my vibrator, and coming until I collapse."

He lifted a brow. "You think so?"

"I know so."

"I *do not* give you permission to come, Sheridan. Remember that."

She flipped him off, snatched her purse from the table, and stomped to the door. "Are you going to open this damn thing or not?"

"Yeah, give me a sec."

He returned to his bedroom, her shout of annoyance loud and clear in his ears. He tugged on dark jeans and a black t-shirt, stepped into his black sneakers and made his way back to her.

She had her phone in her hand. He reached out and snatched it, disconnecting the call.

"Come on, Sheridan, I'll take you home. You don't want to be out in a cab this time of night."

"Oh, like you're any safer?" She shoved his chest and grabbed her phone back. "I'll take my risks with the crazy drivers."

He touched her arm with just enough light pressure to still her. "Sheridan," he said, keeping his voice low and even. Soothing. "I will take you home. Please, let me do this."

The furious beat of her heart continued for a long moment as she skewered him with a harsh glare. As the heat left her eyes, her pulse slowed. Weariness etched a frown on her forehead and she finally nodded. "All right. But no funny business, either."

He reached into the hall closet and pulled out a battered leather jacket. One he'd had since...he frowned...well, since forever. "Here, put this on," he said gruffly. "It's a little chilly and you're not really dressed for the outdoors."

"Fine, whatever." She shrugged into the jacket and pointed to the door. "Unlock it and let's go."

"Car's in the garage, past the kitchen. This way."

He headed through the house, listening for her light footfalls behind him. He opened the door and waved her by, snagging his keys from the cabinet hanging in the laundry room. The car he'd left on Dorchester Street belonged to the precinct. He sure hoped Leopold had taken it back by now. No telling what kind of damage vandals would do to it otherwise. He should call dispatch and make sure the car was secured. He just reached for his phone when Sheridan's low whistle hit him.

She stared at the car then back to him. "Wow," she said, voice losing more of its edge. "Is this a '65 Mustang?"

He rubbed a non-existent spot on the gleaming black hood and nodded. "Yep. All original parts, too."

"How long have you had it?" She rounded the car and gingerly eased herself inside.

He watched her with bemusement. Sheridan Aames was a muscle car buff? Interesting.

He got in the car and cranked the engine.

Sheridan's gasp was filled with admiration. "Sounds beautiful. My dad and I used to re-build old cars like this," she said, tone now way more relaxed, almost friendly. "So, how long?"

McCallister punched the button to open the garage door and laid his arm over the bench seat, fingers gently, deliberately tickling her nape. "A while," he hedged.

No sense telling her he'd bought the thing brand new in '64.

But something must have tipped her off because she inhaled sharply then turned her head to look out the window.

He noticed she didn't move away from his hand, though.

"Where we going?" he asked.

She gave him directions to her house and he was surprised to find she lived not very far from him.

That could prove very convenient.

They rode in silence but he could feel her mind whirling, processing, trying to figure out what had gone on this evening. As much as McCallister wanted to probe and find out what she was really thinking, he didn't. He wanted to earn her trust and compliance the right way, not by sneaking into her brain.

As he idled at a light, he looked at her. "For a reporter, you're awfully quiet. I'm surprised you haven't bombarded me with a thousand more questions by now."

She blushed and tugged her skirt down, though the material didn't go much further than mid-thigh. "Sorry, I've had other things on my mind."

He grinned. "I know."

She gave a derisive snort. "Not you, egohead. I'm trying to decide if you've completely blown my cover or not."

He pulled into her drive and killed the engine, stepped out and was at her side before she could even gather her purse and reach for the handle.

He opened her door and helped her out. "You're not going back there, Sheridan," he said flatly. "Someone knew about you long before I showed up."

"Why do you say that? Where in the hell are my keys?"

"Because someone shot at you, remember? Just what are you chasing?"

"Nothing that has anything to do with you." She frowned as she looked up at him. "Well, except for the name but that's it."

"What name?"

"Forget it, copper. The last thing I need is the fuzz busting my informants before I can get the scoop. Damn it. Keys!"

She shook her small purse and finally fished out her keys. She fitted one to the door, twisted, and moved through.

He started to follow, but she put a hand up to stave him off. "No," she said. "You are most definitely *not* invited in."

McCallister managed to maintain his calm façade, but internally he winced. Despite his earlier claims bashing vampiric lore, an invitation was usually better to have than busting into someone's space.

The Uninvited generally tended to be a bit more vulnerable.

He also might have overstated—outright lied—about that mesmerism thing, too. McCallister loathed using that particular skill, though. Too many bad memories associated with being helpless and guided by someone else's desires.

He banished the past by cupping her cheek.

He stroked his thumb along her bottom lip.

He wanted to kiss her again, wanted to delve into her body and explore all of her.

Instead, he allowed his hand to drop away. "Lock your doors, Sheridan."

She hesitated then slowly, eyes still locked with his, stepped back and closed the door. He waited until he heard the tumblers roll, securing the house.

McCallister headed back to his car. He opened the door and leaned over the roof, staring at her standing at the window, curtains peeked open just enough to show her sleek silhouette.

"Don't forget what I said, Sheridan. You are not allowed to come."

Despite the distance, he caught her growl of indignant anger, the curtain twitched shut, and she snapped off the light.

He chuckled as he slid into his car. "Sweet dreams, Sheridan."

CHAPTER FOUR

"What the hell do you mean someone shot at you, Aames?" Steve Dennison yelled across his paper-strewn desk. "Why in the hell are you just now telling me about this? Why didn't you call last night?"

Sheridan rubbed the back of her neck and tried to come up with a good excuse, but nothing clicked. She was a horrible liar.

"I ran into a cop and he helped me out of the jam." *Mostly true.* "By the time it was over, I just wanted to go home, take a hot bath, and go to bed." *Definitely true.*

She'd luxuriated in her garden tub, inhaling the soothing scents of lavender and chamomile while she tried to get Detective Sexy out of her mind. She'd even put on her favorite episodes of the old Dick Tracy radio show.

For a little bit she'd succeeded. Sort of. But when she finally made it to her bed and tried to pleasure herself, she was horrified to hear his voice in her head just as she was about to come, denying her. Telling her to stop.

She never did orgasm. Five tries and not one blasted time could she come.

Bastard.

Sheridan refused to dwell on exactly why she couldn't come, preferring to chalk it up to nerves instead of some vampire hocus pocus. Mostly.

"Look, Steve, I'm positive my informant was right about that deal going down last night. Those guys in the Caddy were trying to shill that Vampire Dust to some unsuspecting druggies. I just know it. That's why I got shot at. I got too close."

Sweat pooled on Steve's forehead and slithered down his neck. He shook his head and droplets splattered the papers in front of him. He smelled a bit, too. Like sardines a few hours overripe.

Behind her, she could hear the clacking of keystrokes on computers from the newsroom and the creak and buzz of conversation. Snippets of words echoed in her ears as if the speaker stood right next to her. She turned her head only to find no one there.

Then everything returned to normal.

Sheridan held her breath. *What the hell just happened?*

"Exactly why you need another assignment. I don't need you hurt, Aames."

She rose and planted her palms on his desk, towering over him with a glare. "I'm not giving this story up, Steve. I'm in already. I just need to shift my disguise a little bit. I have a few more stool pigeons I can hit up for information."

He still looked like he would refuse then his shoulders crumpled. "You always were too damn stubborn for your own good. Or mine. Fine." He waved his hand. "Get the hell out of my office and run your story down."

She smiled. "You're a gem, Steve. A real gem."

He shook his head. "You've been listening to that 30's detective show again, haven't you?"

She laughed but was puzzled. "Dick Tracy. How'd you know?"

His smile was genuine and his eyes twinkled a bit. "You always spout the lingo. I guess it seeps into your brain."

Sheridan shook her head, waved goodbye, and high-tailed it to her desk to grab her purse. She wanted out of the newsroom before he could change his mind.

"Going out again, Sheridan?" Bobbi, the Metro's uber-efficient receptionist asked. Her syrupy voice was a holdover from a lifetime spent in the Deep South.

Sheridan learned quick enough Bobbi's personality was just as sugary. Bobbi—with an i, thank you—was as Southern as the General Lee, sweet tea, and barbecue. She'd met and married her husband in college and broke her mama's heart when they moved to Boston from Gumlog, Georgia. The young woman was a genuine breath of fresh air, though, and Sheridan really liked her.

"Yeah," she replied. "Running leads."

"Did you clear your phone? Your mail box is full. Again."

Sheridan winced. "Sorry," she said and pushed the button for the elevator. "I'll do it when I get back. Take messages for me? Please?"

Bobbi sighed dramatically even as she winked. "Sure thing, darlin'."

The elevator opened and Sheridan squeezed out into the lobby of the downtown high rise that housed the Metro.

"Miss Aames," the concierge called.

She swung mid-stride and headed for him. "Hi Bert, what's the good news today?"

He gave her a dour look. Bert was one dodgy old coot, but he always had good leads and knew just about everyone in town, from deadbeats to the mayor. She trusted him implicitly. The old man had never steered her wrong. Didn't hurt he was also a dear friend who shared her passion for old time radio dramas and decadent full-sugar, full-fat, full-everything ice cream.

Bert's brows furrowed with worry. "Heard you were shot at last night."

"Well, that traveled fast. How'd you hear?"

"I have my sources. They also said you vanished with a vampire cop named McCallister." He gave her a stern, we're-gonna-discuss-this-right-now-young-lady look.

Sheridan went cold. *How in the hell did Bert know about vampires? About McCallister?* She wanted to pepper him with all the usual W questions: who, why, when and how, but her attention was grabbed by a low murmur. She tucked a lock of hair behind her ear and looked sideways at the bustle of people in the lobby. Her skin crawled for half a second and, just like upstairs, she could suddenly hear voices, only this time the conversations were crystal.

She definitely heard her name and *grab her.*

Fuck.

"I don't have time to talk about that, Bert, but please, don't repeat it to anyone."

His brown eyes went wide. "Shit, are you serious?" The green porter's cap he wore jiggled with the motion of his brows.

She nodded. "Look, I need to take a powder. Can I hop the freight elevator down?" Another prickle at her nape. She looked over her shoulder.

Among the bustling lawyers and corporate raiders, two men stood out. Both looked as if they should fit in. Tall, broad, heavily muscled. Despite the nice suits— probably Armani—she knew a goon when she saw one.

These Brunos could have worked for Flattop Jones.

"You still after that new street drug? What's it called? Dust?"

She pulled her gaze back to Bert, but watched the warped images of the two men in the brass plate behind the old man's green-cap topped frizzy head. "Yeah. I need some info, too. My last snoop probably won't have the time of day for me now."

"We'll talk about your encounter later." He hesitated a heartbeat, brown gaze scanning her with speed of a laser. "You're okay, right?"

His sincere concern warmed her. She grabbed his hand. "Yes, I am. Thanks."

"Yeah, sure, kiddo. I still got questions, though. Tons of 'em."

"I don't know that I can answer everything, Bert," she said. "I don't really have a clue what's going on."

"I know that feeling. Here." He slid a card across the marble counter. "Ask for Sullivan Alexander. Tell him I sent you and that you need information and fast. Now, get. They're about to head this direction."

Sheridan snatched the card and inched past him. Just as she reached the brass lattice doors of the freight elevator, she heard a ding and they slid open. She stepped inside, jabbed G, then the Close Door button.

The doors swooshed shut, and she leaned against the wall with relief.

In the garage, she scoped out the area, listened for sounds of footsteps in the stairwell, then sprinted to her car.

Though the small VW Bug wouldn't win any awards for appearance, Tess got her where she needed go. Her once-red paint was chipped and faded and the interior cloth seats were in dire need of repair, but every bit of sheet metal, every bolt, every gear, and every inch of her engine were pristine.

"Come on, Tess," she muttered as she cranked the engine. "We need to jet. Now."

The car roared to life, and she reversed and sped out of the garage. Only when she made it onto the freeway did she take a solid, relaxed breath.

As she drove, Sheridan pulled the card from her pants pocket.

Glossy black and etched in blood red, the card read *Vesper's Bite. Open shadowfall to pre-dawn.*

"What the hell?" *Shadowfall? What is that?* She flipped it over, but no address was on the back. How was she supposed to find the joint without an address?

Damn, sometimes being a reporter was a pain in the ass. She should have been a detective.

Which brought up thoughts of McCallister and his damn sensual aura. The way his hands roamed her body and made her feel sexy and wanton. The way her body froze just before coming at the insidious whisper of his voice.

She growled and forced him from her mind.

Sheridan tossed the card to the passenger seat and checked her rearview mirror, relieved to find no one following her.

Just as she pulled into the parking lot of Copley Place shopping mall, her phone clanged. She quickly found an out-of-the-way spot, checked the number—one she didn't recognize—and answered.

"Sheridan Aames."

"I hear you want to know about Dust."

The voice was smooth, educated, urbane. British? Definitely cultured. The voice of someone raised with a silver spoon in their mouth and gold in the bank.

"Who is this?"

"Identities are overrated, Miss Aames. Suffice it to say we are both working to achieve the same end."

"Sorry, bub, I don't work with anyone who won't give me his name. Call me back when you're ready to do that."

Silence.

"I suppose you're going to insist?"

"I am."

"Very well. I am Paxton Barrett."

Sheridan's eyes went wide and she pulled the phone away, stared in disbelief at the call screen, then replaced it at her ear. "Are you serious?"

"Indeed. I would like to discuss this matter in more depth. Are you available this evening?"

Paxton Barrett—old money millionaire, medical invention pioneer, and as reclusive as Howard Hughes. No need to ask how he gained her number—the man could have anything he wanted.

Again her eyes narrowed. "Pardon my distrust, Mr. Barrett, but what in the world do you need *me* for?"

She heard the smile in his voice. "You wouldn't believe me if I told you, Miss Aames, but I will try to explain this evening. There's a club at which we can meet called Vesper's Bite."

She started at the name of the club, her gaze zeroed in on the glossy black card she'd tossed away. Slowly, she picked it up, grabbed a pen and flipped the card over.

"What's the address?"

His chuckle was disconcertingly low and oppressive. "There is no address, Miss Aames. Show up at Fifth and Carter exactly at 6:17 and look for the door. Don't be late. I despise tardiness."

The line disconnected and she hit the end button and slumped back against Tess' seat. Slowly, she flicked the business card.

"All right, Mr. Barrett, let's see what you're all about."

† † †

At 6:15, Sheridan sat in her car, parked in the pay-as-you-go lot facing the corner of Fifth and Carter. She touched up her makeup in the rearview and wondered if she'd gone a bit too heavy with the black eyeliner and copper shadow. Her eyes *did* look kickin' hot, though. And showing up to a club, any kind of club, only half-assed dressed was the kind of rookie mistake that could get a dame out for the scoop, iced.

She giggled nervously. Steve was right, she'd been listening to way too many Dick Tracy programs.

6:17. *Showtime.*

She popped open her door, grabbed her small red velvet purse, and stepped out of the car, gaze glued to the corner of the street. It was a non-descript building. Beige and red brick from the turn of the last century. Crumbling in a few places, boarded up in others. A dark green grill covered a doorway and a huge padlock bolted the door shut. Everything else on the street was dark and lifeless.

Sheridan scanned the corner again.

Nothing.

She hip-shut the door and started forward, though she kept a vigilant and wary eye to either side of her.

Was this some sort of weird joke?

A sudden wind kicked up a discarded newspaper which wrapped around her leg. She grimaced and bent to peel the slightly sodden paper—the Metro, of course—off. Wadding the day old print, she tossed it into a trash can then looked back at the corner.

Her breath stilled.

The green door now sparkled and stood wide open. A burly man with shoulders wider than a Mack truck lounged against the brick. He was tall and broad all over with skin the color of dark chocolate, right down to the dull glare on his bald head. A large diamond winked from his right ear and she caught the glitter of a gold necklace peeping out from his black T-shirt. He reminded her of an ancient Nubian soldier guarding the palace from infidels. He didn't so much as acknowledge her existence when their gazes met.

Sheridan swallowed and tugged down the hem of her black leather skirt, then started forward.

The Nubian shoved away from the building, a frown creasing his ebony skin. Sheridan pasted her best vacant, party girl smile on, adjusted the sway of her hips and sauntered so close she could see the bristle from his five o'clock beard.

"Hi," she said, channeling Breathless Malone. "I'm here for Mr. Barrett." She winked slowly. "He's expecting me."

Not so much as a twitch. Hell, if anything, his expression grew more stone-like than the building he was in front of.

Sheridan bit the inside of her lip and pondered the wisdom of trying to barrel past him.

"You won't make it," he said, voice low and slow like cold honey. "Got a card?"

"Uh, yeah, I do." She pulled the now bent and slightly tattered black business card from her purse and handed it to him. As he reached out, she gasped and yanked it back, staring hard.

Vesper's Bite was still prominently displayed, but the card now also blared a shifting set of words. She caught Barrett's name, hers, McCallister's—what the hell was that about?—Sullivan Alexander and Bert's. A shiver raced over her.

Was she getting into something too deep here?

The black guardian plucked it from her fingers, studied it closely, whistled then nodded and stepped aside, handing her the card.

"Barrett is in the Red Room. McCallister's at the bar. Alexander will be there, too. Not sure where Bert is tonight. Interesting company you keep."

"McCallister? What's he doing here?" Was the big lug following her or something?

The bouncer didn't respond, just tipped his head toward the door.

Obviously, he wanted her inside and out of his non-existent hair.

Fine.

She shoved the card back into her purse and stepped forward, muscles tensed and braced for God only knew what.

As soon as she passed the threshold, sound exploded around her and she clapped her hands over her ears. Eyes watering, she frantically looked over her shoulder, but the doorway was gone, replaced by a solid wall.

The enormity of her what-the-fuck situation hit her, and Sheridan sucked in a shuddering, panic-filled breath.

She had to get out of here.

Except she had no idea where *here* was. People crowded the hallway in front of her and through the dim lighting, she glimpsed a larger, open room. Rows of bottles lined the far wall and a tall, good looking blond man stood behind the red-and-black patchwork bar.

She wavered, tempted to head that direction. *I could use a drink right now.*

But the Nubian said McCallister was in there and she wasn't ready to face him just yet.

The big vampire cop was still on her shit list for last night's confusing debacle. Sheridan squeezed her eyes shut and concentrated on pushing the noise from her ears as if the sounds held physical mass. McCallister's eerie green eyes and incredible lips filled her vision.

The sounds lessened.

His lips moved but she didn't hear anything. Frowning, she shook her head and concentrated on his face. Her anger at his arrogance, the sudden halt to their lovemaking, his ridiculous command not to come all faded, melding into an oasis of need and desire. The realization that now all she wanted to do was pull his head down to hers and kiss him as senseless as he'd made her made her scowl.

McCallister's mental image chuckled and he tapped her on the nose, winked, then faded from sight.

Sheridan's eyelids popped open, and she breathed a deep sigh of relief because the noise was gone. Only the normal sounds of being in a club with a hundred other people, a great bassline in the background, and the clink of glasses filled the air.

"Interest you in a shot, ma'am?"

Sheridan looked down. A petite, young woman with hair the color of a fire truck and eyes as big and dark as coal, lofted a silver tray containing several shot glasses.

Despite the temptation and the need, she shook her head. "Maybe later." *Definitely if I run in to McCallister. I'm gonna need something strong to deal with him tonight. Why did I picture kissing him instead of smacking him?*

The woman nodded and pushed past her. Sheridan reached out and touched her arm.

The waitress spun so swiftly, the alcohol sloshed in their glasses. The sweet, smooth face had gone wild and fangs protruded from her mouth.

"Whoa!" Sheridan jerked her hand away.

Once more her gaze darted around the bar and this time she realized there were many, many sets of fangs on display.

She swallowed hard.

Fuck this. I'm out of here.

"I'm sorry," the waitress said. This time *her* hand curled over Sheridan's forearm. "I didn't mean to startle you. Are you a new Consort?"

Sheridan shook her head even though she had no damn idea what that meant.

The waitress's expression went wary. "You have a card, right?"

"Yes." Sheridan cleared her throat and forced her unease away. McCallister's claims from last night were the only thing keeping her in this damn place.

Well, that and I can't find the blasted exit.

"I'm here for Paxton Barrett. The big guy outside said he was in the Red Room. Do you know where that is?"

The redhead nodded slowly. She pointed to the left with her chin. "Down that hall, second door on the right." Her head tipped as she narrowed her gaze. "Mind if I look at your card?"

Since she had no intention of being anyone's dinner snack or causing any trouble at all, Sheridan dug the black card out and handed it over.

"McCallister?" The waitress flicked her with a glance that held both envy and tension. "He's in the bar. I'll get him."

"No," Sheridan yelped and grabbed her card back. "I'm here for Barrett. I don't know how McCallister's name got on there, but it's wrong."

The waitress held out a shot glass with liquid as green and bright as McCallister's eyes. "Take it," she said softly. "I have a feeling you're going to need it."

Sheridan wavered then reached out for the glass. "What is it?"

The girl smiled. "It's called a Mad Scientist. Rum, melon liqueur, and a dash of water. It's McCallister's favorite."

If the drink hadn't already been at her lips, Sheridan would have put the shot back on the tray. Instead, she slugged the burning liquor down and savored every drop.

"Tasty. How much?"

"Nothing," the waitress said. "My treat." She hesitated then grinned. "Actually, McCallister's treat. That one was his."

"Damn it," Sheridan muttered. "Why did you give it to me?"

"I don't know. Just seemed like the thing to do all of a sudden."

Sheridan dug in her tiny purse and pulled out a five then tossed the bill on the girl's tray. "I pay my own way."

"It's too late but thanks." She turned and melted into the crowd, offering drinks to chatting vampires.

Sheridan shuddered away the realization she was surrounded by a building full of vampires.

One she could handle. Sort of.

An entire building of them?

Let me out.

"I should have asked her where the exit was instead." Sheridan fiddled with the strap of her purse and looked over her shoulder. Still no doorway.

She peered down the mostly empty hallway the waitress had indicated.

"I'm here. No sense wasting the opportunity to meet the reclusive Paxton Barrett." She was also curious as to why the man was in a bar full of vampires. Had he known they existed all along? That question moved up to her number one spot. Several more investigative questions surged in her brain and helped her to regain her bearings.

Sheridan tugged on her tight teal shirt and wished it was just a smidge longer. Her tummy felt oddly exposed.

Not that any of them were looking at her. She peeked at the crowds again and saw, to her surprise, they were all hanging around chatting, drinking and laughing. Just like regular people in any bar.

This is so weirding me out.

Sheridan headed down the hallway. Her steps only faltered once when the overhead lights flickered as she passed beneath.

Total coincidence.

As she made the last turn, she caught sight of a faint glowing sign above a doorway: Red Room. Okay, that made her smile even as she grimaced. Vampires had black humor. Who knew they had *any* humor? She didn't know whether to knock or just go in. Her decision was made when the door soundlessly whooshed open.

"Come in, Miss Ames."

The voice, no longer distorted by cell technology, sounded even more cultured. Sheridan peered into the room, scoping it out as fast as she could.

Two empty upholstered wingback chairs sat in front of a fire, a burgundy leather chaise with only one arm, also empty, sat along one wall, and a fully stocked bar complete with stone faced bartender against another. She sized up the lean man in traditional white and black server's garb and lifted a brow as she stepped inside, cockiness rising once more. He didn't look old enough to be a medical pioneer, but she appreciated a good cover when she saw one.

"Didn't expect you to pose as a waiter, Mr. Barrett."

The guy's upper lip quivered.

"Do you always jump to erroneous conclusions, Miss Aames? Not good practice for a reporter, I would think."

She pivoted on her heel and gasped, stumbling backward. From the shadowed corner near the chaise stepped a tall man, impeccably dressed in a muted gray suit that matched his hair. His eyes were dark, almost black but compelling. Sheridan found herself drowning in their seemingly endless depths. Once more McCallister's face popped into her line of sight and she inhaled deeply, breaking whatever oddity held her in stasis.

Barrett had high, chiseled cheekbones and a sharp, long nose that flared over thin lips. His skin held the pallor of Swiss cheese left unprotected overnight. Slightly yellow and oddly brittle.

"My apologies," she said and held out her hand. She felt like an idiot. Of course Paxton Barrett was going to be an old man. He had tons of money and influence and had been in the news for what seemed like forever.

He stared down at the offering then lifted his lip in a half-sneering smile. "I don't shake hands. Too many germs. I hope you understand."

His tone really said he didn't give a damn if she understood or not, he wasn't going to contaminate himself.

Fine by her. Rapid panic rose within her and she stared at his mouth. His thin lips pressed together then peeled back revealing what she thought she'd seen.

She stumbled backward, clutching her purse to her chest. "You're a vampire?" she said on a strangled gasp.

He inclined his head then slowly returned to his seat. Glided down. Like a fricking paper airplane drifting through the air.

Oh, God. Him, too? Am I the only human left on earth?

Hysteria didn't just threaten—it was knocking at her psyche with a battering ram.

"You look in need of a drink, Miss Aames. Ernest will get you what you want."

She nodded but didn't move, just continued to stare. She couldn't pull her gaze away from him. Studying him helped slow her racing heart and give her a much-needed moment to regain her equilibrium. She should have known. *Seriously.*

She wanted to ask how he managed to bite anyone being a germophobe but when she thought about it, her neck itched, making her blanch. The difference between this vampire's frail appearance and McCallister's fitter-than-fit physique was astounding.

Just thinking of the cop somehow helped her re-establish her normal sense of self. She even relaxed a little bit and smiled at Barrett.

She turned back to the bartender who'd been eyeing her butt. She winked at him and he smiled in return, his blasé façade finally cracked. "Can you make me a Zombie?"

His eyes widened and it looked like he was strangling on his tongue. Sheridan shrugged. "Sorry, I know it's an old drink. Three kinds of rum, some pineapple and papaya juice..."

"Yes, ma'am," he interrupted. "I know what's in it." His gaze shot over her head for a half second before returning. Color flared in his cheeks. "It's just I've never had anyone actually ask for one."

"Get the lady her drink, Ernest." Barrett's voice slid around her and the bartender snapped to, filling a shaker with the fixings immediately.

She wasn't ready to turn around and look at Barrett again, so she watched, feigning fascination as Ernest made her Zombie.

When he strained the liquid into a chilled glass and passed it to her, she gulped greedily, savoring the sweet and sharp bites of rum.

"How much?"

He waved a hand.

"All the drinks are on the house at Vesper's," Barrett said. "Come. Sit with me."

She frowned. *Didn't that waitress say McCallister paid for the shot she swiped? Maybe Barrett is just being a gentleman.* Sheridan debated ordering another.

"Now. Miss Aames, you really must improve your listening skills if we are to work together."

Now *that* caught her attention and she whirled, careful to contain the sloshing liquid. "Who said anything about working together?"

He was seated in one of the chairs and waved at the other. "Sit."

She didn't move.

"Please."

Though he'd offered the word grudgingly, Sheridan was satisfied. She wasn't some pushover dame, and she'd often found it best to get that straight from the start.

Once her drink was safe on the table beside her chair, she dug into her purse and withdrew a small notebook and pen.

"All right, Mr. Barrett, let's talk Vampire Dust."

CHAPTER FIVE

"Leopold tells me you had an interesting experience yesterday," Brooks Wingate said as he sat down, tumbler of Scotch in hand. The billionaire looked as urbane and elegant as ever. He wore a dove-gray suit tailored to perfection complete with a maroon tie and matching handkerchief peeking from the breast pocket.

McCallister couldn't remember a time when he'd ever seen Brooks looking less than refined and in total control. He sipped his dark German beer then flicked a pointed glare at Leopold who grinned.

"It was a stake-out," he hedged. "Those are never interesting."

"You know that's not what I'm talking about."

"It was nothing," McCallister said. He hadn't had enough time to process everything that happened with Sheridan Aames the night before. He sure as hell didn't feel like dragging it out in the middle of the bar so Brooks could analyze it.

"Bullshit." Brooks leaned forward, his blue eyes intense and focused. "This could be vitally important if it's true. There hasn't been an actual first-hand account of a vampire experiencing Sine Qua Non in over seven hundred years."

McCallister shook his head and sighed. "How is it possibly important? It doesn't exist. Vampire soul mates are the kind of stuff desperate teens and gothic poets write about. Life Legend? Give me a break." He took a swig of the dark beer and wiped the foam from his mouth. "Don't you have a mega-corporation to run?"

"I delegate. What do you know about the legend?" Brooks asked.

He shrugged. "Same as anyone else." He rolled his eyes. "A vampire's one soul mate will be identified by a particular fragrance, known only to the vampire. Blah, blah, blah, emo bullshit."

Leopold chuckled, but his golden eyes were serious. "There's more to it than that."

"A lot more," Brooks said. "The fragrance is their pure Essence. It's the hallmark of their soul and a part of yours. That's why you, and only you, can identify the scent. On the other hand, it doesn't always happen that way. Every pairing is different."

McCallister frowned. He'd never heard this bit of the story. "What do you mean, it's part of my soul?"

Brooks sipped his Scotch. "I have some texts on it at my house. You can read them to get a better idea but this is what I know. At the moment a human turns into a vampire, his soul dies and splits in two. Part of it returns to the vampire but the other half fades into the universe where it waits to be reborn. As a human. From that life to the next, there is only one goal—find the other half of its soul. In other words, find the vampire to which it belongs."

McCallister rolled one of his shoulders to displace the building tension. Despite his protestations about the idiocy of the legend, he was beginning to think it might have some merit.

"You said from that life to the next," Leopold said. "What happens when they find the vampire they share souls with?"

"That's where the power comes in. In a regular Consort Joining, there is a small exchange of powers. The vampire feeds his human Consort a tiny bit of one of his powers. Most often it's a psychic link between the two of them. The human gift is life, of course. They don't really have anything to offer a vampire other than that." Brooks cleared his throat and leaned toward the middle of the table. "In a Sine Qua Non Joining, the exchange is greater and more powerful. The human Consort will imbue her vampire with a part of her soul. The part that was lost when he was turned."

McCallister shifted in his chair. "I don't know, Brooks. It sounds too fantastic to be believed."

Brooks' face was grim. "You haven't heard the worst of it. If the vampire recognizes the Sine Qua Non but fails to claim the Consort, he will rapidly age until he dies."

McCallister frowned. "How rapidly?"

"The upshot? Dead within a year. The Consort will also die and both souls will be lost."

Unease licked at McCallister. A vision of lively, vivacious Sheridan shriveled and dead filled his mind. His chest ached like a giant hand reached in and grabbed hold of his heart and squeezed without mercy.

"Evening, gents." Sullivan Alexander pulled out a hardback chair, flipped it around and straddled the table. His dark gaze immediately speared McCallister. "'eard yer dovey is fated. Right barrel o'crap 'at is, guv."

McCallister winced at the language mangling. "For God's sake, Sullivan, drop the damn Cockney shit and speak like a civilized person."

The shaggy haired man gave him a dour look. "Jeez, you take the fun out of everything. Sometimes a man has to get back to his roots, you know?"

"You were raised in boarding schools, not the mean streets of London. Your roots are servants, silver spoons, and sacks of money," Leopold said dryly. "You only choose to be a thief now."

Sullivan grinned. "Beats sitting around jacking off to horrible porn."

The club, filled with all manner of vampires and their associates — servants, familiars and Consorts — roared loudly for a moment before an unnatural hush descended. The air around McCallister stilled and though he saw Sullivan's lips still moving, he heard nothing. Nothing save the almost familiar heartbeat of Sheridan Aames. He pushed up and away from the table, noted the slow reaction of his friends and spun around.

A pink and white path shimmered among the throngs of people, tinted with the softest overlay of roses. He followed the faint trail until it flared around Becky, a Vesper's Bite waitress.

McCallister grabbed her arm. "Where is she?" he demanded. The words were swept away in a sudden rush of heartbeat, blood, and terror.

Sheridan!

The waitress frowned, said Red Room then pointed to her left. McCallister looked down the hall and spotted the pink and white path. He gave a curt nod and headed in that direction.

Becky stopped him. "I gave her your drink."

The words filled his ears slowly, but when he understood, he smiled, spun and made for the Red Room.

At least Sheridan would have a bit of protection, however small. He hoped. Since he didn't technically offer her the drink he wasn't sure how well it would cloak her.

Damn, all this Sine Qua Non was a jumble of confusing bullshit.

He continued down the hall, around a bend and into a deeper portion of the club until it dead-ended at a closed door. Like a sudden splash of water, everything returned to normal.

Noise, movement, jostling all happened in real time.

Sullivan and Leopold appeared behind him. Sullivan's jocular expression replaced by a grim determination and Leopold's golden eyes gleamed with the scent of the chase.

"Brooks?"

"Got held up," Leopold said.

McCallister nodded and looked up at the nameplate above the door. "Red Room."

A frisson of alarm skittered along his nerves. McCallister reached out and touched the doorknob, twisted slowly.

Locked.

Again the unseen wind billowed and his eyes widened as Sheridan's scent blew through him. He gritted his teeth against the ever-increasing odds that it wasn't just a sweet aroma. He was smelling her Essence.

Sine Qua Non.

"She's in there," he said tightly. "I have to get in."

He yanked his gun from his shoulder holster and aimed at the lock.

Leopold hissed and grabbed his arm. "Not like that, you idiot." He tipped his chin at Sullivan. "Let the damn thief earn his keep. Sullivan."

"Right-o," the other man said with a cheeky grin.

As he bent, he pulled a small set of tools from his back pocket, selected a thin piece of metal and inserted it into the lock. Seconds later, he winked up at McCallister. "Done."

Sometimes, it was good to have friends with unusual, albeit illegal, abilities.

Holstering his gun, McCallister shoved the door open then barreled in. "Sheridan!" he bellowed.

Dimly aware of Leopold and Sullivan streaming in behind him, McCallister swept the room, nearly overpowered by her Essence. The scent flowered from every surface, impossible to pinpoint. Her heart pounded in wild abandon, further compounding the problem. Pink and red streaks zig-zagged around the space like a graffiti artist gone wild. The room appeared empty, but he knew better. Two chairs flanked a fireplace, a slightly angled chaise sat along one wall. A wilting potted plant stood in the corner.

"McCallister, here," Leopold snapped.

He spun, took in the disarray of shattered glasses, tipped over and dripping bottles, and strewn chunks of ice before he caught sight of a pair of legs protruding from behind the bar. He leapt over and landed beside the figure in one lithe move.

Ernest, the bartender, lay sprawled on the floor.

Dark, unseeing eyes pointed toward the ceiling. Leopold, hand at the man's throat, shook his head.

"Dead." He closed Ernest's eyes then put a palm over the bartender's forehead as though taking his temperature. Leopold jerked then stiffened before surging upward. Fury etched lines into his already rugged face. "Barrett."

"Oh, hell," Sullivan whispered.

An unnatural calm settled over McCallister. "How long?"

"Couple of minutes, no more."

He turned back to the room and checked it out again. The angle of the chaise was definitely off. McCallister walked toward it, veering around the end and into the darker part of the corner, near the plant. Hooking his foot around it, he shoved the container away.

"Sheridan," he whispered and dropped to his knees.

She lay curled in a ball, hands over her ears and tears streaming down her face.

"Honey, it's me."

She flinched when he touched her then her eyes flew open. They were wild and scared as shit, her skin as pale as a British vampire. He caressed her hair. "Sheridan, did he hurt you?"

She whimpered then launched herself at his chest. She wrapped her arms tight around him and buried her face in his neck. Hot tears immediately soaked his collar and slid down his skin.

He surged to his feet and clamped her close. Sheridan's legs dangled for a moment before she enfolded them around his waist.

Sullivan whistled.

McCallister ignored him, trying to calm Sheridan's racing heart. He could feel her blood surging and roiling and it was proving quite a distraction.

"Did he hurt you?"

A small shake of her head. Her heart began to slow as she took in a deep breath.

"Do you know where he is?" He was going to rip Barrett limb to limb. How dare the bastard touch her?

Another head shake.

"Why don't you put her down so she can actually talk?" Leopold suggested.

McCallister glared and squeezed her closer.

She let out an "oomph" and leaned her head back to look at him. "I'm better now," she said, voice whispery and tremulous.

"I don't want to let you go."

She gave him a watery smile. "Really, it's okay. I'm not usually such a namby-pamby, but that man, that *vampire...*" Another tremor rocked her.

McCallister grunted then slowly eased her to the floor, pleased when she stayed cuddled under his arm as she turned to survey the room. Her cry of dismay when she spotted Ernest's body tore at him and he kissed the top of her head.

"Don't look."

Leopold stepped in front of the body.

Sullivan bowed and held out his hand. "Sullivan Alexander, you lovely dish, a pleasure to meet you. The glowering lad over there with the glowing golden eyes is our Hunter, Leopold."

She stiffened, one hand flying to her mouth briefly. She flicked a glance at McCallister then placed her fingers in Sullivan's outstretched grasp.

McCallister felt a growl well deep in his throat. He did *not* like Sheridan being touched by anyone else.

Especially another vampire.

Sullivan winked at him. "Easy there, big guy. Just making introductions."

Sheridan pulled her hand away and nodded. "Hello." She looked up at him, haunted fear shadowing her normally bright blue eyes. "We need to talk." She shivered. "Not here, though."

"Let's go back to my house," he said.

"Not a good idea," Leopold put in. "We'll convene at Brooks'."

"Who is Brooks?"

"A friend of ours." McCallister shared a long look with Leopold, trying to decipher the man's inscrutable face. He got nothing.

Sullivan was already out the door and McCallister put his hand to Sheridan's hip and steered her from the room.

"I'll take care of Ernest," Leopold murmured as they passed him.

They wound their way through the thinning group of vampires and ended up in the Altar Bar where Brooks and a raven-haired woman sat.

"Holy shit," Sullivan murmured. "That's Calliope Jones."

McCallister whistled. "Damn, she rarely ventures out. Wonder what's going on."

The couple looked deep in conversation. Tension and disapproval tightened Brooks' mouth. He looked up at their approach, his hand covering Calliope's fingers. She stilled, then rose and nodded at them before disappearing into the crowd.

"Don't ask," Brooks growled before he could speak.

"Later then."

"We need to leave, McCallister." Brooks studied the room with intensity. "Barrett might be here."

McCallister growled. "He *was* here. He killed one of the bartenders."

"Damn," Brooks muttered, his gaze sliding the direction Calliope had taken. "He must not have known you were here or there'd been even more bloodshed."

"I don't know. He's not that dumb or naïve," Leopold said. "I suspect this was deliberate. Not a trap, though. Something...more."

McCallister couldn't squash the same notion. Barrett was cunning. Orchestrating something like this was right up his alley.

Brooks finally turned his attention to Sheridan. "This your girl?"

Her head lifted. "What? No. I just know him, that's all." She lightly punched his side. "Tell him."

"Yeah, she's mine."

A smile chased briefly over Brooks' face. "Good."

McCallister felt Sheridan's heart give another kick, but whether from annoyance or pleasure, he wasn't sure. If he were a bettor, he'd place odds she wasn't exactly thrilled.

Too damn bad.

"You're right, we do need to get out of here and to your place," McCallister said shortly. "Get Valdór, too, if you can find him. Leopold is cleaning up a little mess and I think Sullivan is informing management about a small incident in the Red Room."

Brooks nodded. "All right. See you there."

He faded into the crowd, following the same route Calliope had taken.

McCallister looked down at Sheridan who wore a frown and a mulish set to her jaw he was coming to realize meant she was about to be stubborn.

He was glad to see the shock had faded from her eyes.

"Hold tight, little one," he said, folding his arms around her.

"What—"

He misted before she could speak further. Though he was slightly more prepared for the extra burden of transporting another person this time, when they re-materialized at the corner of the street across from the club, he staggered and gasped.

"Whoa, there, big guy." Sheridan steadied him and he blinked a couple of times, trying to filter away the shadows still lingering.

"Where's your car?" he asked.

"Lot across the street."

She didn't seem winded or shaken by the mist experience. A good sign.

"Great, let's go. I'll drive."

Her low, sultry laugh vibrated from his head to his balls. He liked the sound. A lot.

"What's so funny?" he asked as they stepped into the street.

"You'll see."

Even before they reached the other side, McCallister sensed the shift in wind. He grabbed her and tried to mist, but he was too weak to do more than waver their bodies. "Fuck," he muttered.

She struggled against him, pulling away and shoving her hair from her face. "What's that about? I thought we were driving."

"Get down," he gasped, bending over and trying to keep his beer from coming up.

A loud screech of rubber on pavement and her eyes went wide. She dropped, pulling him down with her.

Nano-seconds later, three pops whistled the air and glass shattered over them. The squeal of brakes, the clunk of heavy metal doors opening and leather soled feet scraping over graveled street.

McCallister gritted his teeth, seeking strength.

Sheridan's fingers curled around his neck, her sweet lips pressed to his ear. "Don't do anything stupid."

A surge of energy flitted into his tired body.

A deep, rumbling voice broke the night. "Get back in your car, boys. This is not an area for you to play in."

The Guardian.

Relief swept McCallister.

"Where's your car?" he whispered.

"Two to the left," she replied softly.

"We ain't got no beef with you, man," an unfamiliar, rough-edged voice called back.

"Let's keep it that way. Good evening, gentlemen."

The men murmured for a moment then seemed to reach a consensus. The footsteps retreated and McCallister caught the squeak of springs as they returned to their car. The doors shut and they drove slowly away.

"What the hell trouble are you in now, McCallister?"

Strong hands hauled him to his feet. He shrugged them away and sucked in a deep breath, grateful his equilibrium returned quickly.

"Guardian," he said with a nod.

The big black man lifted Sheridan with much more gentleness, and she gifted him with a thankful smile.

Made his damn fangs hurt.

He unclenched his jaw.

"Nothing for you to be concerned with, Guardian. I'll take care of it."

"Uh-huh. The Brigade wants to talk to your lady friend about Ernest."

"No."

The man's grin flashed white in the shadows. "Yeah, figured you'd say that. Tell me what happened."

"I don't know but I'm trying to find out." He knew they would not be able to leave unless the Guardian allowed them to. "All I know is Barrett's involved. He killed Ernest."

"You're sure?"

"Paxton Barrett killed him," Sheridan said. "I watched him, though I didn't know what was going on until it was too late. It was a message." She shivered.

The Guardian shifted his attention to her, and McCallister felt her shrink away from the ebony gaze. Her fingers curled into his, and she tried to squeeze herself into him. He sighed and wrapped his arm around her.

"What kind of message? And to whom?" Guardian asked.

McCallister shook his head. "I'll give you and the Brigade a full report when I have it."

The taut silence stretched long and tense until the Guardian gave one sharp nod. "Before you deal with Barrett," he said, "we must have the facts."

The hell with that.

"Fine."

The black man rolled his eyes in disgust. "You always were a lone wolf, McCallister. Be careful."

He silently vanished, re-appearing across the street, once more guarding the green door to Vesper's Bite.

McCallister looked down at Sheridan. She wore a contemplative look and he saw the wheels turning in her mind, trying to put all the pieces together.

"Come on," he said. "Let's go."

"You *are* going to explain all of this, aren't you?"

She dug out her keys and handed them to him, that damnable smile still kicking up her sweet lips.

"Yes."

"I'll hold you to that. Here we are." Her voice held a wealth of mirth.

He looked down at the small VW Bug. "You've got to be kidding. I can't fit in this toaster."

She shrugged and held out her hand. "The passenger seat goes way back. I'll drive, you direct." She lifted a brow. "Unless you have another way to get there? Where's your car?"

McCallister growled. He hated giving up control, especially in the driver's seat. "It's at home." He dropped the keys in her hand then swept her against him and covered her mouth with his. He kissed her hard, taking in her surprise, her small moan then the warmth of her hands when she clutched his neck.

He'd sought to prove his dominion over her and instead found himself drowning in her Essence.

He pulled away and stared into her brilliant blue eyes. "Fine," he said. "You drive."

CHAPTER SIX

"Jeez," Sheridan muttered as she pulled up to the iron gates. "This isn't a house, it's a damn mansion."

McCallister's chuckle was dark and sexy, just like him. Distracting, too. More than once during their drive her attention had wandered, filled with the vampire beside her. He invaded her every sense, nearly overwhelming her capacity for coherent thought. She had serious doubts about his claims regarding vampiric lore— specifically the mesmerizing thing. She just wasn't the kind of girl who got involved with guys like him.

Dangerous men didn't appeal her. She liked 'em sweet, biddable and ... boring.

Sheridan eyed the handsome scoundrel taking up all the space in her car. The only thing he'd have in common with boring would be deep into her body with his magnificent cock.

"Yeah, Brooks has done all right for himself. Owns a few companies. Or thirty."

The gate swung open and she pressed the gas, forcing herself to remain mentally on task. If that was even possible, which she doubted. Tess lurched and purred her way up the long drive. Sheridan pulled into a parking spot just off the side of the house and waited while McCallister unfolded himself.

He banged his knees on the dashboard and his head on the roof. She giggled as his curses filled the air.

"Laugh it up, little one," he said, suddenly beside her, his hand firm and heavy at the nape of her neck. "I'm going to take it out on your sweet ass later."

A rush of sensual awareness sped through her, pooling between her legs and tightening her breasts even as her mind rebelled. "I told you, I don't play those games."

She shivered as an unspoken *yet* filled her ears. Was that his voice or her subconscious?

She hated admitting he'd intrigued her with his questions about bondage. Piqued her curiosity in ways that had her panties in near-constant dampness. Which was weird considering the many fetish balls and parties she'd once covered as a reporter for her college's alternative lifestyle paper. Never once had the action turned her on.

So, then, why did McCallister's sensual discipline threat have her squirming with anticipation?

"Damn," he hissed, turning her to face him. He lowered his head and nudged her cheek with his nose, dotted light, sweet kisses along her forehead. His fangs glinted in the moonlight when he pulled away. "Do you have any idea how much I want to take you? Right here. Now?"

Sheridan shuddered at the sexual threat threading his words. She swallowed and nodded. "Yeah," she whispered. "I think I do."

A flood light glared over them. "Time for canoodling later, kids." A man's humor-tinged voice floated on the air from another speaker near the front door. "We've more important things to discuss right now."

"Screw you, Sullivan," McCallister said.

He traced her lower lip with his index finger, setting off another round of super-sensitive shivers. Her nipples tightened almost painfully against her red bra.

"We should go in," she whispered.

"Damn it."

She drew a deep breath, trying to clear her head from the sensual fog he'd created. It did little good.

"McCallister," snapped a new voice. "We're all here. Waiting on you."

She watched his green eyes flare dangerously then narrow as irritation creased his brow. "Keep your shirt on, Brooks, we're coming." He lowered his head and kissed her, nipping her bottom lip sharply with his fangs.

She gasped and clutched his chest for support, knees weak and trembling.

"You, little one, just might come later. If you're a good girl."

The arrogance of his words took a moment to sink in. When they did, she huffed and shoved away from him, heading for the brightly lit front porch of the mansion. But beneath her affronted irritation, a new sense of excitement built and swirled.

Trying to play with herself last night had been a disaster. His words, his voice denying her had wracked her incessantly. It'd been both exasperating and intriguing. But mostly it just ticked her off.

What kind of damn hold does the vampire have on me?

McCallister caught up with her just as she reached the door, which swung silently inward.

A man of indeterminate age, sporting an immaculate tuxedo and matching black hair, waved them inside. "Please, come in.

Master Wingate and company await you in the billiards room."

She hesitated at the threshold, but McCallister's big, comforting hand wrapped around her arm and gently tugged her forward.

"Don't worry, little one, I'm the only one allowed to bite you."

Sheridan bucked. "Anyone ever tell you the size of your ego is astounding?"

"All the time." He stopped at a set of oak double doors, one hand at the brass knob. "And I notice you didn't dispute my claim. Good girl."

Again, the odd phrasing felt... *right*, for lack of a better word.

Sheridan had the sensation of being mired in sexual quicksand. She wasn't entirely sure she wanted out.

He pushed open the door and escorted her inside.

The room was immense. Like Grand Central Station big. Three separate pool tables were scattered about. A vaulted ceiling towered over them, a brass and teardrop crystal chandelier dangled from the two-story drop. Bookcases so tall ladders were required lined two walls. A natural stone fireplace jutted from one corner near a row of stained glass windows. In front of the crackling fire were several large chairs and a sofa, each the color of cream-tinted cocoa.

Forget Dick Tracy, this place is straight out of The Great Gatsby.

As McCallister dragged her toward the area, she studied the people—vampires?— seated and staring at her. She'd met all but one, however briefly. Leopold with the golden eyes, Brooks, the one with the cool, reserved demeanor, and Sullivan the shameless flirt. He was also the man Bert told her to look up at Vesper's Bite, though she had no idea how the two even knew each other.

That, of course, had been before Barrett got hold of her. Sheridan shivered and instinctively stepped closer to McCallister.

His warm fingers tightened around her shoulder and she relaxed slightly. She didn't want to delve too deeply into why he made her feel safe, but he did.

The fourth man sat at the farthest chair, closest to the fire. He studied her as they approached, his fingers held out to the crackling flames. He looked a little strange. Almost blue, as if he'd been in the cold too long. He wore his silvery-brown hair tied in a queue and she could see the tail end peeking out near the middle of his back. His square jaw was emphasized by a close cropped gray-shot beard and mustache that only served to make his light blue eyes shine like silver. He was burly, broader in shoulder and chest than even McCallister, and he was one big dude.

"Valdór," McCallister said as they reached the group. "This is Sheridan, she's mine."

The firm words made her gasp and she slugged him again.

He lifted a brow and bent his head. "You do realize I'm keeping track every time you do that, right? There is a consequence."

Sheridan ignored him and held her hand out to Valdór. "Hello."

He looked startled and slightly mistrustful, but eventually he dwarfed her hand in his and shook it once. "My lady."

His accent was heavy, even in those two words. Definitely not American. Slavic? Nordic? Viking?

She clamped her lips over the wild giggle which threatened. If she lost it now, she might not regain her sanity. She was in a millionaire's house, who just happened to be a vampire, surrounded by three other vampires and accompanied by a man who made no bones about wanting her in his bed. Oh, and he was a vampire, too.

When had she fallen through the bloody rabbit hole?

"Please sit down, Miss Aames," Brooks said. "Would you care for a refreshment?"

"No, thank you." She started for one of the vacant chairs, but McCallister hauled her onto his lap as he sat down on the sofa. She pushed futilely at him. "Let go," she hissed.

"No," he said pleasantly.

Intensely aware of all eyes on her, Sheridan crossed her arms and sat up ramrod straight. Beneath her skirt, his strong thighs cradled her butt. If she inched back any further, she knew his cock would be just as hard.

Her pussy moistened.

"Relax," he murmured in her ear, pulling her back to his chest. "And quit thinking dirty thoughts. At least for right now."

Gravity compelled her backward and she grunted as his muscles stopped her fall.

He looped his arms around her waist, covering her hands. "Comfortable?"

Sheridan bit her lip, refusing to admit just how snuggled she felt.

"Miss Aames, please tell us what happened tonight with Barrett."

With that simple request, she shuddered and sank further into McCallister's embrace. "I received a phone call from him this afternoon. He claimed to have information about a story I'm working on. I knew who he was, of course. Who *doesn't* know Paxton Barrett?" She tossed her head a little, amazed at her own naiveté. As a reporter, she really should have known better. Should have checked him out before agreeing to meet with him. But, she'd been dazzled by his reputation, his power. To be truthful, all she really thought about was how she could parlay a meeting with him into much more than just information on her drug angle.

"How did he know about your story?" McCallister asked.

"I don't know. I didn't ask. He told me to meet him at Carter and Fifth. I did. Jeez, imagine my surprise when the building went from dump to jumping." She twisted to look at McCallister. "What's the dope with the card, anyway? I looked at it one second it was black and red, the next it showed all kinds of names on it, including yours."

"Shows your connections and appointments. It's a way to ensure you're legit and not some damn Hunter—sorry Leopold— ready to lay waste to the vampire population once you got in."

"Oh. I see. I think. Anyway, I met with him in the Red Room, which by the way, you guys have a wicked sense of humor. I chuckled when I heard it. Well, until it actually happened, that is."

"Why?" Valdór asked. He seemed genuinely puzzled.

"Uh, Red Room. Redrum? Murder? *The Shining*? Look, I had no idea the guy was going to ice Ernest. Or me, for that matter."

McCallister's body went rigid beneath her and not the good "I'm-so-hard-I-could-fuck-you-through-my-pants" kind of rigid. His fury swept over and through her, stealing her breath. She gasped and plucked at his arms, seeking air.

"You're smothering the girl," Leopold said.

The pressure in her chest eased and the shadows faded from the edge of her vision. She glared at him. "More vampire crap?"

"Yeah. Finish your story. I'll behave. Mostly."

She had her doubts and scooted to the side. "I'll sit on the couch next to you so there's no chance of a recurrence."

He refused for a long moment, then grumbled under his breath and eased her down, but maintained a solid grip on her shoulders.

She clasped his hand and continued her tale. "I went in, got a drink from Ernest, and sat down to talk Vampire Dust with Mr. Barrett. He had good information, stuff I'm definitely going to follow up on, but that discussion took all of five minutes."

McCallister jerked and stared down at her. "Did you say Vampire Dust?"

She frowned at the shocked ferocity of his tone. "Yeah. It's a new street drug and it's pretty damn vile. It's killing a lot of people and no one has any idea where it's coming from. The cops are stumped."

Sheridan narrowed her gaze and contemplated him. Her investigative radar screamed like a tornado siren. "Well, the human cops are puzzled. What do you know?"

"Not much more than you apparently. It's killing humans in droves but we don't have any information on it. No leads on its manufacture or distribution." His face clouded over. "I don't want you on this story anymore. It's too dangerous."

She snorted. "Screw that shit, McCallister. No one tells me how to do my job." She'd had enough of that back home in Texas. She wasn't about to put up with it again, even from a sexy hunk of man—vampire—like McCallister.

"You two can discuss that later," Brooks put in. "Barrett?"

Sheridan gave McCallister another short glare to let him know she meant what she said then squeezed his fingers. "Well, what Barrett really wanted to talk about was McCallister. And someone named Callie, whom he said was his daughter."

"Fucking bastard," Brooks hissed, surging to his feet. "He won't touch her. I will not allow it."

"Settle down, Brooks, and get your damn ass in line. Barrett is mine," McCallister growled. "We all know he's been after me for more than a hundred years."

Sheridan's eyes widened and she had to remind herself to physically pull air. "A *hundred* years? When the hell were you born?"

"Doesn't matter," he grunted.

"It sure as hell does."

"Why?"

She opened her mouth on a hot retort, only to find silence. "It just does."

"Typical woman answer," Sullivan said.

She glared at him. "Okay, for now I'm going to ignore that last part about how long and ask *why* he's after you. That man has some real hatred in his heart for you. It's not natural."

An almost oppressive silence blanketed the room. Sheridan waited, looked each man in the eye, but no one would respond. She twisted out of McCallister's grip and rose. Hands on hips, she glared down at him. "What's the problem with you two?"

He reached up for her, but she danced out of his reach, head shaking. "Not until you tell me what I want to know."

Sullivan's laugh was sharp. "You've got your hands full with that one, McCallister. I suspect she'll not be an easy submissive."

"Shut up, Alexander," McCallister snapped. "The short answer, Sheridan, is he hates me because I refused to turn him."

"Turn him?" She tipped her head and pointed to her neck. "Like into a vampire? But he is one. I saw it."

The cop's eyes were haunted, the bright green sheen a troubled emerald. "Yeah. He found a way."

Something in the way his shoulders tensed, coupled with the tight brackets at his mouth, made her want to wrap her arms around him and soothe him. "How?"

Brooks cleared his throat. "I don't think this is the time."

"Why not?" Leopold demanded. His golden eyes blazed with fire-crackling fury. "That bastard is using her to get to McCallister. Don't you think she has a right to know why?"

McCallister's chest rose. "Leopold's right, Brooks. The more she knows, the safer she'll be."

The suave, raven-haired businessman shrugged nonchalantly but Sheridan saw the irritation flash in his midnight-blue eyes.

"Will someone please fill me in? I don't need the entire world history. A highlight reel will suffice," she said.

McCallister reached out and grabbed her hand. She looked at him. Sorrow shadowed his eyes even as fatigued lines creased his brow. His jaw was tight and his lips flat in a line of suppressed anger. Each emotion seemed rooted in the past he struggled with. Sheridan leaned forward and cupped his jaw. "Trust me," she whispered. "Please."

His expression went blank. He pulled away from her and stared at the fire. "In 1898, Paxton Barrett was the only friend I had left." McCallister's gaze skittered to Leopold. "The only *human* friend, I should say."

Another dart of pain crossed his features but this time she didn't dare reach out to him. Sheridan didn't know why he'd pulled away but the slight brought her armor up and she wasn't ready to pull it back down. Instead, she settled against the couch, offering silent comfort by pressing her thigh to his.

"Why was he your friend?" she asked.

McCallister's green gaze touched on her before flicking away.

The grief she glimpsed toppled her hastily erected emotional barriers like wet tissue. She pulled his hand into her lap. She didn't say anything, just stroked his arm until his muscles began to relax.

"I was away for awhile. Five years, actually. My family had given me up for dead. When I returned in 1893, I was changed." His lips flattened. "At first, I didn't tell them what happened to me but my sister suspected. I'm sure the fact that I hadn't aged a day in those five years gave her some sort of idea. She confronted me one night and demanded the truth. By then, I was learning to control the vampire side. I was trying to regain my humanity." His short laugh was humorless. "I told her everything. My father was outside the study, listening to our conversation. I could hear his heartbeat. With every word, it sputtered then sped up until I thought he might just explode. I waited for him to confront me but then a few days later, my brother died in a horse riding accident. The old man showed some genuine emotion for once. Got himself rip-roaring drunk and stumbled into my room with a silver cross and a sharpened wooden stake."

This time when he looked at her, his mouth quirked up just the tiniest bit.

"You mean he was going to try to kill you?" she whispered with horror.

The brief glint of humor disappeared. "Yes. I didn't really sleep in those days. I knew the second he entered my room. I felt him standing over my bed. His heartbeat was fast and loud in my ears." He swallowed again and Sheridan blinked back the tears threatening.

"Stop," she said and looked around the room. She didn't want him baring his soul with all these people just sitting and watching. It was too much, too heart-rending. Such private agony shouldn't be put on public display.

"No," he rasped. "You need to hear it. To understand how serious this is. They know all the details anyway."

Sheridan studied the assemblage again. Really looked at them. This time, she saw the pain and empathy on their faces. They weren't the cold-blooded and emotionless beings as movies would have her believe.

"I was going to let him," McCallister said.

He had her full attention again.

"What?" she asked with a gasp. "You weren't going to defend yourself?"

"No. I thought it would be better for all of us if I was gone. But he couldn't do it. I opened my eyes and told him to kill me. I begged him to do it. Instead, he dropped the stake, threw the cross at the fireplace and stormed from the room. We never spoke of it again. Two months later he put a gun to his head in the same study. That's when Georgette and I learned we were nearly bankrupt."

"My God, McCallister."

He shrugged. "I'm past that now. I worked hard and was able to save our home and some money. Georgette had a knack for the stock market and we recouped our monies. But the stigma of Father's bad dealings and suicide hung over us. Of all his so-called friends, only Barrett remained close to us." McCallister's free hand fisted on his lap. "The next few years passed in a haze of worry and determination. Barrett was there to guide us through all of it. Without him, Georgette and I would have found ourselves in much more dire circumstances. Out on the street and doing God only knows what to survive. He and I grew close. I looked up to him. He was my mentor, my guidance and eventually, my confidante."

"You told him what you were?" Sheridan guessed. Her heart tightened because she already knew the answer.

"Yeah," he confirmed. "His reaction was very different than my father's though." McCallister sighed and looked at her. "He told me he was dying. Asked me to turn him and give him eternal life." Anguish crossed his face. "I couldn't do it, Sheridan. I couldn't bestow this curse on him, my trusted friend and partner. He didn't know the horrors I endured on a daily basis, even ten years after being turned."

She shuddered as her imagination went crazy filling in those horrors.

"What did he do?"

"He cursed me and stormed from the house vowing he would find a way." He looked at Leopold and nodded.

The golden-haired Hunter rose and took over the story. "Barrett knew all about McCallister's transformation, including where the event happened. He went there, to Desdemona's, and begged her to turn him." A satisfied smirk passed over his lips. "The bitch turned him down and told him he was too old and frail for her to waste her time." His eyes narrowed to glittering slits of hatred. "That vicious whore only takes youth who will serve and service her until she's done with them."

"Or they escape," Brooks murmured.

Sheridan's eyes went wide and she bit her lip. Another part of McCallister's murky past fell into light. She wanted to bow her head and weep for what he'd endured.

"Too bad Barrett was more desperate than McCallister knew." Leopold's furious expression chilled her. "That bastard took his twenty-three year old daughter Calliope to Desdemona in exchange for turning him."

Sheridan gasped. "My God."

"There was no God involved here, Sheridan. That vampire bitch is pure evil. She took the deal without blinking but true to her nature, she meant to kill Barrett. She turned them both, chained Barrett to her prison wall and tortured him for a few days. Ironically, it was Calliope who saved his life. She helped him escape but she remained trapped in Desdemona's private hell."

"How did she escape?"

Leopold's eyes brightened and this time his grin filled with grim satisfaction. "McCallister and I found out and planned a rescue mission." He tossed a wink at Brooks. "That's where we ran into this guy. He was on the same mission as we were. We broke her out and set fire to that damn place once for all."

Sheridan was enrapt. "What happened to Desdemona? I hope she burned with the house."

Leopold shook his head. "She didn't. She's still out there and her hatred for us is as strong as Barrett's for McCallister."

A chill wound through Sheridan and she contemplated crawling back onto

McCallister's lap. "You mean Desdemona could attack you at any moment?"

McCallister tugged his hand free and wrapped it around her shoulder. She burrowed into his strength. His lips brushed the crown of her head.

"Don't worry, little one. I won't let anything happen to you. Desdemona is probably on a different continent by now and Barrett is only after me."

"I wouldn't count on that," Brooks said.

McCallister tensed.

"What do you know?" The question came from Valdór. His accent put a *v* on *what* that Sheridan found charming.

I'm pretty sure this guy was a real Viking at one time. She made a mental note to corner him later and find out who he was and where he'd come from. She was already this deep into McCallister's unbelievable world. Might as well find out everything she could about it.

She briefly wondered if Steve would let her write a story about them.

As soon as the thought crossed her mind, she squashed it. They'd managed a modicum of secrecy for over a thousand years. She wasn't about to out them.

Brooks reclaimed her attention. "Calliope says Barrett's dabbling and experimentation is getting out of hand. She hasn't yet been able get into the lab to find out exactly what he's working on."

"Is she living with him? How could she?" The idea of forgiving such a betrayal as the one perpetrated by her father was unthinkable.

"No," Brooks said. "She stays as far away as she can but she does a bit of surveillance when she can. Keeps tabs on him for us."

"She sounds remarkable."

"She is," Brooks said with a soft smile.

Sheridan wondered if he held a torch for the woman.

"What does she suspect Barrett is doing?" McCallister asked.

"She's not sure but what notes she was able to find mentioned some sort of human gene that resists deterioration. Those humans who have the gene seem to be fairly small in number."

"I wonder how he's identifying them," Sheridan murmured.

Leopold leaned forward, hands clasped between his knees. "All humans give off some kind of marker to vampires."

He grinned and winked and she suddenly felt very vulnerable. Sheridan scooted deeper into McCallister's arms. "What do you mean?"

"It's hard to explain but think of it as color coding, in a way. For example, someone with a debilitating disease such as cancer or AIDS gives off a slightly different vibe than a healthy human." He studied her intently, nodding the entire while.

She shifted on the couch. "What?" she demanded then cringed at the defensiveness in her voice.

Leopold shook his head. "Nothing. Just messing with you."

She glared at him. "Well, knock it off. It's creepy."

McCallister chuckled and hugged her tight. "She's mouthy, huh?"

"Very," Leopold said. "Got your hands full with this one. Not like your usual Consort."

Sheridan twisted around to glare at McCallister. Not that she planned on getting freaky with the sexy vampire but she didn't like the sound of "other Consorts." "What's he talking about? What's a Consort?"

"Later," McCallister murmured.

"Now," she replied. Sheridan pulled away but he quickly hauled her back to his arms.

"Later."

Leopold chuckled. "While this is all very interesting, as ancient history usually is, why don't we get back to the subject at hand? Namely, what did Barrett want with you and why did he kill Ernest?" he said.

Just remembering the ferocity and suddenness in Barrett's attack made Sheridan nervous all over again and her mouth went dry. She looked at Brooks. "Maybe I will have that drink now. Don't suppose your guy knows how to make a decent martini? Hell, right now, I'd even take a Cosmo."

Even as Brooks nodded, the door opened and the tall butler appeared, departing as soon as he was given his instructions.

The odd instantaneousness of it all creeped her out. Just a little bit.

"What kind of information did you give him about McCallister?" Sullivan asked.

It was the first time he'd spoken. His light tone held no censure, for which she was glad. He smiled and winked at her. "There's your drink."

Without a whisper of sound, the butler appeared at her side, a tall, frosty drink dead center on his silver tray. God, the trappings were astounding. She lifted the cold glass. "Thank you," she murmured.

"Certainly, ma'am. I apologize for the lack of alcohol, but we didn't have the necessary ingredients so I made you a Shirley Temple."

He said it with such sincerity, she couldn't bring herself to be annoyed. "Thank you, it's fine. Cold and bubbly."

He bowed and disappeared. Well, not really disappeared, just melted away from the light and out of sight. Sheridan slugged down the drink, sighing in delight as the soda coated her throat.

She eyed McCallister over the rim and finally nodded. "When he found out I really wasn't a good source of information about McCallister, and more likely, when he learned I wasn't going to be used as bait to get to him, he became enraged. Started yelling and cursing. Ernest told him to calm down and before I could even move, Barrett was at the bar, flinging bottles and glasses everywhere." She shivered at the memory of how cold the room had become when Barrett went into his rage.

"One minute, Ernest is standing there, hands up and voice calm, the next thing I know, Barrett has his hands wrapped around the man's throat. He gurgled and dropped. I threw my drink at Barrett when he headed my way but that didn't really do anything." Her heart picked up as fear crept through her again. His eyes had been cold, dead. Like a fish left too long on the sand. "He reached for me, put his hand on my neck. Here." She laid her finger along the now jumping pulse at the base of her neck. "He started talking, telling me I would deliver McCallister, that I was under his protection and command because I'd accepted his invitation, drank from his stores." She blinked and shook her head, clearing the cobwebs of the man's voice from her mind. "He seemed intent on the whole thing, so I played dumb. I nodded and repeated that I'd deliver McCallister." She looked at the detective and tried a smile to defuse the absolutely brittle air surrounding her. "I don't think you'll fit in a gift box, so I'm pretty sure I'm off the hook for that."

The tension radiating from McCallister threatened to knock her over. She looked askance at him but he was staring at Brooks who, to her surprise, had a shocked, speculative look on his face.

Slowly, his dark blue gaze slid to her, assessing, sizing, calculating.

Sheridan leaned into McCallister but lifted her chin. "What?"

"You're certain of his words? Where he said you were under his protection and command?"

She nodded. "Yeah, a girl doesn't forget something like that, especially coming from a guy who'd just whacked someone in front of her."

Brooks tapped his fingers on a trouser-clad leg. "Very intriguing. Did you actually imbibe anything while in his presence? Anything he offered you?"

"Yeah, Ernest made me a Zombie and I gulped that sucker down quick." She shrugged. "I was nervous. Just as I had my second, that's when he got all creepy and weird on me. Barrett, not Ernest," she clarified then clamped down on her runaway tongue. Something, *someone* was making her very nervous and her chattering was driving even her nuts.

Valdór, the odd, burly Viking rose slowly and approached the couch. Sheridan held her breath, trying to quell the rising anxiety.

He knelt on one knee, his massive arms crossed over his leg and regarded her steadily. "My lady, 'tis unheard of for an unclaimed mortal to deflect such a powerful vampire's command once you have partaken of his sustenance."

She looked up at McCallister, sucking in a breath at the blank, hard look cresting his face.

"Why?"

"Offering is everything to a vampire. He, or she, offers you a portion of themselves and you accept willingly. Once that happens, you are Joined. Linked. His will can become yours. His commands your only desire."

"Hey, it was some gin and juice, no vampire parts in there at all."

Leopold growled from the depths of his seat. "Bastard probably lined the glasses with something before you got there. Did your drink taste off?"

Panic swelled and beat at her chest. Tiny pinpricks of pain and lack of oxygen made her heart ache. "It was gin, that stuff kills everything else. Are you saying he put..." She gulped and held her hand over her now-roiling stomach. "Blood or something in my drink?"

The silence was absolutely deafening.

"I think I'm gonna upchuck."

Beside her, McCallister stirred. His arm slid around her waist and he lifted her up and onto his lap, cuddling her to him, one palm spread along her back. She felt secure, safe. Her own palm splayed wide against his chest, taking in the re-assuring, if slow, thump of his heart.

Another bit of vampiric lore proven false.

"It doesn't matter what he did," McCallister announced, voice deep, measured and tinged with rage.

Slowly she lifted her head and met his shining green gaze head on. Her lips were suddenly as dry as sand and her mouth twice as gritty. "Why not?"

"I claimed you first."

CHAPTER SEVEN

"You're coming home with me," McCallister said as he crammed himself into Sheridan's lunchbox of a car. "Christ, next time we're taking the Mustang."

She snorted as she revved the engine. "I don't deal well with commands or autocratic asses, haven't you figured that out yet? I would have thought the whole episode with Barrett proved that."

He cupped his knees against the hard plastic dashboard and gave her a half-smile. "Yeah, you're a bit prickly in some areas. But in others, sweetheart, you're perfectly made for obeying."

"Forget it, McCallister."

But there was no heat in her voice. Indeed, he was pretty sure he caught a hint of grudging intrigue.

"So, how do you know all those guys, er, vampires, anyway?"

"We have the same goals in common," he said.

"Such as?"

He slanted a look at her. "Do you really want to know, Sheridan?"

Her cheeks went rosy. "Actually, yes."

"Then I'll tell you. After the Joining."

She smacked the steering wheel with the palm of her hand. "Typical male. Wait, what the hell is the Joining?"

McCallister's nape crawled and he looked out the window. She'd already taken them far from Brooks' impressive mansion. They crested the back roads, littered on each side by tall, dark trees, some of which bent into each other and covered the street. No streetlights, no illumination from the half-obscured moonlight in the cloudy sky above. Just black pavement and the miniscule beams of her VW's headlights.

Crap, why hadn't he paid more attention? He'd allowed them to be driven into the perfect spot for an ambush.

His nerves stretched tauter and he caught a flicker of shadows running across the road ahead.

A haunting bay wound through the trees and echoed in the tight confines of her car.

"McCallister?" she asked, one hand now on his thigh.

He covered her hand. "It's okay," he murmured, but his eyes never stopped scanning the area ahead.

He figured Barrett's hybridized wolves would likely attack at the next bend—the last one before the road widened into a more-traveled space, lit by the county's tall, steel lamps and occasionally patrolled by the local authorities.

"My bullshit detector is in high gear," she said and downshifted the car, slowing slightly.

"Don't," he hissed. "Go as fast as you can and don't stop for anything. *Anything*. No matter what you see. Or hit."

"Hit?" she yelped and again the car slowed.

"Damn it, Sheridan, I don't have time to explain." The road started to twist and he caught the fast-moving shadow as it launched from the roadside. He gripped the dash and slammed his arm along her stomach, pinning her to the seat. "Give it the gas," he barked.

The car lurched forward with an impressive and unexpected response. A *thunk* sounded and the little car bounced up and down as a pained howl shrieked.

More howls built and swirled around them.

"What the hell is that? *Was* that?" Sheridan asked.

In the light of the dashboard, her knuckles glared white and tight on the steering wheel and dazed determination covered her face.

"Barrett's attempt to stop us."

More shadows darted in and out of the trees, some swiping at the car, leaving behind the sharp rend of claw on steel interspersed with grunts and cries of pain.

"Just a little further, sweetheart. Don't stop. Can this thing go any faster?"

She cut him a glare. "Tess can take on anything. Well, except a semi."

Her voice shook just the tiniest bit and he swallowed a grin of pride. She wasn't the kind to back down, she was strong.

For they were about to face, she needed to be.

He had to get her to his house, finish the claiming. Of course, she had to agree to everything, too. The Joining had rules which could not be ignored.

One of which was complete agreement between both parties.

Sheridan had to agree to submit to him, to become his, to feed him.

And he only had a few hours to convince her.

McCallister looked through the tiny back window. Howls rose and fell as they left the shadows behind and he watched until they no longer moved.

When she hit the freeway, he expelled a sharp, relieved breath and slouched into the tattered passenger seat. "Okay, you can slow down now. We're safe."

She immediately let off the gas. "Why do I get the feeling you're leaving out a 'for now'?"

"Because you're a smart cookie," he murmured.

"Don't forget it, either, buster." The car hummed as they flew down the highway. "What were those things? They looked sort of like dogs or wolves, but not. I saw yellow eyes. And I swear some hands."

"Barrett is obsessed with changelings. Creatures that are half-human, half-something else."

Her head snapped in his direction. "Are you saying those were werewolves?"

"No, werewolves are a much different society." He rubbed a scar on his thigh received long ago during an altercation with one of those damn beasts. "And they most definitely do not obey anyone, especially vampires."

The car swerved dangerously on the road, nearly clipping the concrete zippers in the middle before she stopped, car drunkenly tilted to the side. She fumbled with her seatbelt, popped the door and tumbled out, landing with a pained "oomph" on her knees.

McCallister wrenched himself from the car and bolted around, just in time to see her toss her cookies. Or more likely, the Zombies and Shirley Temple she'd imbibed. Certainly nothing more solid than that.

He whipped out his handkerchief and knelt beside her, wiping the sweat and tears from her face.

She shoved at his hand. "Leave me alone," she grumbled.

"Shut up, Aames, and let me help you." He cupped the back of her head and massaged her nape. "You've got nerves of steel, Sheridan, but you're not Superman. Or Supergirl, either. You've seen and heard a lot of unbelievable stuff this evening and your body is rebelling."

She waved a hand at the still running car. "Water bottle, back seat."

He sighed and looked, but didn't see anything. A flash of white caught his eye and he dug under the floorboard, pulling free a half-full bottle and passed it to her. She sat up with a wince and rinsed out her mouth.

Cheeks full of the water, she looked at him, eyes suddenly wide before spearing the ground in front of her. She turned her head away and leaned down, the water streaming from her lips.

"What, you can't spit in front of me?" he asked with a chuckle.

"Good girls don't spit."

"They swallow?"

She gasped and slugged him. "You're horrible."

But she was smiling, the light and color slowly returned to her face. He rose and lifted her to her feet. With gentle hands, he stroked over her body, brushing away grass and road debris, assuring himself she was all right.

She trembled beneath his touch and grabbed onto his arms. "Is this really happening, McCallister?"

He cuddled her close, resting his chin on her crown. "Yes, it is. I'm sorry you got caught up in all of this, Sheridan. If only I'd known you were meeting Barrett."

"Why would you have? It's not like I was going to call and clear my plans with you or anything."

His heart constricted as all the what-ifs and near-misses bounded in his mind. If only he'd not been an ass and had taken her when she was at his house. Staked his claim fully. Joined with her completely.

If she'd submitted to him Barrett would never have been able to get near her.

Now, with the process only half-complete she was vulnerable.

They both were.

"We need to get to my house. We have a lot to talk about." He hesitated then tipped her chin up, forcing her to meet his eyes. "To do."

Wariness exploded in her gaze and she pushed away, crossing her arms tight to her chest. She shivered. "You're talking about that damn Joining thing, aren't you? What Brooks was talking about."

"Yeah and the side of the road in the middle of the night is no place to get into it."

But she was building a head of steam and barreled on. "So, what, you fuck me and that's it, I'm yours forever? Christ, you must have a thousand women who belong to you, then. Sorry, bub, I ain't a bunny. Got higher standards than to be one egg in a dozen."

His lips quirked. "A bunny?"

She sniffed and he caught a rush of embarrassment. "A dumb girl," she said. "It's something they said in the 1930s."

"I know," he said. "I remember that."

"You remem—? Oh, for fuck's sake, that is it." She tossed her arms and walked in a tight circle, mumbling to herself. He caught a few words, enough to know she was casting aspersions on him, herself and everyone in the known world.

He let her wander a few more seconds then caught her around the shoulders again. "Sheridan."

She looked up, blue eyes glistening with tears, the corners of her luscious mouth turned down and quivering.

"Relax. It'll all be okay. Let's go home, okay?"

She closed her eyes and her shoulders dropped. "You're full of shit, McCallister. How can it be okay when I'm surrounded by vampires, chased by shadowy wolves, and being shot at by thugs because you blew my cover?"

"All very valid and excellent points. But you have to trust me."

"Why? How do I know you're any better than them?"

His anger roared full force at the petulant accusation and she gasped, grabbing at her head.

Her pain echoed in his mind and he struggled to contain his now fully-roused fury. He sucked in several slow and measured breaths, keeping his hands on her shoulders. "Look inside yourself, Sheridan," he bit out. "You'll see the truth."

He spun on his heel and rounded the car. Over the bug's hood, he glowered darkly. "Get in the car, Sheridan. Now."

He felt her resistance, the lingering ache in her head and body from his tidal wave of anger. But beneath it, he sensed her resistance crumbling. They'd partially completed the Joining so a part of him was within her, though she didn't know it yet. He wasn't quite sure why he could *feel* so much of her emotion, though. He'd never experienced it with any other Consort. But then, Sheridan wasn't just any Consort.

McCallister tried to swallow his anger and focus on the night ahead. He glanced at the sky then checked his watch. Roughly three hours until dawnbreak. Not much time to convince this stubborn, independent woman not only was she his pre-destined mate, but being that mate meant she had to willingly submit herself to him.

Kneel before him and obediently allow him to take his pleasure—and displeasure——upon her body.

How in the hell was he going to do that?

† † †

Sheridan clenched her jaw and tried a stare-down over Tess's hood with her tall vamp but found that didn't work. His eyes glittered with impatience, anger and something she couldn't define but which she felt through her entire body. Her whole soul shook with that indefinable pull.

She wanted him.

No, it's more than that. I need him.

She was in deep shit here.

"All right, we'll go to your place. For now." She cast a glance down toward the darkened road from which they'd escaped. "But you've got a lot explaining to do."

His curt nod was not encouraging. He stooped and folded himself into Tess and Sheridan furrowed her fingers into the tangled mess of hair she sported and tugged with a low growl. Damn him and damn this whole freaking thing.

Vampires and werewolves.

"Give me good old fashioned thugs any day," she muttered and slid into the car. She slammed the door, ground Tess into gear and shot off toward McCallister's house.

His anger continued to bathe her in simmering waves and she bit at her lip. She had known as soon as the words left her mouth they'd been both unfair and untrue.

She owed him an apology, but damn she hated saying them.

"So, are these werewolves like you guys? All urbane and stuff?"

"Most of them."

Terse and curt.

She sighed. Loudly.

He didn't respond.

"Silver bullet types or is that a bunch of crap, too?"

"It's crap."

"How did the movies get it all wrong? I mean, they've got you guys lethally allergic to garlic, invisible in mirrors, compelling us poor innocents with your wicked mesmerism and sleeping in dirt-lined coffins."

"They got some of it right." Curt. Taut. Pissed.

She doggedly continued trying to draw him into a normal conversation. *If talking about vampire lore with a real vampire could be considered normal.*

"Which parts?"

McCallister's green eyes lasered on her with enough irritation to cook a steak. "Dirt."

She blinked, swung her head in his direction and gaped like a fish. "Excuse me? I've seen your bed, remember. No dirt there."

He shrugged. "I have several places I keep it. Boxes, vials, safety deposit box in the bank."

This last was said with a tiny bit less anger and hope bloomed. Her mouth had a tendency to run ahead of her brain. Maybe she could talk her way out of her insensitive idiocy.

"Why so many places?"

"We don't have to sleep in coffins but we *do* need to keep a bit of the dirt from our graves near us. It helps to balance us, keeps us strong."

"Huh." Her mind turned this over and over. "It's in the long box on your dresser, isn't it?"

McCallister started. "Why do you say that?"

"Makes sense. You don't have much in there and it was sort of in a prominent place. Plus the box is locked."

"Good point.

"I have them sometime. What happens if you don't have dirt? I mean, surely not every human who is turned into a vampire is actually buried, right? What about them?"

Another small release of tension from the car and she breathed even easier, relaxing into Tess' worn but comfortable seat.

"It's difficult to explain. I was never actually buried. My sister placed a marker atop an empty coffin for me. When my stone was erected, the dirt became imbued with a kind of ethereal energy and I was compelled to take some. I hear it's the same for most vampires. I've also heard of other totem items being substituted such as clothing, jewelry, and hair. Like everything it's different for each person and it continues to evolve as we do."

"That is just bizarre. If it's not important why were you compelled?"

"I didn't say it wasn't important. It's just not like it's a kryptonite for us or anything."

"That's interesting. Hell, this whole situation is interesting." Sheridan glanced in her rearview and squinted at the overly bright headlights coming up behind them.

Coming up *fast* behind them.

Too fast.

"What's wrong?" he asked.

"Car."

He twisted in his seat, bonking his head on the low roof and cursed.

This time she didn't giggle.

The car slowed as it approached, then darted around and in front of them and slammed on the brakes before letting up and easing forward again.

Sheridan swerved to the right, dropped into fourth and nearly blew her RPMs into the red as she shot past the dark sedan.

She kept the pedal all the way to the floor until she saw a multitude of lights ahead and none behind.

"Why'd they give up?" she asked, thoroughly rattled.

McCallister pulled his cell phone and jabbed at the keypad. "Pull a stunt like that again, you dick, and I'll stake you myself." He ended the call and dropped the phone between his legs.

She peered at him. "Uh, what?"

He met her gaze, his liquid green eyes still fuming, but thankfully not nearly as hot as before. "That was Sullivan being an ass. I recognized his car. Explains why I didn't get any kind of warning, too. He meant us no harm."

Instant indignation swelled in her and she smacked the steering wheel. "Yeah, well, the next time I see him, I just might mean *him* some harm."

McCallister's small chuckle broke her last stubborn defense.

"I'm sorry," she said quietly. "I didn't mean what I said. I was just jingle-brained. Shocked. I know you would never hurt me."

"How?"

She exited the highway and thought about it. "I'm not sure," she replied honestly. "But I know I can trust you implicitly. Know you'd never hurt me."

"That's technically not true," he said.

She was relieved his voice was even once more and she no longer was buffeted by waves of his anger. "How's that?"

His hand slid over her thigh, along her bare skin. His fingers stretched and nudged the lower edges of her crotch.

Sheridan swallowed hard, but remained still, concentrating on the street traffic.

McCallister slowly increased the pressure on both her thigh and pussy lips until she jerked and pushed back into her seat.

"I want to hurt you," he said.

The silky sensual threat beaded between her legs, searing her clit and causing a low ache to begin in her lower lips.

"I want to watch your skin turn red and mottled because I've used my hand on you. Or a flogger. Or a whip. I want to see you bend and arch because I've caned you. Disciplined you. Brought you to the brink of orgasm and denied you the pleasure until you beg and plead for it."

His voice melded with the unbelievably realistic images in her mind and she barely realized in time she needed to turn on his street. With a wide jerk and squeal of tires, she made the turn and bumped into his driveway.

Killing the engine, Sheridan remained still, hands gripping the steering wheel, legs gripping his fingers.

"I want to hurt you until you beg me for more, Sheridan. But I want to pleasure you as well. Torture you with my hands and tongue and cock. Fill every orifice, take every part of your body. Brand you as mine. Forever."

She heard the *snick* of his fangs, was surrounded by the blanket of sexual need swamping the small interior of the car.

God help her, she wanted it, too.

She panted and closed her eyes, then settled her hands over his and pressed him deeper into her wet crotch.

"I'm not the kind to serve, McCallister. I have a brain and a backbone. Kneeling and obeying are not in my blood."

"Yes," he whispered and leaned closer. "They are. Submission does not mean pushover. It doesn't diminish your strength, it highlights it."

His lips found the wildly beating pulse at her throat and she groaned then gasped as his fangs scraped along the tender spot.

"You are the perfect submissive, Sheridan. Passionate, powerful, independent. You will be a joy to break."

"I don't—" her voice cracked and she cleared her throat. "I don't want to be broken, McCallister. I don't want to lose myself."

His teeth sunk a little deeper into her skin, scoring her with a hint of pain. Her clit jumped and she moaned.

"You won't be lost, Sheridan, you will be re-born."

Something in his words shook her to the core and she pulled away, her hand covering his mouth. "I don't want to be a vampire, not that. Never that."

His eyes glittered with a sexual power so deep she forgot everything but him. His heartbeat echoed in her ears and she could smell his arousal.

Taste him in her mouth.

She licked her lips and struggled for words. "I will not be turned."

Something akin to pain washed over his face. He nodded. "If that is your wish."

Sheridan couldn't stop herself from cupping his jaw. "I'm sorry but I want to live out my life as a normal, ordinary girl."

He covered her hand. "You were born extraordinary, Sheridan Aames."

Her heart melted a little more. She closed her eyes and leaned her forehead to his shoulder. A vision of herself as he described burned brightly in her mind and shot to every erogenous zone in her body.

She licked her lips. *What would it feel like to be whipped by McCallister? To be taken? To submit?* Overwhelming hunger and curiosity filled her and suddenly she burned to know. The need to give control to him became a sudden aphrodisiac she felt powerless to resist.

Her eyelids flew up and she jerked back to look at him. "Did you do that?"

His brow furrowed. "Do what?"

McCallister's puzzlement was genuine. Sheridan's heart kicked wildly. "We should go inside," she said.

He studied her for a long, intent moment before nodding. He opened his mouth and she put her finger over his lips.

"No, hush," she ordered softly.

His brow rose and the shadows in his gaze lessened. He nipped her finger. "You have it all backwards, sweetheart. Come on, let's go inside where I can show you just what I'm talking about."

Sheridan waited for him to come around the car and open her door. She loved his show of manners, but more than that, the time gave her a moment to breathe and compose herself.

She fully admitted she wanted him, was attracted to McCallister more than she'd ever been to anyone in her life.

What shook her even more, though, was the urge to go inside, fall on her knees, and let him control her completely.

While the thought scared the hell out of her, it also turned her on like nothing ever had.

CHAPTER EIGHT

"Come inside," McCallister's deep voice invited.

Said the spider to the fly.

Sheridan crossed the threshold of his front door, breath held. She wasn't sure exactly what she'd expected—maybe a supernatural jolt of some sort—but nothing happened.

As soon as she moved past him, the door clicked shut, tumblers rolled over and a warm whoosh of air swept through the room.

His house hadn't changed since last night and the couch caught her attention. Her nipples hardened as she remembered vividly lying against McCallister, her body pressed so tightly to his she could still feel the imprint of his desire for her.

"Sheridan, come here."

She pivoted, fingers running over the gold chain of her red handbag.

"Why?"

His lips twitched. "You're going to be difficult about this, aren't you?"

"I told you so." Her heartbeat sped up as he padded toward her, all power and sensual intention. She lifted a palm and stepped backward. "Hold it, McCallister. We need to finish our discussion."

He didn't stop until he'd invaded her personal space and she refused to budge any further. *Start off as you mean to go on.*

"So talk."

She cleared her throat. "I want to know more about this Joining and *why* you're so insistent I have to submit."

He sighed and his gaze flicked to his watch.

"What? Are we on a timeline or something?" she joked.

His expression didn't alter but she caught the subtle tensing of his shoulders. Her breath whooshed out. "Are you freaking serious? How long?"

"That's not important," he said. The tension radiating from his taut body belied the mellow tone of his voice.

Sheridan sank onto the couch. "If your expression is any indicator, I have to disagree. Talk. Fast. Apparently I have a decision to make."

McCallister settled next to her. He turned his big body so he faced her but didn't make any effort to crowd or touch her. She didn't know if that bothered her or not.

"The Joining is your choice, Sheridan. For all your worldly ways and journalistic stories, I don't think you quite understand the power you have in this partnership."

She snorted. "Partnership? It sounds more like a 'Mongo, do what I say or get smacked' situation."

He choked on a laugh as he raked a hand over his face. "Oh, Sheridan, you are something else." McCallister stroked her cheek and sighed. "There isn't enough time to explain everything."

"Let's start with the basics. What is the Joining?"

He picked up her hand and smoothed his fingers over her knuckles. The small caress felt good. Sheridan realized it was also helping her relax.

"In the normal course of things, when a vampire takes a human Consort, it's a mutually beneficial agreement. The human is gifted with a small portion of their patron's strengths."

Sheridan squirmed on the sofa. "What sort of strengths? What does the vampire get in exchange?"

McCallister squeezed her hand. "Each vampire has a different skill set. We don't really know why but I think it has to do with who their *Sator* was."

"*Sator*? What's that?"

McCallister's brow wrinkled. "Uh, closest thing to an explanation is their sire, I guess. A *Sator* is the vampire who turns a human into a vampire."

Sheridan mentally cringed. She wasn't ready to think about that. "What strengths do you have?"

He shrugged. "Speed, hearing, and, to some extent, a sort of psychic ability. I can hear thoughts sometimes but that really depends on the Consort."

She sat up."Really? Hearing the thoughts of others. Boy, could I use that when I'm talking to an informant. I'd never get shafted again."

He laughed. "It's not a guarantee, Sheridan."

"Well, damn. That sucks."

"Sorry."

"You don't sound sorry." She took a deep breath. Her nerves clamored as loud as marbles in a tin can. "So, what do you get from me?"

His fingers tightened as his expression turned a little dark, almost sorrowful. "Life."

The simple word hit her with the force of a two-ton truck. She reeled backward and flopped to the sturdy couch back. She understood, of course. Everyone knew that vampires had to drink human blood in order to survive. Hearing the reality of it, though, was something of a shock.

"Oh." Brilliant response, but the best she could do.

McCallister pulled her to him, nestling her against his side. He brushed his lips over the top of her head. "I wish it were different, Sheridan. I wish I could tell you something magical would happen but it doesn't. Humans feed vampires and keep us alive."

She looked up at him. The pain on his face went back hundreds of years. She cupped his jaw. "I understand." She grinned weakly. "Hey, finally, the movies got something right."

He smiled. "Yeah, imagine that."

Being the reporter she was, another question reared its head. "If *any* human will do, then why is it so important that it's *me* who feeds you?"

He winced. "You're right about any human. In our world, the more human blood we drink, the slower we age from the time of our turning. Any human Consort will give a vampire that necessary life."

"Which doesn't answer my question at all, but brings up another one—how old were you when you were turned?"

His face went granite. She didn't have to be observant to read the sudden "Do Not

Trespass" signs he'd thrown up around himself.

She held up a hand. "Okay, okay, question withdrawn. Back to the original. Why me?"

"Sorry," he muttered.

This time he actually sounded contrite.

"Well, it's nice to know even vampires can get touchy."

He snorted and tugged on her hair. "I don't have all the reasons why you're so important, Sheridan. I only know that you are. Whatever Barrett knows about you is driving him. I don't want you hurt. By fully becoming my Consort, I can protect you. He can't have you."

She frowned. His words sounded too carefully chosen, as if he were omitting something of great importance. Or that could just be her own building hysteria hearing things. "But if he did get a hold of me? Could he turn me into a vampire?"

McCallister hugged her tighter. His heart beat as hard as a runaway bull. "No," he whispered. "You will be under my protection and he can't break that to turn you." His chest expanded as he took a deep breath.

Uh-oh. "What aren't you telling me?"

McCallister caressed her cheek again, then cupped her shoulder before sliding his hand down her back. Each touch sent shivers of awareness and safety through her. Despite the seriousness of their discussion, she felt herself relaxing more and more.

"He can't turn you, but he can kill you."

She bolted up and away from him. "That's so not reassuring."

His face was shadowed by regret. "I know. But all I can tell you is that I'll protect you with my life."

Sheridan slumped back down. Confusion and defiance fought for dominance inside her. She should walk away from the entire situation. Wash her hands of McCallister, Paxton Barrett and the lot of vampires.

Her soul chilled at the thought, nearly paralyzing her with fear. She was already in too deep. She had to see this to the end, no matter what end that was.

Sheridan had no rationalization for her feelings but a soul-deep certainty propelled her forward.

A tiny whisper echoed behind her, she turned behind her but no one was there. The words came again, softly whispered but strong and insistent. She concentrated on them but they made no sense.

"What's wrong?" he asked.

She frowned up at him. "I don't know. I heard something. Like a soft voice talking behind me."

He tensed. "What did you hear?"

"I'm not sure. It's weird but they sounded like a foreign language."

His body went ramrod straight.

She grabbed at him and leaned back. "You know what it is, don't you? What I heard?"

His emerald eyes shuttered. "It's not possible."

"You keep saying that, McCallister," she muttered. "Two days ago, *I* didn't think vampires were possible."

"Good point."

"Yeah, I'm full of 'em. What did it say? And who said it?"

"I don't know who's whispering you. It's very rare."

Sheridan frowned. "Whispering to me?"

"No," McCallister said. "Not *to* you. Just the barest hint of sound in your head." He studied her like a bug under a microscope. He looked like he was fighting an internal battle and wasn't happy about it. Finally, he cursed and exhaled sharply. "Sine Qua Non."

Her eyes widened and she gasped, grabbing for his shirt. "Yes," she yelped. "Yes. That's what I heard."

He closed his eyes and leaned back against the couch, shaking his head. "What the hell?"

Sheridan tugged on his shirt. "That's what I want to know."

McCallister shifted on the sofa and drummed his fingers on his thigh. He looked a little uncomfortable. "In our world, I've always heard stories about something called Sine Qua Non. I always thought it was bullshit thought up by desperate vampires to snare the woman they lusted for."

Her lips twitched.

McCallister slid closer and took her hand. His long fingers tangled with hers and squeezed. Heat spread up her arm and across her chest in a slow and sensual crawl. The air grew heavy with anticipation.

"You see, Sine Qua Non is supposed to be the calling card of a vampire's soul mate."

"Soul mate," she said on a low gasp. His fingers tightened and she gripped back, needing the stability of his strong presence. "What do you mean?"

His smile was gentle. "Exactly what I said. If a vampire recognizes the Sine Qua Non of another person, they are destined to be soul mates. If the vampire doesn't act on the bond, then he, or she, will wither until they are no more than dust and ash."

Her heart spasmed painfully in her chest. "And I have this Sine Qua Non?"

He nodded and reached up to caress her cheek. "The first time I saw you I smelled it."

"Smelled it?" she asked. Her mind raced as fast as the pulse pounded in her veins. "McCallister, are you saying I stink?"

"No jokes, Sheridan. Your Sine Qua Non is multi-layered and incredible. Lavender and roses mixed with brilliant hints of pink and white lights. I see the strength in you and it calls to me."

She frowned. "Wait a minute. If you thought Sine Qua Non was crap then why all the fuss about us Joining? Don't other vampires do that, too?"

"I knew you were smart," he said with obvious approval. "Joining is a different bond from Sine Qua Non. When a vampire takes a companion, there is some sharing that goes on but it's not to the extent that a soul mate bond will create." He smiled ruefully. "Granted, all of that is hearsay since I've never known any vamp who's actually had a Sine Qua Non partner."

"Have you had many Consorts?" She could have slapped her hand over her mouth when the question popped out. She sounded defensive with a twist of haranguing fishwife.

H shrugged. "I'm a guy with big appetites, Sheridan. I've had my share."

She struggled to tamp her annoyance. *The past is the past.* She didn't want to reflect on why it irritated her. She also didn't want details but she felt compelled to ask about them. "How were those bonds with them? Do you still have them?"

He shook his head. "No, my last Consort died over thirty years ago."

"Did you love her?"

"No."

His short flat answer pleased her and that made her frown. She shouldn't be happy he hadn't loved the woman who shared his bed.

"The bond was plain and simple. I accepted their submission, I took their blood. I never turned one, though." He gave her a meaningful look. "Turning someone against their will is very dangerous. It manifests a lot of anger and hate that can turn the vampire into something truly evil."

"Vampires aren't evil inherently?"

"No."

A clock in the house started to bong loudly and he stiffened then sat straight up. He caught her face between his hands and kissed her softly, sweetly.

Her toes curled as hunger revved low in her belly.

His breath came in heated gasps when he released her. "Sheridan, we're almost out of time. The Joining must be complete." He rose and held out his hand to her. "Please, trust me."

She stared at his hand then up at him before slowly standing. "I'll play your game tonight, McCallister. I'll let you bind me and do what you want, but tomorrow I expect all the answers."

Elation surged through McCallister. The noise in his head roared to a near-deafening crescendo of elation and he fought to tamp it back.

She gasped and staggered a bit. She had a pained look on her face. He caught her shoulders.

"What's wrong?" he asked, worried she'd already changed her mind.

"The noise is so loud. It's hard to concentrate."

He was amazed she'd heard it since their Joining was not yet complete. Perhaps it was one more way her possession of Sine Qua Non changed things.

"Concentrate on me, Sheridan. I'll teach you to block it out later."

He stepped back and looked her up and down. Her black leather skirt showed off her long, lean legs to perfection. The tight teal shirt fitted against her breasts like cling wrap on a bowl of Jell-O. He already knew the beauty of her body. Now, he was going to have the beauty of her soul.

"Follow me." He turned and stalked to the bedroom. His mind whirled with all the things he wanted to do to her. To do *with* her.

Too damn bad I don't have that much time. Tonight.

McCallister stopped by the bed and motioned her forward. "First lesson is position."

Her glance jumped to the bed and she gave him a saucy grin. "I think I know that one."

He smothered a chuckle and schooled his expression into serious implacability. "I'm talking about presentation position. It's the first thing all new submissives learn when dealing with their...Dom." He was going to say Master but figured she'd throw a shit fit about it. That could come later. If they wanted it to.

"Take off your clothes, Sheridan. I'm not looking for a sexy show. You entice me enough as it is without being seductive."

"Thank you," she murmured drily.

A grin slipped through his stern facade. "You're welcome. Clothes and shoes off." He didn't wait to see if she would obey. He turned and opened the closet door. Inside, he opened a drawer of the built-in dresser and pulled out a small section of hemp rope, a nylon flogger, and a small set of nipple clamps. He stared at the blindfold for a long moment. The very idea of being in the dark made his skin crawl as usual. Good thing the blindfold wasn't meant for him. McCallister closed the drawer without picking up the black satin mask.

When he turned around again, she was totally bare. His dick contracted painfully and his fangs deepened with the instant, savage need to sink into her.

He fought himself and the urges down.

One step at a time.

He laid the implements out on the bedside table. He ignored the minute tremble in his fingers as they straightened the flogger. Stroking her beautiful skin with it was going to be an erotic challenge to his self-control.

Hell, *she* was a challenge.

McCallister sat on the edge of the bed and motioned her forward.

Sheridan's full breasts swayed with her steps and his mouth dried in response. He licked his lips.

Amusement drifted over her face and she lifted a brow. "Something wrong, Detective?"

Her sauciness shot another anticipatory zing through him. Teaching her was going to be an invigorating experience. She would push back at him every single time and he couldn't wait.

"On your knees, Sheridan. Hands clasped behind your head and elbows up."

The amusement disappeared and a fire sparked in her blue gaze. She regarded him with steady, calculating eyes and he was sure she was going to refuse. But then her knees slowly buckled and she dropped in front of him. Her long, elegant arms lifted and cupped the back of her honey-colored, wavy hair. She tipped her head back and met his gaze.

"Now what?"

McCallister's blood heated even more. Sheridan was a paradox. Her position was typical submissive but her eyes shone with authority.

His palms itched to cup the silken curve of her ass while bent over his knee even as his dick ached to plunge inside of her where he could lose himself completely.

"Spread your knees. Your body will always be available to me."

She shivered and her nipples peaked.

Ah, I was right. The minx is not unaffected

Relief hit him in the solar plexus. Far from having to coerce her, it would seem Sheridan's innate sensuality was going to help him guide her to her own submission.

His mind rippled with whispers of her desire and fractured, confused needs. He picked up one distinct impression—she liked the image of herself being spread and open. Her brain thrummed with words and phrases that coincided with the excitement surging in her body but not enough to get a clear vision. He was going to have to test the waters but at least he had a general direction.

"When we are engaging in submission scenes, you will always greet me in this position." He stood, picked up the flogger, and walked around her. Her head swiveled to the right. He tapped her lightly on the shoulder with the butt of the whip. "No moving. You will be still, legs spread and arms up just as you are now. Do you know why?"

She shook her head.

He tapped her again. "Speak when spoken to."

A small growl echoed in his head and he grinned because she couldn't see him.

"No, why?"

McCallister slid the flogger strap over his wrist and straddled her spread legs, careful not to step on her feet. He bent over and cupped her shoulders. She jerked lightly but didn't break position.

"Good girl," he murmured.

A flare of pleasure rolled through him but he couldn't tell if it was his or hers.

He let the flogger throngs dangle against her back as he slid his fingers down and around her breasts. He cupped her tits and lifted upward with his fingers, tweaking her still-hard nipples.

"I want you spread out and available to me when I walk in the room."

She swayed in his grip and her fingers loosened from the back of her head before she re-clasped them.

"Good girl," he said again.

Another, deeper rush of pleasure. This time soft pink light wrapped the emotion. He didn't have a clue how that even was possible. He'd never experienced it before.

McCallister rolled her nipples between his fingers. He pulled them outward until her flesh stretched before letting go.

"Jesus," she said on a gasp.

"If I want to fondle your beautiful tits, then they're already up front and ready for my pleasure in this position." He scooted back a little bit and squatted down. He ran his fingertips down her back to the swell of her ass. She went rigid.

He heard her catch her breath.

Her butt was round, taut, and as firm as a basketball. Here the skin was lighter and scattered with tiny freckles. He traced a pattern in the small dots and she shivered with each one. "You feel like velvet," he said.

He leaned forward and kissed the base of her neck. She immediately stiffened again. He smiled against her skin and licked her.

She shuddered.

"If I want to play with your lovely ass, then I will." He eased back and gripped both cheeks in his hands and wrenched them apart.

She toppled forward and he had to let go to catch her. Her hands wrapped around his arms and she twisted to look up at him. Shock covered her face.

Lust filled her eyes.

"What the hell?"

He set her upright. "Resume your position. I am not done with my inspection."

"I'm not a freaking horse," she grumbled. But her hands went up and behind her head again. "Not to mention, this shit hurts. Do you have any idea how much agony my leg muscles are in right now?"

He ignored her complaint. He was much more interested in why she'd nearly fallen over. "That was a strong reaction, Sheridan." He looked down at her ass. She clenched so tightly he saw deep dimples in her buttocks. He slapped lightly and she gasped as she swayed forward. "Relax. Your ass is my property as much as your lovely tits and hot pussy."

White-hot lust ramrodded him. Pink explosions of demand, desire and denial all coalesced in his brain. McCallister strained to separate her emotions from his.

How am I supposed to Dom her if she keeps knocking me off-kilter? He was surprised by the strength of her will. He'd never encountered anyone as strong in all the years he'd been alive. *And dead.*

He forced her desire back and cupped her butt again. This time, he slowly spread her and let his fingers dip into the valley of her ass.

"McCallister," she said on a groan.

His cock was so hard he could have hammered nails with it. The aching tone of her voice reached around and squeezed him by the balls which shot to the head of his dick. Pre-cum leaked out.

He nuzzled her neck again. "Sheridan, have you ever been fucked in the ass?" The guttural question thrilled him. He loved talking dirty. Loved the way words like fuck, ass, pussy and cunt sounded in the sensual atmosphere.

Her butt clenched in his hands. She remained quiet.

The buzz of her emotions spiked and ebbed as if she were trying to control them.

McCallister scraped his front teeth along the soft part of her shoulder. "Sheridan? I asked you a question."

Goosebumps rose where his mouth touched and her heart picked up speed. The steady thumping turned into the rapid tattoo of a 40-yard dash.

"Yes," she whispered.

He blinked. He hadn't expected that. "Did you like it?"

Another pause. "Yes," she said.

His cock surged upward and nudged her spine.

She let out a gasping laugh. "Guess you liked that answer, huh?"

He let go of her ass and petted her soft butt cheeks. "You could say that. I wish I had time to stretch you out tonight, but I don't." He glanced at his watch and cursed. Only two hours left before midnight. For both their sakes, he had to get this done before twelve. They would be too vulnerable afterward.

Time to pick up the pace.

McCallister rose and stepped back. His mind ricocheted in a thousand different directions. He found himself dodging Sheridan's emotions and swirling thoughts, too. He was again amazed at the depth of their connection. He'd never felt anything stronger with any companion.

McCallister swished the flogger behind her just close enough to her beautiful back for her to catch the waft of air but not so close he actually touched her.

Sheridan's head turned.

"Eyes forward," he barked.

She hesitated then slowly looked forward once more. Her spine was taut and her arms shook. He could feel the fatigue growing in her shoulders.

"You've done well holding the position so long, Sheridan. Just a few moments longer."

"Hurry up," she muttered. "Before I keel over, savvy?"

McCallister let the throngs of the flogger brush against her back. She arched and he caught her soft moan.

"What I understand is you've got a lot of learning to do. This is a nylon flogger. Tonight I'm just going to introduce you a little to the feeling of being whipped. It won't hurt much, if at all."

"Then why bother?" she asked.

He paused and considered the question. She didn't sound sarcastic, merely curious.

"Pain is just one sensation, Sheridan. Flogging can be very pleasurable."

"For whom?"

He laughed. "For both of us."

"Why do you enjoy it?"

McCallister swished the flogger again and moved left for better access. "I enjoy knowing you're giving control of your pleasure to me. You are trusting me to take you to the highest peak possible yet I get to determine the way I want to do it." He tightened his grip on the handle and pulled back. "Your pleasure, my way."

McCallister struck her between the shoulder blades, pulled back and brought another blow lower.

She arched and her hands fell to her knees. Her head bowed and he saw the shivers wracking her lush body. The aura around her flared hot pink then exploded into white light and the floral scent of her Sine Qua Non crawled up and around him, grabbing him in a fierce vise grip of need.

"Hands up," he barked.

The blue-eyed glare she shot him was as poisonous as a Cobra's venom yet she couldn't hide her excitement from him. Gone were the darts of pleasure. They'd been replaced by giant, sledgehammer swings of lust and desire.

"Keep your head up and still," he ordered. "I'm going to walk around you. You'll taste the flogger on every inch of your delectable body before we move on. Not a word, Sheridan." He flicked her buttocks. She tensed but didn't drop her hands or make any comments. "Good girl."

A rush of pink-tinged happiness blew through him. The sensation was immediately followed by a confused mish-mash and the haunting refrain, "*What am I doing?*"

He wanted to reassure her, but didn't. He needed to gain absolute control of her and babying her would not be productive.

McCallister twirled the flogger and ran its soft throngs up and down her back, her thighs and the soles of her feet.

Her toes clenched tight and caught some of the polyester strands. She let go when he tugged and McCallister made a mental note to explore just how ticklish she was later.

He moved to her left and trailed the flogger up and down her sides and her arms. The whip motion never ceased as he walked around her. He didn't want to give her even an instant to breathe.

He was barraging her with sensation after sensation. When he stepped in front of her, she tipped her eyes up and met his gaze head on. Sapphire fire flickered wildly in her eyes. Panting lightly through her luscious, full lips, he saw her nostrils flare even as a pink blush crawled along her cheeks.

McCallister kept his eyes locked on hers as he flicked the flogger at her tummy. She flinched but otherwise remained still. He increased the speed and force of the blows and moved the licks up her abdomen until he reached her breasts. Her nipples strained outward in tight points hard enough to cut glass. Once more he upped the strength behind the blows. Soft red streaks appeared on her tits. Her nipples hardened even more and she sucked her bottom lip between her teeth.

More. Harder.

His stroke faltered at her demand for a half-second before his own lust burst forward. He drew back and swung the flogger harder and harder. Each blow scored her beautiful skin and the soft whisper of the throngs exploded with sharp raps of thunder.

Her eyelids lowered to half-mast and her chest heaved. McCallister could smell the sweet gathering of her juices and knew she was close to coming.

Fierce happiness pierced him. It was exactly what he wanted.

He twisted his hand and laid the flogger with lighter force along her right side and the underside of her arm. She moaned and tried to twist her body.

McCallister immediately stopped flogging. He dropped the whip to the floor.

Her eyes widened. "Why did you stop?" she asked with sharp, staccato breaths.

"You were too close to coming."

The blush deepened and she lowered her gaze to the floor. "I know."

The confession sounded like it came from the very depths of her confused soul. McCallister knew he'd made a major breakthrough.

"You want me to flog you until you come?"

She shrugged then cleared her throat. "Maybe?"

He picked up the nipple clamps. "Not your choice. Stand up."

Her mouth tightened but she rose. Her body was awash with stripes and splotches in degrees of red. McCallister traced a line around the tip of her right breast.

She leaned into the soft touch and he wondered if she'd realized she'd done so.

"Lift your tits."

Again a small hesitation, even tinier than the last one. Hands cupping her tits, she offered them to him. McCallister bent and took her right nipple in his mouth.

"Oh, fuck," she moaned and pushed against his lips.

He flicked her pink nipple with his tongue then bit lightly. She shuddered.

He pulled back and took a second to admire the gleaming wetness of her flesh before bringing the clamp up and around her nipple. He tightened the screw until he could let go of the weight and it hung from her round breasts.

"McCallister," she said with a gasp. "What are you doing?"

"Attaching nipple clamps," he said then bent his head to lave her other breast.

"I know what they are," she muttered. "God, I never knew how they felt, though."

He pulled back and slipped the clamp around her nipple and tightened it. "What's it feel like?"

"Like your hand is perpetually around my skin. Squeezing with no relief." She shifted her feet and her fingers drummed along the bottom of her tits where she still cupped them. "It's sort of like little ants running pell mell across my skin but in a frustrating, almost-pleasurable kind of way."

He grinned. "Let go and shake your shoulders."

Slowly her hands released her tits and she moved her shoulders. The motion was small but effective. "Holy crap," she whispered.

"Better?"

Her smile was a bit surprised. "Yes and no. The pressure is greater and the sensation deeper but it's still frustrating. I feel like I'm just on the edge of something but can't get over."

"Good to know."

"Why?"

He tapped her nose. "You'll find out soon enough."

A quick check of his watch showed he had roughly an hour to complete their Joining.

Damn it. I want to take my time with her.

He silently promised both of them the next time would be a slow, sensual torture that would leave them exhausted and sated.

"Remember the other day when I told you not to come?"

The bemused happiness left her face. Her glare was dark and indignant. "Yes. Not cool."

"I thought it was fun."

"You're a sadist, then."

McCallister choked on a laugh. "This is the last step of our Joining, Sheridan. This is where you give up your control to me entirely."

"Gee, you mean I haven't done that yet?"

"Hell, no. You've been mouthy and fighting me all night long. We're about to change that." He dangled the blindfold in front of her. "Come here."

She scowled. "I don't need that."

"Starting your tally of spankings all over again, I see."

Her mouth screwed into an adorable moue and he felt her rush of lustful interest. That pleased him. He knew he'd been right about her.

"Fine," she finally said on a huffy breath. "I just don't know why I can't watch you while we do the deed."

Sheridan closed the distance between them, crossed her arms, and jutted her chin out as her eyelids fluttered down.

McCallister tapped her nose until she looked at him. He had the odd desire to explain to her just why he wanted the blindfold. Tell her how knowing she couldn't see anything, that she was totally dependent on him and her other senses for her pleasure gave him a high unlike few others. But he wouldn't. He never did.

"Turn around," he ordered.

Her eyes narrowed but she pivoted slowly.

He dropped the blindfold over her head and settled it against her eyes. "Can you see anything?"

"No, there's a damn blindfold on my face," she muttered.

"Two." He tied the strap securely then misted in front of her and waved his hands under the edges of the mask. She didn't flinch.

He took her hand and she gasped. "Damn it, I thought I told you to quit doing that."

"Climb on the bed and get on your hands and knees," he told her. He guided her to the tall mattress.

Despite the mask, she clambered onto the bed with graceful, sensual ease. He couldn't help but admire the lean line of her thighs and ass. She scooted gingerly to the center of the bed and stilled.

As she took her position, he stripped off his jeans and t-shirt with a speed borne of lustful determination. His naked body bobbed at the sight of her luscious ass and buoyant tits as she took her place on his bed.

"How's this, oh high and mighty commander?"

He eased up behind her and slapped her ass. She jumped with a tiny squeal. "It's fucking beautiful, Sheridan." The huskiness in his voice wasn't the least bit faked. She took his breath away with her beauty, inside and out. He'd never felt such a strong connection to any Consort in his entire lifetime.

Even as the thought crossed his mind, the scent of mixed florals deepened in the room. McCallister grabbed her hips to steady himself against the onslaught.

He was running out of denial about Sine Qua Non. He swallowed hard and caressed her butt.

She started to sway in time to his touch. "Your skin is soft beneath my fingertips." He glided over the globes of her butt to the taut muscles of her thighs and down to her rigid, cut calves.

Must be from all those heels she wears.

Soft little moans escaped her. "I like it when you touch me," she whispered.

He scooted closer until the tip of his cock brushed along her butt. She jerked forward then ground back against him.

McCallister groaned. "I can smell your arousal, Sheridan." He flatted his palm along her back and pushed down so his cock slid along her slick lower lips. "You are so fucking wet. You liked being flogged."

She didn't answer verbally but he felt her agreement in his every pore.

"Are you going to fuck me or what, McCallister?" Her saucy, demanding tone made him grin.

He smacked both of her butt cheeks with loud, heavy force.

She jumped again and her breath rushed out on a long moan. "Damn."

McCallister fitted his cock to her pussy and slowly eased inside. Her muscles were tense and her hot walls grabbed at his head like a tight, sensual fist.

"Oh, hell," Sheridan muttered. Her head tipped down and her shoulders hunched. "I don't remember you being so big."

He slid a hand up her back and caressed her shoulder until she relaxed. "You will take every inch of my cock, Sheridan."

With each word, he eased deeper into her snug sheath. She clamped around him and drew him inward. He struggled to maintain the slow pace. He wanted to drive her crazy so she was on the very edge of insanity before he let her come but if she kept milking him with her pussy, he was going to be the one to go over the edge first.

Again, not something that he ever allowed to happen.

McCallister cupped her butt then eased his thumbs to the edges of her wet outer lips and pulled outward, opening her even more.

"Fuck!" she yelled. She shook her hips and writhed on his dick.

The movement seated the last bit of his shaft all the way inside her pussy.

"There," he said on a deep rasp. "You have every inch of my hard cock, Sheridan. How does it feel?"

"Huge," she whispered then waggled her butt. "Amazing."

He scooted his legs a little further apart and clamped his hands on her hips. "But?"

"It's not enough," she said.

He heard the shocked laughter in her voice and grinned. Slowly, he pulled out.

She groaned and bounced, her breath escaping in tiny little gasps.

McCallister popped the head of his dick in and out of the tight ring of her entrance until she quivered beneath him. Her pussy grew hotter and wetter with each movement.

Tiny pink flashes shimmered around her body for a second then dissipated. McCallister closed his eyes and concentrated on filling her body with his. Feeling every inch of her sweet pussy drawing him in and out and pushing his desire higher and higher.

A soft hint of roses invaded his senses, followed by hydrangea, then lavender. He stilled.

"No," she yelped. Her head came up and twisted around. The black mask covered half of her face but he still made out the sexual irritation in her. "God, don't stop now. Fuck me, McCallister."

The sweet curve of her lips around the dirty words made him swell and throb inside of her. They both gasped and she nodded. "Yes. Yes. Like that. Fuck me. Fuck me, hard."

"Careful what you ask for, little one," he said even as he started to piston his hips back and forth with ever increasing force.

"Oh yeah." She sighed. "Damn, like that, yes."

Her hips jerked and ground hard on his dick and he gasped at the inferno suddenly enveloping him. He was caught in a maelstrom of pink and white lights, the heady floral combination and the wetness of Sheridan's body. Her mind buffeted against his and he heard her continued silent litany.

Fuck me. Fuck me. Fuck that pussy. God, yes. You're so fucking big. Pound my pussy, McCallister. Fuck me hard. Like you own me.

Her internal dialogue paused on a moment filled with surprise and he couldn't help the guttural groan that ripped from his throat or the sudden, savage need to claim every inch of her, inside and out.

He reached down and tangled her hair around his hand and jerked her head up. She arched against him, seating her juicy pussy even further on his throbbing dick.

He swelled and pulsed inside of her. His balls tightened.

"McCallister," she yelled in demand.

"Fuck, Sheridan," he said on a gasp. She pulled him to orgasm with every twitch and pulse of her body. He had the devil's own time controlling the urge to spill his seed deep inside her.

She would come first. That was the way of the Joining. He reached around and cupped her still-clamped tit.

Sheridan's moan ripped through him and he tugged the clip off.

"Ah, Jesus, that hurts!"

He rolled her nipple and kept fucking her, never giving her a second to breathe.

McCallister pulled her off her hands and flush against his body. He wrapped his hand around her chest and plucked at the other clamp.

"Enough," she said. "I want to see you." She reached for the mask, but he caught her hand.

"No," he said. "My bed, my rules. You want to come, you obey me. In all things."

Her body quivered. Her mind rebelled. *Fuck you.*

"I am fucking you," he muttered into her ear. She shuddered again.

"Get out of my head," she demanded breathlessly.

"Do you want to come, Sheridan?" He toyed with the clamp, flipping it in tiny movements that made her dance against his chest.

He continued to slowly slide in and out of her pussy, careful not to break contact with her sweet heat.

She whimpered and nodded.

McCallister pulled the clamp off and she slammed against him so hard, he nearly fell over backward.

"Hurts?"

"Hell, yeah," she muttered.

He brushed the flat of his palm over her stiff nipple with both speed and pressure.

Within seconds, she was panting and groaning but she didn't ask him to stop.

"I think you like pain," he murmured.

He didn't need her internal agreement to validate his supposition. The need in her reached out to him with a force he couldn't escape.

She was the most exciting partner he'd ever had. He wanted to sink into her body and fuck her forever.

His cock swelled again.

McCallister pushed her back to all fours. He re-wrapped her hair around his hand and started riding her sweet pussy with hard, furious thrusts.

His breath came in floral scented gasps and green lights flashed in his peripheral vision. Pink and white dots quickly melded with the green. Her pussy clamped down hard and she stiffened then groaned.

"Damn it, McCallister. I was so close!" She tried to drop her head. "So damn close. Why can't I come? It's there. I feel it."

McCallister tugged her head back up. "Ask me, Sheridan. Ask me for permission to come." He slowed his pace, torturing them both with slow, full thrusts that had him at the very brink of orgasm. He stroked her back. "That's all you have to do. Ask me."

No!

She shuddered and clamped hard on his dick.

He gasped. He was so close to coming. "Ask me, Sheridan," he said with a low, demanding growl. "Ask me to come."

She whimpered. "Please?"

He increased his pace and dropped his fangs. He was so close. He didn't know if he was going to make it. "Please what?"

He laid his chest along her back and tipped her head to the side. Her pulse beat rapidly against her creamy skin like a butterfly trying to escape its cocoon.

"Please, McCallister. Let me come. Please."

A rush of colors, scents and pleasure buffeted him. He kissed her neck then nipped her ear. He pulled his cock to the very edge of her pussy.

"Come now, Sheridan."

He plowed all the way into her cunt and she exploded around him. Her inner muscles grabbed and throbbed around him with the force of an earthquake.

Yes!

"Ah, fuck, yes! McCallister. Oh, my God."

As she thrashed on his dick, he fitted his lips to her neck and gently pierced her vein.

She stiffened. "McCallister," her voice was soft and hazy.

Her blood exploded on his tongue in a frenzied conglomeration of tastes, scents and sensations. Flowers, sex, and honey all combined into one aphrodisiac he couldn't resist.

He stiffened and sucked even as he shot his seed deep inside her body. His entire focus was on the incredible joy filling him. He felt whole and strong with a will too great to be denied.

"McCallister."

Her weak voice jarred him back to reality. He pulled his mouth free of her neck then withdrew his cock.

He collapsed to the bed and drew her into his arms. She immediately cuddled into him, her arms wrapping around his waist with a grip as tight as her pussy.

He pulled the mask from her eyes and she blinked at him then smiled.

"What happened?" she asked.

He sighed with relief at the rapidly returning strength in her voice. He kissed her long and deep, savoring every bit of her eager response.

"We are Joined."

CHAPTER NINE

Sheridan woke slowly. Her head was a fuzzy mess that felt like she'd had a few too many margaritas. Except she hadn't had one since she'd left Texas. Besides, she never got hangovers. Never got sick. Never even had a cold sore for that matter.

"Good, you're awake."

McCallister's deep voice sounded from her right. She cracked an eyelid and turned her head to stare at him.

He hadn't changed. Tall, sexy, and still as mysterious as the moment she'd met him. The only difference was now she knew what a fantastic sexual arsenal the man had at his disposal. Not to mention, he knew how to use every erotic weapon in ways she doubted any other person on earth could even imagine.

"Hi."

She cringed. *Hi? Seriously? What, are you, in junior high?*

His lips twitched and she opened her other eye before slowly sitting up.

When his gaze dropped and his expression grew dark with hunger, she looked down and found herself naked as a jaybird. She grabbed the sheet and hauled it to her neck.

My neck.

Gingerly, she touched the spot where he'd bitten her. *Fed from her.* The entire surreal situation was still unbelievable.

"I told you to stay out of my head," she muttered. "Where are my clothes?"

"In the washer."

She groaned. "You put leather in the washing machine? Good God, McCallister, who taught you how to do laundry?" She pushed the pillows to the headboard and scooted up against them, careful to keep the sheet at chin level.

"I figured it out on my own. Of course, I had a ton of pink socks and briefs for about a year before I realized I should separate clothes."

His grin was infectious and she tried to keep herself from responding.

No such luck. He was irresistible.

Sheridan winked. "As I recall, last night you weren't wearing any underwear."

His nostrils flared. "Mmm, so I wasn't."

McCallister wasn't the only one getting turned on. Memories of the night before flooded her mind and within seconds, her pussy was equally drenched.

"Oh, damn, don't do that," he said. He checked his watch and grimaced. "I have twenty minutes to get to work and it's a twenty-five minute drive."

Sheridan's eyes widened. "Work. Holy shit! What time is it?"

"Eight thirty-five."

"Damn, damn, damn." Sheridan looked down at the sheet then back at him. "I was supposed to be at work at eight. Steve's going to be worried and then, when he finds out I'm okay, he's going to kill me."

McCallister's wavy brown hair rustled as he shook his head. "Nah, you're good. I called in for you."

She froze, all thoughts of how silky and sexy his hair was, flown. "Excuse me?"

She did *not* hear him correctly. She *better not* have heard him correctly.

"I called and told Steve you weren't going to be in today." McCallister grinned. "You have the whole day to just relax. You can catch up on your soaps or whatever."

She tossed the sheet aside and jumped from the bed, landing in front of him with a loud boob to chest slap.

He grinned and she jabbed him in the chest with a stiff, and hopefully painful, finger. "What a lamebrain thing to do. What in the hell were you thinking? Crap,

I can only imagine what he's thinking. I've got to call him."

Sheridan whirled around but came up short when McCallister caught her by the waist. The naked waist.

Heat immediately flared where his palm cupped her bare flesh.

She tried to push her response away but it was difficult. All she could feel was McCallister. He surrounded her and made her thinking less than clear.

She shook off his hand and stepped out of reach. When he started to follow, she raised her palm. "Stay there."

"Even after last night, you still think you're in charge?" he asked.

Humor lit his eyes and threaded his voice.

She scowled. "This is different. Besides, last night was an anomaly. I couldn't help doing what you wanted because I really wanted to come. You used my body against me."

His smile widened.

"Oooh, you are maddening. Where's my phone?"

She stomped from the room. Unlike the night before, when he appeared directly behind her, she knew.

That knowledge made a cold chill break out on her shoulders. She didn't want to think about *how* she knew.

Her purse was on the table and she snatched it up, riffling through the small compartment until she found her phone.

"Sheridan," McCallister said.

She turned as she put the cell to her ear. "Just a minute," she whispered to him. "I have to fix this."

"Steve Dennison."

"Steve, hi!" Sheridan interjected as much enthusiasm and pep into her voice as a high school cheerleader.

"Aames? I thought you were taking the day off."

Her mouth dropped open and she glared at McCallister who shrugged.

His hair was now tied back in a ponytail, making the angles of his jaw and chin more prominent.

She shook her head and looked away. Now was not the time for distractions, regardless of the big, sexy package they came in.

Her pussy clenched. Her teeth followed.

"No," she bit out. "I am not taking the day off. There was a miscommunication. I'll be in the office by ten."

"Are you sure?" Steve sounded dubious. "I agreed with McCallister that you needed some downtime after what happened with that shooting."

"You agreed with him?" She worked to keep her incredulity out of her voice. Apparently, she didn't do a good job.

"Yeah," Steve said defensively. "He's a cop, Sheridan. You should listen to him. Take some time off. I can re-assign the story to—"

She stiffened and spun back around, shooting daggers at McCallister. "Oh. Hell. No. You are not giving my story away, Steve. I don't need a break and I sure as hell don't need to be coddled. I'll be there in thirty minutes." She snapped the phone closed before he could protest again.

"You're safer here," McCallister said softly.

"I'm a grown woman, I know how to use a gun and I have a taser. I'm good."

She was so angry right now completing sentences was a major accomplishment. "This was a mistake, McCallister." Pain dropped in rivets down her spine. She rubbed at her back. "Don't get me wrong, the sex was great. Hell, it was awesome. I don't mind telling you it was the best sex I ever had since I doubt your ego could get much bigger. But it's done now. Over with. One night, that's it."

A loud whistle started in her ears, growing in strength and intensity until the pain forced her to her knees.

Suddenly, McCallister was in front of her. His hands cupped her head and the noise lessened.

"Sheridan, focus on me."

His voice warbled to her through layers of the cotton in her ears. She stared at his mouth like a lifeline.

"Concentrate on me," he said. "Think of me. My face. My arms. Holding you."

She struggled to form the images. When she finally re-created the final scene from the night before, when he held her in his arms and kissed her softly, the noise abated. Ceasing as suddenly as it'd begun.

She squeezed her eyes against the tears that now threatened.

He hauled her into his arms. A fine tremor wracked him.

Sheridan tipped her head back. "What's wrong? What was that?"

His jaw pulsed and his crisp apple green eyes shone brightly with the eerie internal light. He looked like he was struggling to contain...something.

"We are Joined, Sheridan. A part of one another. Denying it, ignoring it, threatens our bond."

Brushing away the tears, she sniffled loudly. "You didn't mention that."

"Are you sure? It's kind of important."

She glared up at him. "Yeah, I'm positive." But she wasn't. Not really. Ever since meeting the vampire detective, her mind had been in a whirl of sensation overload. He probably could have told her she'd be queen of Norway at some point and she doubted she'd remember. "I think you need to tell me every single thing of this Joining."

He looked at his watch again. "Tonight, I'll tell you everything."

"But—"

He laid a finger over her lips. "I promise, Sheridan. I'll tell you everything."

She sighed, realizing she didn't have a choice. McCallister was as stubborn as she was. "Are you going to tell me what you just did to stop that noise?"

He wiped away a stray tear. The light in his eyes had lessened but the green glow was still pretty strong. "I didn't do anything, sweetheart. You did it all. I just gave you something to focus on." He rubbed her back lightly. "If it happens again, hell if *anything* like that happens again, do the same thing. Concentrate on us and you should be able to block whatever it is."

His big palm sweeping up and down her back felt heavenly. She still frowned. "Wait a sec, are you saying that someone is going to try and invade my mind? Someone besides you?"

His expression tightened. "It shouldn't be possible now that we're Joined. I'm just telling you as a precaution. You have my protection, Sheridan. You're not invincible, but you're stronger than you were."

"Huh."

McCallister lightly slapped her butt. "That doesn't mean you can go out and do something foolish."

"Wouldn't think of it," she assured him.

"Bullshit," he countered. "You just did."

She laughed. "Guilty." Sheridan pulled away from him. "I need to borrow some clothes so I can drive home. Don't wanna do it naked, you know."

McCallister remained tense for a moment before she felt him relax. "Naked looks good on you, sweetheart. In fact, I'm going to go ahead and say whenever we're home alone, you should be naked." He grinned. "Yeah, starting tonight."

"Wait a sec, who said I was coming back here tonight? I have a place of my own, you know."

"I know, but I'm not done exploring you." His mouth quirked upward. "Please come back tonight, Sheridan."

It was the please that got to her. She had a feeling he didn't use the word often. McCallister definitely demanded, expected, and commanded instead of requested.

"Okay," she said and smiled up at his surprised start.

His eyes darkened and a languid, lush desire built between her legs. Sheridan inhaled sharply and leaned into him, lifting her head for his kiss.

His mouth met hers in a sweet, soft embrace she felt all the way to her toes. She grabbed at his sport coat and held on with both hands.

Open for me.

She parted her lips and his tongue slipped inside. He stroked her tongue, retreated, then claimed her again before breaking the kiss.

She couldn't help but feel branded by his taste, the pressure of his mouth, and the slick slide of his tongue.

He invaded every pore.

Left her wanting more.

Called to her soul.

Sheridan rose on tiptoe and kissed him lightly. She feathered tiny, quick kisses to his lips. Just enough to tease but never enough to satisfy either of them.

He growled in his throat. His hand tangled in her hair and pulled her head backward. "You're a temptation, Sheridan Aames. Do you have any idea how much I want to take you back to bed?"

She ground her hips to his. "Yeah, I have an idea."

"Minx," he whispered. His eyes gleamed as he lowered his head. A whisper of a kiss brushed her lips then traced down to her jaw. He tipped her head and softly trailed his mouth along the column of her neck until his lips settled on the tender point where he'd claimed her the night before.

He flicked the tip of his tongue over the spot then clamped his teeth down.

Goose bumps erupted over her arms and down her thighs. He didn't pierce her but the erotic sensation of his teeth coupled with the soft suction made her knees weak and her desire ratchet even higher. Too damn bad prudence reared its logical head. She pulled back and held her hands up.

"I have to go to work."

McCallister lifted a brow. "After I make love to you," he said.

The sensual words clamped around her with the force of a vise grip and she wavered. *What's a few more minutes? Or hours?*

"No," she muttered. Sheridan raked talon stiff fingers through her hair from sheer frustration. She wanted to stay but needed to go. He might be one potent vampire with wicked control over her body but while they weren't in bed, she steered herself. The niggling fear that he was using sex to keep her home—and safe— refused to leave her mind.

She couldn't allow that.

"Sorry, McCallister, we'll have to pick this up later."

His expression went hooded and a storm brewed in his grass green gaze before distinguishing with a ragged sigh. "I knew you were too clever."

She inhaled at his unwitting confirmation. Blood beat an angry rhythm against her temples. "You need to learn something about me right now or this *thing* will never work."

He crossed his arms.

"I'm not a wilting lily, not a woman waiting to be saved, not the kind of dame who sits on her kazoo and hopes her guy will show up and make the scary go away. I kick ass and take names all on my own. I always have, always will. If this whole submissive thing means I have to become that kind of woman, we're sunk. It'll never happen."

McCallister's cool, steady regard didn't waver. Soft whispers fluttered against her mind like butterflies caught in a net. She pushed them away. His lips lifted.

The murmuring grew louder, harsher, more demanding. Sheridan fisted her hands, spread her legs and lifted her chin. She would not give in. The wail grew stronger. The image of a tower shield, the kind carried by Templar Knights, sprang to her mind. She clung to it, gathered the noise into a ball and pushed back with the shield as if she were throwing a fastball right down the pike.

McCallister whistled and the noise stopped. He shoved his hands in his pockets and surveyed her with a new appreciative gleam. "That was interesting. How'd you know to do that? I told you to think about us."

"That was you? What were you trying to do?"

"Distract you. It didn't work. I'm glad. You can hold your own, Sheridan." McCallister sauntered forward, tipped her chin up and pressed a soft kiss on her mouth.

She pursed her lips and kept them firm. Her silent form of protest.

He laughed again. "You're a tough cookie, I get it. And I shouldn't have tried to trick you into staying all day, in bed, naked and orgasming."

Well, when you put it that way...

"Is that an apology?" she asked, all the while trying to get her knees to solidify and her pussy to quit clenching.

"It is. I understand your job is important to you, Sheridan. Don't begrudge my worry for you."

His soft words burrowed into her heart like ants on a Twinkie. She cupped his face, rose on tiptoe, and kissed him.

"I don't, but don't begrudge me my independence. I've had to work hard to get where I am professionally. You've already taken away my choice in the sex matter, McCallister. Let me adjust to one thing at a time."

He closed his eyes and hauled her into a tight hug. "I'm sorry," he whispered.

She stayed within the comfort of his arms for a long, satisfying moment before pushing away. "I need some clothes."

"I've got some sweatpants and a T-shirt you can borrow."

She smiled her thanks.

He moved to the dresser, fished out a pair of navy sweats and a matching shirt. He also tossed her a pair of socks. "Sorry, you're SOL for shoes unless you wear your heels." He winked. "You just might start a new fashion trend."

"Ugh, no thanks. It's not that far, but it's too far to drive bare-assed." She stepped into the pants and pulled the drawstring as tight as it would go. The large sweats hung precariously on her hips. She tugged the shirt on then the socks. "Okay, I'm ready."

His lips twitched madly and she didn't need any kind of psychic connection to know she looked like a homeless rodeo clown.

"Can it, McCallister," she muttered as they headed back to the living room. Scooping up her purse, she fished out her keys. "What time will you be done with work?"

He locked then checked and re-checked the doors as they stepped into the garage. "Probably eight or so." He pushed the automatic lift button and caught her around the waist as the wide door shuddered upward. "I can come home sooner if I know you'll be here naked and waiting."

She winked and shimmied out of his arms. Skirting the Mustang, she pressed the unlock button on Tess' fob and opened the door. "You never know, Detective." She sank into the driver's seat then popped back out and laid her hand on the hood of the car. "Wait! How do I get in the house if you're not here?"

His grin was what her daddy would have called "shit-kicking" and smug. "Are you going to freak out if I tell you to just ask the door?"

She shuddered.

"Okay, that's a yes." McCallister pulled out a brass key and gave it to her. "I'm just messing with you anyway. We're not *that* advanced."

"My bullshit detector is going off left and right," she said, dropping the key into her cup holder. "I'm not saying I'm all domestic and stuff but I can cook up a mean pot of chili if you're interested."

"Sounds good. I've never had real Texas chili before."

"Holy crap, you guys do eat real food?"

McCallister gently pushed her into the car. "Yes. I can see we are really going to have to have that talk tonight. Otherwise, you're probably going to imagine the worst and craziest in every situation."

She laughed but her fingers shook as she tried to find the slot for the car key. "Yeah, you know us writers. Always blowing things out of proportion."

Tess purred to life. The tall vampire shut the door, tapped the hood, and stepped back.

Sheridan reversed down the drive, shifted into first and left a thin coat of rubber as she sped away. She looked into the rearview mirror and her heart clenched. She didn't see McCallister in the mirror's reflection. She looked again.

His black Mustang rolled out onto the street and she nearly sagged with relief.

"Get a grip, girl." But really, who could blame her? She was just a Texas girl living in a Yankee world and thrown into utter chaos by being bitten by a sexy vampire.

"Everything's normal," she said in a sing-song voice.

The sound snapped her out of the slightly hysterical mania gripping her.

Am I nuts? Everything is most definitely not normal. She replayed every moment she'd experienced with McCallister from the first meeting when he'd saved her then scared the hell out of her with his magical mystery ride to his house to the last few hours when he'd made love to her on a level she'd never before experienced.

"Except it wasn't love-making. It was fucking. Pure and simple." Her nose tingled and she blinked the sudden moisture from her vision. "Pure. A good word for it."

The self-analysis threatened what little sanity she had left. Concentrating on the road home seemed the much better, safer solution. The topic of McCallister, mind-blowing sex, and saving the world needed to be examined much, much later. Setting aside the turmoil of thoughts, Sheridan flipped on the radio and sang along to every tune that played in the ten minute drive to her house.

Once inside, Sheridan dashed into her bedroom and tugged off McCallister's clothes. She left them in a pile on the floor and dug in her closet for something clean.

Laundry hadn't been at the top of her to-do list for a couple of weeks.

"Crap," she muttered. "I hope I have some clean underwear."

She plucked a pair of black slacks from a hanger, paired them with a sleek turquoise vee-neck pullover that sported only a tiny bit of bling and grabbed her favorite black sling backs. Digging through her dresser yielded a canary yellow bra with awesome lift and separation and,—thankfully—a pair of clean undies. Who cared if they were her giant, comfy, period panties? She'd just have to remember to take them off before McCallister got home to see them.

Sheridan dressed with as much haste as possible then ran into the bathroom and brushed her hair. She was debating taking five minutes to do her makeup when she noticed the small bruising on her neck.

Gripping the sink, she leaned closer to the mirror. "Shit!"

Peeling back the edge of her shirt, she stared closer at the two blue pinpricks dotting her neck. She ran her finger over the spots, grimacing at the tenderness and rough scabbing. "Damn it, McCallister."

She grabbed her tin of mineral make-up and brushed some over the bite mark. *Still visible.* Adding more just made the area look oddly discolored. With an irritated growl, she washed the make-up off then returned to her closet. The Metro's offices were usually one of two temperatures— sweltering or frigid, but no one ever knew which it would be. Showing up in a turtleneck wouldn't raise that many questions. *Probably*. But what if it were one of those hotter than hell days?

Sheridan riffled through a hanging bag filled with shawls, hats and scarfs. "Aha! Come to mama, you pretty thing." The long, satin scarf was a mixture of yellow and blue flowers. She could add dangling sunflower earrings and matching bangles and no one would be the wiser.

After donning her accessories, she revisited her image and was relieved to find she looked absolutely normal. *Even if I feel anything but normal now.*

The clock on the bathroom wall showed nine thirty. Steve was going to have her butt on a platter. "I'll be lucky if he doesn't bump me to classifieds."

Tossing her red clutch into her larger black-and-white tote, she slammed her door, locked the house up tight and hauled ass through Boston traffic, arriving at the Metro in a record-tying twenty-eight minutes.

No sooner had she stashed her tote in the bottom drawer of her desk than Steve's salt-and-pepper head poked out from his office and he bellowed her name.

"Coming," she yelled back. She scooped up her lined steno pad—she preferred pen and paper to computers or tablets when writing—and casually walked down the long hall to his office. The usual jaunt seemed to take mere seconds.

"Hey boss," she said as she walked in.

"That was fast. What the hell are you doing here?"

She blinked and sank into the chair in front of his desk. "I'm fine, thanks for asking. Good to see you, too."

"Cut the crap, Aames. Detective McCallister was pretty clear he didn't want you out and about being a target."

She fisted her hands, crinkling the cover of her pad. She smoothed the cardboard out as she tried to form a response. "I'm surprised, Steve."

He glared at her and paced the small area between the wall, his desk and the office door. His hands flailed at his sides as he walked. "By what? That you're still alive? Me, too."

"No, that you just took his word for everything without even talking to me."

Steve stopped walking and turned slowly to look at her. His brown eyes were absolutely huge and shock covered every inch of his face. "He was lying?" The editor's gaze narrowed as he shook his head. "No, he's a cop. I checked him out. He's totally legit."

Sheridan swallowed a snort and looked away from her boss. She wasn't about to touch that ridiculous statement. She knew if Steve had a freaking clue just what kind of cop McCallister was, the presses would be stopped and tomorrow's headline would read something sensational like *Vampire Invasion* or *They Walk Among Us*.

Yeah, Steve liked his drama.

"He's a cop all right," she finally said. "But I'm not in imminent danger, no matter what he said."

"Right. 'Cause those bullets aimed at your head were made of bubble gum."

She shrugged. "I told you, I'm getting close. I have new information, too. This is big, Steve. Something unusual is going on here and we need to keep the pressure up."

Steve leaned a hip on his desk. "I was hoping you'd consider taking a break. I've got a piece on a new lab opening down at Longwood that looks pretty promising. It's a genetics lab doing some amazing stuff—"

"No."

Steve scrubbed his hand over his face then through his hair sending the thin taupe strands in all different directions. "I should have known you were going to be difficult. Fine. Just be careful."

She jumped to her feet. "I'm always careful."

He snorted. "What's the latest word on the drug?"

"Not much, though I'm beginning to suspect Detective McCallister is chasing the same guys I am."

"Why do you say that?"

She rolled her shoulders, choosing her words carefully. No sense letting Steve know the "Vampire" part of "Vampire Dust" was real. "He's investigated a few deaths that present with pretty much the same symptoms. Curled hands, shriveled bodies, leftover husks of humans."

Steve blinked. "Humans? You say it like aliens are behind the drug."

A nervous laugh escaped her and she fiddled with her yellow and blue scarf. "Don't be silly. Aliens. Seriously."

He gave her an odd look and she clamped her lips together to prevent any more idiocy from escaping.

"Well, if he is on the same track, that would be good for you. You two ought to compare notes. Maybe you could help each other out. Think he'd be up for that?"

"Maybe? He's kind of recalcitrant but I'll do my best." She turned to leave again.

"Sheridan."

She stopped at his door and looked over her shoulder. "Yes?"

Steve's face held real worry and she felt bad for not telling him everything. "If you go chasing any more leads, I want the names of your informants, where you're meeting them, and a phone call when you're done, letting me know you're okay."

She bristled at the strictures. Seemed everyone wanted to constrain her these days. She nodded. "You got it, boss."

"Go on," he said gruffly. "I'm not paying you to stand around yakking."

Hurrying down the carpeted hall back to her desk, she wondered at his unusual concern. Steve was not exactly known for being touchy-feely, warm and fuzzy.

She dropped into her chair and grabbed the stack of pink memo notes on her desk. The orange light on her phone glared brightly at her.

Four of the five messages held the same phone number but no name and a generic *please call* scrawled on them. The fifth was a reminder from one P. B. about the promised delivery. She growled, crumpled the paper up, and threw it into her trash can.

"What's up, Aames? Nice neck wear. Trying to start a trend?"

Sheridan had been reaching for her phone but pulled her hand away at the words. She forced a smile to her face. "Hello, Brian. Just looking for a change."

His slimy smile repulsed her almost as much as the sheen of his overly gelled hair and carefully waxed brows. The guy took his manscaping way too seriously. "I got a couple of tickets to a great dance party happening tonight. You interested?" He lowered his head and waggled his too-perfect brows. "It's a private party with some high-profile celebs. Lots of good contacts."

"Gosh, Brian, thanks for the invite, but I have to pass."

Brief annoyance flashed on his face, just like it did every time she turned him down. Which was every time he'd asked her out. She'd stopped counting after ten. The twenty-something had perseverance, she'd give him that. It was part of what made him a great reporter. He was a smarmy guy, but one hell of a reporter.

"Come on, Aames. There's a chance you might get some info on your Dust story."

"How much of a chance?" She wasn't buying this line for one second.

He spread his hands. "Information is everywhere, why not at a sexy lingerie party with models, actresses, and some smoking hot centerfolds?"

"Gee, Brian, I'm thinking having me along will ruin your chances for hooking up with any of those ladies. Definitely better I don't go. But listen, if you do hear something about Dust, pass it on and I'll make sure you get some byline coverage."

He sighed and straightened up. "I had to try. It's going to be at The Basement Brawler on Sixth Street if you change your mind."

Sheridan made a production of writing down the address. "Got it, thanks. What time?"

"Nine til dawn tomorrow."

She dutifully filled in the numbers then laid her pen down and reached for her phone. Giving him a patently unapologetic look, she waved the receiver at him. "Sorry, got some messages to return."

He nodded and walked away without another word. Sheridan sighed as she punched in her voicemail code. No wonder there'd been so many pink messages, her mailbox was completely full.

She listened to the first ten messages with some confusion. They were rambling mutterings of odd phrases that didn't have a lot of meaning and no names she could identify. Each number the automated receptionist recited before the message played was different, too. At the end of the tenth, she heard a garbled sigh and the word Dust.

She replayed it but couldn't pull anything useful from the words.

The next five were all from Paxton Barrett. Each was a little more menacing than the last even though he didn't actually threaten her. But she knew. He'd killed a man in front of her with no remorse or thought at all.

He'd been trying to scare the hell out of her and it worked beautifully.

"Don't forget, Miss Aames, out of sight does not mean out of mind. I'm sure you now understand."

She wished she didn't, but the message came through loud and clear. He was watching. She barely resisted the urge to look over her shoulder. Sheridan swallowed hard and replaced the receiver gently. Her fingers shook like she was in a wind storm.

The phone rang and she jerked her hand back. The display read Bobbi, the Metro's receptionist, and she gingerly answered.

"Hey, Sheridan."

"Hi, Bobbi."

"Honey, you've been as popular as the winner of Bacon County's Porcine Princess Pageant today."

Sheridan smiled. "Come on. No way. Bacon County and Porcine Princess?"

"I swear on my mama's blue ribbon recipe for strawberry jam. You just can't make this stuff up."

"I guess not. Sorry about all the messages, I've been working on a big story."

"It's all right. Gives me something to do besides my nails. Now, who is that lovely man with the divine voice? He sounds like one of those old time actors from England. Just made my toes curl."

You have no idea.

"Just a, uh, an acquaintance," Sheridan said. "He's got information for me. Is he on the line?" She held her breath, praying the answer would be no.

"No."

Thank you, God.

"I'm not calling about him, I was just curious. Bert said he can't get through to your phone, so he called me. He wants to know if you can come down and see him."

She smiled. "Tell that old coot I'll be right there."

"Will do, hon!"

The elevators were running swiftly, so it took only a few moments for her to make it to the bottom floor of the Metro Building. Bert stood at the concierge desk, his green and gold cap perched at its usual jaunty angle on his silvered head. His emerald jacket fit his trim body snugly and he kept it buttoned all the way to the neck. Bert despised sloppiness and kept all the building's valets, porters, and service staff on their toes with his surprise inspections.

He'd worked in the building forever. No one could seem to remember when he'd started, he'd always just been there.

There were a couple of people crowding his curved brass and green marble desk so Sheridan hung back and studied the architecture of the building. They didn't make them like this anymore. Tall ceilings, beautiful columns and delightfully creepy gargoyles poking out from random spots around the area. *Who puts gargoyles on the inside of a building, anyway?*

She wondered what the building used to be before it became home to the various companies now housing it. She knew the Metro took up six floors of the eighteen but didn't know much about the other residents.

"Sheridan!"

Bert waved her over to his now empty area. A thundercloud of disapproval suddenly covered his face and she slowed her pace.

"What's wrong?" she asked cautiously.

"He bit you."

CHAPTER TEN

Sheridan gasped and clapped her hands over her neck. "How can you tell?" she whispered. "I covered it up."

The old man shook his head. "It's written all over your face. You've got the Consort glow."

Her eyes bugged and she bent to look at herself in the brass. "I glow? I'm going to kill him." Her heart skipped several beats as she stared at her reflection but she didn't look any different. "I don't see it," she said. She jerked her head up. "Wait a second. You said Consort glow."

Bert nodded slowly. "Yeah, I did. Hang on a second." He picked up the phone, punched a couple of numbers, then spoke rapidly before hanging up. "Carlson will be here in a minute to cover for me."

"Why? Where are you going?"

He waggled his finger at her. "You and I are going down to the coffee shop where we can have a latte and talk."

He looked disappointed and resigned and for some reason, both those emotions hurt. "We don't need to talk, Bert. I know what I'm doing."

Ha! Lie of the century.

"No, you don't. I'll bet you a dollar to a doughnut he didn't tell you half of what you need to know. He's like that."

Sheridan pursed her lips. "How do you know what he's like? For that matter, how do you know Sullivan Alexander? He doesn't seem like your usual kind of acquaintance."

Humor briefly usurped Bert's annoyed expression. "He and I came across each other in the middle of the night. More specifically, while he was cracking the safe in my apartment."

She gaped. "He did what?"

"Oh yes, Mr. Alexander is a first-class thief. He'd heard a rumor I kept some excellent jewels in my safe." Bert smiled again. "That was back in the days when I was a first class jeweler. Ah, good times."

She smiled in return. "What happened? Did you stop him?"

Bert's lips twisted. "Sort of. He was very polite. Apologized for getting caught in the cookie jar, as it were. Said it hadn't happened to him in quite a while. He seemed genuinely crushed and upset that I'd walked in on him. We got to talking about what tipped me off, the quality of the safe, and what I really had in there. He's a very curious man."

"That's for sure," Sheridan said.

Bert chuckled. "I'm not exactly sure how it happened, but he opened the safe, looked at the jewels, then closed it up tight without taking a thing. The rest of the night we spent at my dining room table trying to drink each other under it and swapping wildly exaggerated stories of gem intrigue."

She looked at him with new eyes. She would never have pegged Bert for having a wild past.

The freight elevator behind Bert dinged and a tall, skinny teenager stepped out. He gave Sheridan a wide, friendly smile. "Good morning, Miss Aames."

"Hi Carlson, how's it going? How's school?"

"Pretty good, thanks. Finals are coming up next week then I'm free for a little while."

"No time for chit chat. We have to go. Keep an eye on things." Bert removed his hat and jacket and stowed them under the desk. His black slacks were perfectly creased and his dress shoes would make the shine on a diamond weep with envy. She blinked twice as she realized her old friend was packing some serious guns beneath his concierge's uniform. He looked in ultra-toned condition.

He shrugged into a white button down shirt, tucked the ends into his pants, and came around the corner. "Let's go," he said.

"Bye, Carlson," she yelled as Bert hustled her to the door. As soon as they were on the street, she tugged free from his surprisingly strong grip. "What's with the bum's rush?"

Bert inhaled sharply. "Give me a minute here, Sheridan. I'm trying to come to terms with all this. Let's go inside and sit." He waved toward a building.

"Inside? It's six blocks down the street, we're not even halfway there."

A smile touched his lips as he pointed. "Yes, we are."

Sheridan followed his finger. BB's Coffee House. She swallowed and looked over her shoulder at the crowded sidewalk then back at him. "What just happened?"

"More of what McCallister didn't tell you." Bert opened the door and waved her inside.

Sheridan stepped through and inhaled the delicious aroma of freshly ground coffee, decadent sweet cakes, and freshly baked cookies. "I'm gonna need something a lot stronger than a latte," she muttered.

They ordered—double espresso for her and a light chai latte for him—then took the last booth in the most remote corner of the coffee shop.

Sheridan studied the old man as he sipped his drink. His silver hair, combed back in a modified pompadour, looked as thick as McCallister's dark mane. In some ways, Bert reminded her a little of Dick Tracy with his no-nonsense attitude and gruff determination. After his third silent sip, Sheridan cleared her throat.

"Okay, spill it."

"When did it happen?"

She thought briefly about denying it. "Last night. Why?"

"Of course. You weren't marked earlier."

Resisting the urge to look at her reflection in the window took all her willpower but she did it. "You said that before. What are you talking about?"

Bert played with the cardboard ring on his coffee cup. "Consort Joining is a sort of commitment, Sheridan."

"Yeah, he mentioned that."

"He did? Well, I have to give him credit for that. What else did he tell you?"

She shook her head. "No way. You tell me what you know and, by the way, just how the hell you know it."

Bert blew air through his lips in a near raspberry. "All right, kiddo." He unbuttoned his shirt and pulled the collar away. "I'm a Consort."

Sheridan stared at the two tiny dots marking his skin. She cupped her hand over her neck where McCallister had bitten her. "I'll be damned."

Bert smiled and re-fastened his shirt. "Probably. But it's not like you think. Vampires are not inherently evil. They have souls and hearts just like humans do. They just happen to have a few extras we don't. Their body chemistry has been altered for near immortality and they've adapted in other ways over the years since they were created."

Trying not to look as shocked as she felt, Sheridan slowly nodded. "McCallister told me the first vampire was a Templar."

"It's a long and involved history. Some day when we have more time, I'll be happy to tell you all I know."

"That would be cool." She took a drink of her espresso. "So, how long have you been a Consort? And who's your vampire?"

His smile widened. "Are you sure you want to know?"

"Yes?"

"You don't sound so sure."

"Listen, Bert, I don't know up from down and in from out right now. You being a part of this whole wacky assed world is just one more what-the-hell moment. I know my name and that's about it. But, yes, I want to know about you and the other stuff you were talking about." She checked her phone. "Steve thinks I'm running down leads on my Dust story, so he won't be looking for me for at least an hour." She hoped. His last admonition to keep him updated as to her whereabouts at all times rang in her head. "I have a billion questions."

Bert winced. "Shoot."

She opened her mouth then closed it. "Hell, I don't know where to start. I don't have enough information about what's going on with this whole world to even get a decent one out."

"That's usually how it goes until you've been around for a few years."

"Great. I hate being in the dark."

"All right, let's start with me. I was born in 1905. I led a boring, ordinary life until the mid-70s." He sighed and smiled big. "Disco was king, polyester suits were in, and excess was the name of the game. I was hitting my second mid-life crisis and boogieing my shoes off at nightclubs. That's where I met her."

"Her, huh?"

He snorted. "I was having a mid-life crisis, not a sexual identity crisis. I spotted her at a little disco in Chicago. We hooked up." His cheeks reddened. "Well, you can imagine."

Sheridan shuddered. "I can, but I won't."

Bert's laugh was a little wheezy. "Gee, thanks. Anyway, Allison and I dated for a while before I even found out what she was."

Sheridan was intrigued. "How did you find out?"

"We were at her house, it was the middle of the night, and there was a commotion from the kitchen. I stumbled in and saw her milking the neck of a young woman."

"Holy shit."

"Pretty much. There was a guy there, too. Another vamp and apparently the one who brought the girl to Allison. We all stared at each other for a very long, awkward, and silent moment then I turned around and went back to bed. Fifteen minutes later, Allison joined me. She turned on the light and asked me if I was leaving her. I told her hell no." He grinned and leaned closer. "Actually what I said was 'Hell no. A great pair of tits beats a pair of fangs any day.'"

Sheridan choked. Hearing such blue language from Bert was unheard of. "Boy, you must have been some kind of player back in the day."

He blushed again. "I never had any complaints. That night Allison explained her turning, what a Consort was and that she was currently without one. I promptly volunteered."

"And then she bit you? Just like that?"

"No, and that's why I'm going to have a little chat with McCallister. She and I talked for days about what was going to happen, what the perils and pitfalls were as well as the benefits to both of us."

Sheridan frowned. "Wait. You were, what, seventy back then?"

"Yep."

"But, but—" She waved her hand at him. "You still look seventy, actually a little younger."

"Thank you."

"You're welcome but that wasn't my point. That was almost forty years ago."

Bert grimaced. "You see why I want to talk to him, huh? Consorts are still human but our aging slows considerably and there are ways to almost completely stop it."

"By becoming a vampire," she whispered.

"No, actually."

"Then how?"

"I'm not sure you're ready to hear that."

"Bert," she said through gritted teeth, "quit pussyfooting around."

"All right, all right." He winked at her. "I can see why you're so good at your job. The aging process for a Consort is slowed by accepting the blood of your vampire."

She jerked backward. "Ew, gross!"

"It's not as bad as it seems."

"I'm sure it's worse."

"It doesn't take long to get used to the taste and it doesn't take much. Accepting their blood also increases the abilities you gained from them."

Her brow furrowed. "Okay, he sort of mentioned that but not a whole lot."

"Jeez, that idiot."

She straightened up. "Hey, we were a bit pressed for time."

"Don't make excuses for him, Sheridan. Not explaining the whole process is bogus. During the Joining, there is a small exchange of powers between human and vampire. You gain a tiny bit of his and he gets his life sustained by you."

She patted her arms, chest, and legs. "He said that but I don't feel any different. Maybe it didn't take."

Bert cocked a brow. "Don't you remember how quickly we arrived at BB's?"

Her mouth went dry as realization dawned. "McCallister said speed was one of his special talents. Are you saying I'm like Speedy Gonzales now?"

"Yep."

"Huh." She finished off her espresso. "Now, that's kind of cool." She smiled widely. "Yeah, I dig that. Although, I was kind of hoping for his nifty mind reading ability. Boy, wouldn't that kick ass during an interview?"

"There's more, though. He might be able to pinpoint you psychically, using your heartbeat as his guide. He hears it in his head all the time and he can find you by tracking it."

"Hm." She wasn't sure she liked that. "How do I turn it off?"

"You don't, Sheridan. Ever. You are now Joined to him until you die."

All the air left her body and she shook like a leaf in a hurricane. "That can't be right. What happens if someone decided they made a mistake and don't want to be someone's Consort anymore?"

He blinked. "It's never happened."

"Never?" She scoffed. "I find that hard to believe. Do you know how high the divorce rate is? This Joining stuff can't be that different. Are there any books in the vampire world? They have their own cop shop, I'm assuming they have other entities, too. A society like that can't be lawless or uneducated."

Bert nodded. "Good Lord, yes. There are more rules for the vampires than any other country on earth. It's actually kind of ridiculous. They are governed by a body called The Brigade which is made up of one

Precept from each of the nine vampire factions."

Sheridan shook her head. "Sounds complicated."

"It is. The Brigade has its own army called the Guardians."

She remembered the big black man standing outside Vesper's Bite and shivered. "I met one of them."

Bert's eyes narrowed. "Out at the Bite?"

"Yes."

He smiled. "That Guardian has been there since the beginning. He's very protective. Anyway, they have all sorts of professions. They actually are with us and around us all the time. Most of the myths out of Hollywood are things made up by screenwriters. I never could figure out why they decided sunlight could hurt a vampire."

"Maybe it was more light and dark representing good and evil, not anything scientific."

"I guess. It's dumb. They get some of it right but McCallister will have to tell you what. I can't do that." Bert rubbed at his neck. "Why did you say you were running out of time?"

She cleared her throat and squirmed until his steady stare. "I got into a little trouble with Paxton Barrett when I was at Vesper's Bite."

He stilled. "Barrett. What happened?"

"He called me. I met him. He wanted McCallister and told me to bring him. I declined at first, then he went bat-shit crazy and killed Ernest the bartender. I agreed after that. He was very strange, too. Kept talking about accepting his favors or something like that."

"Did you have anything to eat or drink in his presence?"

She waved her hand. "I've already been through all that with McCallister and his gang." She frowned. "What do they call a group of vampires, anyway? Something cool, I bet. Like a bunch of crows is a murder. A bunch of vampires is—?"

"Focus here, Sheridan."

Obviously the old man wasn't in the mood for levity. "I did but it didn't have any effect." She coughed and looked down at the table. "Apparently because McCallister and I had sort of started this whole Joining thing, it didn't take effect." She sure as hell wasn't about to tell him that McCallister "claimed" her first. "After that whole mess, we went back to Brooks' mansion. Have you seen that place?"

"No. The Joining, Sheridan."

"We went back there, talked about what happened, then we headed to McCallister's place and uh, you know, finished. End of story." She licked her lips. She wasn't really as nonchalant about the whole thing as she was trying to appear. "He said I had his protection and that Barrett couldn't turn me. Is that true?"

Bert nodded and she sighed with relief.

"But you still have to be careful. He can hurt you, especially if he doesn't get what he wants. Barrett has always been on the fringes of the vampire society. I've heard rumors of his experiments and theories."

"Like what?"

Bert licked his lips, looked around, and lowered his voice. "He's got some yahoo idea that he can become the most powerful vampire ever. Finally harness every power they have. He's also been developing an army of hybrid creatures and experimenting on humans."

She frowned. "I ran into one of those beasts leaving Brooks' mansion last night. Sort of a wolf but on two legs and seriously ugly though I didn't get much of a glimpse."

Bert's eyes widened. "Wow," he said as he sat back hard. "I didn't really think those rumors were true. I just always pegged him as one of those not-right-in-the-head kind of guys." Bert lunged forward and grabbed her hands in his. The strength of his grip pulsed painfully in her veins. "Be careful, Sheridan. Be very, very careful."

She slipped her hands free and gently covered his age-spotted fingers. "I will, I promise. Besides, McCallister doesn't want me going off doing anything crazy."

"Boy, does he have a lot to learn about you." Bert slipped free of her grasp and checked his watch. "I'm going to have to get back. Here's the upshot, Sheridan. You are now Joined to McCallister, to the vampire society, and to all other Consorts. There are rules and laws you have to follow and not knowing them is no excuse. The Brigade is pretty harsh about lawbreakers."

"You're scaring me here, Bert."

"Good. You should be scared. McCallister needs to sit down and go over everything with you. I mean everything, too. All the rules, the laws, the legends, the rumors, everything."

One word grabbed her attention. "They have legends?"

His smile was soft as he rose. "They are the remnants of a great company of knights, built in the era of chivalry, pageantry, and over-the-top codes of honor. They are only slightly different now than they were in the fifteenth century. Of course they have legends."

She really wished she had her pad and pen with her. They walked out the door and onto the street. She touched his arm.

"Let's take this the old-fashioned way, okay?"

He patted her hand. "Sure. And before you ask, when you're moving like that, normal humans don't see you. You're a blur in the corner of their eye, even if you're walking right in front of them. It's one of those abilities vampires adapted to cloak themselves."

"Good to know." She smiled at a woman coming toward them. The older woman—she was probably in her sixties and dressed as stylishly as any model—smiled then slid an appraising, flirtatious glance at Bert.

Hello, handsome. Sheridan's eyes went wide and she gasped, looking over her shoulder as the lady passed. *Did I really just hear her say that?*

"What's wrong?" Bert turned to look, too.

"Nothing." She wasn't ready to talk about that. If she did have the ability to hear voices, it just might have been worth having to beg McCallister to let her come. *Although, that was pretty fucking hot.* "I still have a ton of questions, you know."

"Not shocked," Bert said. "We can discuss it over the next few years. Even you can't learn everything in one day."

She laughed. "I can try." They stopped at a red light.

Bert tapped his foot as they waited for the cross signal to turn white. "I can probably answer one or two now."

"Do you love her?" Sheridan blinked at the question. That wasn't the one she'd intended to ask.

"Allison?"

"Yeah."

"Love? That's a very strong emotion. We are bonded. I know everything about her. She's intensely sexual, even after all these years. I would be distraught if I lost her. Is that love?"

"Sounds like it to me."

"Then I guess so."

Sheridan didn't like his uncertainty but she only had a couple more blocks. This time she asked the right question. "What's their greatest legend?"

He pursed his lips. "Oh, that's a tough one."

"Why?"

Bert grinned. "Depends on what kind of legend you want. There's the one that talks about The Corrupt Apostle and how he's still alive and the head of the Brigade. There's the one about the frozen vampire thawed back to life and about how Vampires are evolving into the perfect human being."

She laughed. "That's an oxymoron, don't you think?"

"Yep. There's the one about soul mates, probably thought up by a hoard of love-stricken vampire poets."

Sine Qua Non. Sheridan fought to keep her expression placid. She didn't really feel like explaining to Bert why she knew all about that particular legend. And how she was apparently McCallister's Life Legend. "Good Lord, are there emo vampires?" she said instead.

"I'd say so," Bert said. "It seems when a human is turned, they sometimes stay in the mindset they had at the time. I've met vampires from the Victorian period who are still painfully uptight. Stoners from the seventies who can't go one day without a toke. Suffragettes from the twenties who continue to rally for all kinds of rights."

He opened the door to the Metro building. Sheridan could hardly take it all in. "Please tell me they have a library. Someplace I can go to read about all this stuff."

Bert grinned. "Absolutely. Ask McCallister. He'll take you."

She hugged the old man tight. "Thanks, Bert."

His arms wrapped around her then let go quickly. "Don't worry, kid. I got your back. I have a feeling you're going to need all the help you can get."

Sheridan laughed as she headed for the elevator. "Oh, come on, what else could happen? I'm protected remember?"

CHAPTER ELEVEN

McCallister cruised down Dorchester Street for the tenth time. He'd been searching for that souped-up Caddy for the last three hours and he was growing more irritated with each pass, so he was grateful for the reprieve when his cell phone rang.

He didn't recognize the number on the caller ID.

"Hello?"

"McCallister? It's Calliope Jones. I must speak with you."

Shock blistered through him. "Calliope?"

"Yes." Impatience slid down the phone. "It's urgent, please. Can you meet me at Brooks' house right away? Leopold, Sullivan, and Valdór are on their way as we speak."

The fine hairs at the back of his neck stirred like tufts of grass being buffeted by wind. He turned his head and spotted the Cadillac easing from the cover of a darkened alley.

Shit.

"I can be there in an hour," he said.

"No. Now, McCallister. This is urgent."

He frowned, watching the purple car slide down the street. It stopped near a flickering street lamp in front of the abandoned hospital. The doors opened and two men unfurled themselves from the interior. Each wore black clothes and hats pulled low, effectively covering their faces.

"Damn it." He pulled to a stop across the street and watched them stride toward the rusted chain link fence.

"Did you hear me?" Calliope demanded.

"What's so hot it can't wait?"

The men didn't even pause as they hit the fence but seemed to melt right through and appeared whole on the other side.

McCallister stiffened so quickly, his head bumped the roof of his car.

"Ow," McCallister muttered, rubbing his scalp with his free hand.

"I know what my father is up to," Calliope said. No emotion, no inflection, no passion. The flat tone pulled his attention from the two guys in black who'd disappeared inside the hospital.

"What?" he demanded.

"Come to the mansion."

The phone call dropped and he cursed as he slammed his cell onto the passenger seat. He wanted to follow the guys into the building but he knew he needed back-up. No way was that happening without a shit ton of paperwork and wheedling. The Other Side thought they had it bad with jurisprudence, but they didn't know half the shit he and his fellow cops had to go through to enter someone's property without permission. A search warrant just didn't cut it.

McCallister glared at the building as he put his car into drive and headed for Brooks' mansion. On the way, he tried Sheridan's cell but it went to voicemail. Her desk phone also rolled over to the auto-attendant and he cut the call off without leaving a message. As he pulled into the drive of Brooks' luxury townhouse on Beacon Hill, McCallister dialed the paper's front desk.

"Boston Metro, all the news you need to know. This is Bobbi, how may I help you?"

McCallister grinned at the professional yet syrupy voice on the other end of the line. Her accent elongated every word into multi-syllabic sounds of lyrical luxury. "Good afternoon, Miss Bobbi. This is Detective McCallister. Is Sheridan Aames available, please? She's not answering either of her phones."

He heard the swift inhalation from the other end.

"Oh my, you sound even better than that other guy. He didn't have that wonderful husky baritone you do."

McCallister's smile dropped like a fifty pound dumbbell. "What other guy?"

"Just some guy who keeps calling her. Sheridan said it's for that story she's working on. I told her he sounds like an English gentleman or something."

Barrett.

It took every ounce of control he had not to crush his cell phone. "Does he call often?"

"Just about every hour for the last two days, sugar. I take more messages for that girl, I swear. Her phone's always full. Want me to ring her desk and see if she's available?"

"Yes," he said. "Thank you," he added belatedly.

"Hold tight, honey."

Some godawful violin version of La Vida Loca started playing in his ear.

"Are you coming in?" Brooks' voice blared from the loudspeaker near the gate.

McCallister jumped and glared upward. He couldn't remember the last time he'd started like that.

Christ, I'm on edge. He knew it was because of Sheridan, Barrett, and not knowing what the bastard was doing. Or where she was.

"Detective? Sheridan was called out to a meeting with an informant. Steve says she'll be back in a couple of hours. Want to leave a message?"

He headed for the house. Every footstep echoed in unison to a deep, pounding throb at the base of his skull. "No, thank you," he said. "Do you know where she is? Maybe I could meet up with her there."

"No, sorry, I can't give you that information." Bobbi's voice turned coolly professional though the Southern charm remained. "Against company policy. Being a cop, I'm sure you understand."

"Yeah, I do. Damn it."

Her chuckle reverberated in his ear. "I can tell you that Steve knows her exact location. Want me to patch you through to him?"

The front door opened and Brooks glared at the phone then him. His square face looked sharper and tenser than he could recall in recent years.

"No thanks, Bobbi. I'll call him after a while if I haven't heard from her."

He hung up, pocketed his phone, and lifted a brow. "What's going on?"

"Calliope has unearthed some disturbing information. Come on." The tall, immaculately dressed vampire turned on the heel of his highly polished shoe and strode down the marble hallway. No one looking at Brooks would doubt he was anything except urbane, suave, and successful. Exactly as he wanted.

McCallister caught up with him and they entered Brooks' large study. A gleaming oval conference table anchored the middle of the room. Valdór, Leopold, and Sullivan were seated around the walnut expanse with Calliope standing at the head. The table was strewn with folders, photos, and various papers.

"Calliope," McCallister greeted softly. Of them all, she was the most skittish and reclusive. She hated what she was, what her father forced her into becoming to save his own skin.

Bile coated McCallister's tongue as memories of that long ago night rose to hound him.

No time.

Calliope met his gaze steadily. She'd swept her curly black hair into a high ponytail. Her porcelain skin was bare of any makeup and he saw the dark smudges beneath her lavender eyes. Despite her reluctance, she'd fed regularly since her turning and she looked only a few years older than the twenty-three she'd been that night.

"We must stop Barrett," she said in that flat, harsh tone.

McCallister strode forward, edging between Valdór and Leopold to stare down at the tabletop. "What did you find?"

He picked up a photograph and grimaced. It was a laboratory of some sort with six gurneys. Each was filled with some type of human or creature, strapped down and connected to various hoses and machines.

"His experimentations have gotten worse," she said. "He's moved from animals to humans as you can see. But take a look at the last table on the right."

McCallister scanned the photo, squinted, and pulled it closer. The air left him as fast as a punctured balloon. "That's a vampire."

"Yes. That's Derek Craft. Turned in the mid 1950s. One of the first vampires of the modern age to exhibit new abilities."

"Like what?" Leopold asked.

Calliope crossed her arms and shivered. "Mr. Craft has the ability to regenerate body parts."

Sullivan whistled. "Handy."

Valdór snorted. "Always with the jokes, Sullivan." He turned to Calliope. "Have you seen this ability yourself?"

Her throat worked. "Yes." The word sounded ripped from the depths of her soul. "Father cut off Mr. Craft's right thumb. He re-grew it within a matter of minutes."

"Mother of God," Valdór muttered, crossing himself rapidly.

McCallister's jaw clenched. He settled a hand on his friend's big shoulder. "Why doesn't Craft mist out? Every vampire has that ability, even your father."

Calliope's shoulders slumped inward. "I believe Barrett has created some sort of device that prevents his escape." She skirted the table and slowly pulled the photo from his hands. Squinting, she lifted the page closer then tapped a long, oval fingertip near Craft's head. "There." The image trembled in her hands.

McCallister studied the area she'd indicated then sucked in a deep breath as a hailstorm of strong, unpleasant memories assailed him. An old, rusted collar cut across Craft's neck.

McCallister's own throat clenched in pain and air suddenly became a precious commodity. He struggled to inhale, struggled to expel the fetid stench of the past, struggled to remain composed and focused. He stared at the photo again, mentally dissected every inch of the collar and the skin it covered. When he reached the tendons of Craft's neck, he saw the deviation he was looking for. A small needle jutted from the iron bar and embedded itself into the vampire's neck.

Hanging below, a small tube funneled a neon green liquid.

"Do you know what he's being injected with?"

Calliope shook her head. "I couldn't get that close. I only had a few moments to root around. Barrett was out meeting someone but left his guard dogs in charge." Her eyes went as hard as diamonds and glittered with rage. "I incapacitated them but only temporarily. They won't remember a thing but I had ten minutes tops in his lab."

She whirled and paced to the front of the room again. She rooted through the stack of papers and pulled out another bunch, waving them in the air. "For years my father's only goal has been to rid himself of the illness still plaguing him. Becoming a vampire arrested the disease but it still resides in him. He often lamented this was why he had few of the powers the rest of us possess. It has eaten away at him every day of his miserable existence."

This was the first time she'd ever spoken of her father in such open terms. Unwanted sympathy wrenched McCallister's heart. He could still hear his old friend's desperate pleas for help ringing in his ears. The hollow of despair in Paxton's voice as he begged for his life. Even now, over a hundred years later,

McCallister ached from that day but he knew he would not change his decision.

"Something has changed?" Brooks asked.

Calliope nodded. "Yes. Father happened across an obscure text supposedly written by one of the Experimentors."

Valdór surged upward so fast, his chair toppled over. "An Experimentor? One of those bastards who did this to us?" The air chilled rapidly and ice crystals formed on his ever-present blue cape.

McCallister's fingers started to burn with the pain of ice and he blew on them. His breath emerged as a cloudy haze. Calliope shivered and stepped back.

Leopold rose and laid a hand on the big man's shoulder. "Easy, Valdór. They are gone now. No more. Sit, old friend. Please."

The chill deepened, the lights dimmed and Sullivan gasped. "Jesus, it's cold. Don't you pay your damn electric bill, Brooks?"

Brooks, looking as collected and in control as always, merely shrugged. "Mr. Valdór, if you please?"

Finally the bulbs grew brighter, warmth returned to the room and Valdór sank back into his seat. "My apologies, sir. I let my emotions get the better of me." Tiny drops of melting ice dropped from his body. He cradled his head in his hands.

Leopold patted the big man's back before taking his own chair again. He nodded to Calliope. "Go on, Callie."

She managed a wide-eyed smile.

McCallister understood her shock. Valdór was one of those rare unknowns. A vampire whose powers were uncharted, unexplored, and seemingly unstoppable. After all, the man had spent three hundred years frozen in a block of ice before being found by Leopold. When he'd been thawed, for lack of a better word, he'd had no memory of his past life save he'd once been alive and his name. Over the years they'd discovered he was a creation of one of the Experimentors, subjected to primitive horrors and attempts at creating vampires. When the Experimentor discovered he could not control Valdór, he encased him in ice to destroy him.

Calliope cleared her throat. "This Experimentor was apparently very old when he wrote the book. The inscription dates it fifty years after the Beginnings and dawning of our age." Her eyes touched on Valdór. "It details all the experiments, including failed ones going back hundreds of years and those after."

McCallister swung his gaze to Brooks. He didn't look shocked. "You knew about this?"

He nodded. "I told you it was disturbing. Listen."

"Father was particularly interested in one section that discussed efforts to combine the traits recognized in different vampires into one being. Those experiments were unsuccessful but I believe it sparked something in him."

"Calliope." Sullivan drummed his fingers on the table. "It's no secret you hate your father, with good reason." His lips compressed and anger flashed hotly in his eyes. "We share your feelings. Knowing this, I must ask how you came to have this knowledge? How do you know what he has been reading and what he has been trying?"

Her smile was as brittle as hundred year old paper. "Father has never stopped trying to regain my favor, Sullivan. He knows where I live. He sends me rambling letters of his trials and triumphs as well as his failures. According to him, he's successfully increased his strength, durability, and speed. He's working on other talents now, including the regeneration shown by Mr. Craft. When I received the last missive three weeks ago, I became concerned and decided to infiltrate his lab. I believe he is the source of the Vampire Dust you are investigating, McCallister. The notes and vials I found are fairly conclusive. He also had a few corpses in the lab bent exactly as we've seen with the Dust victims." She took a deep breath. "There's more, I'm afraid." Her beautiful purple gaze bore into McCallister.

Tension filled him. "Tell us."

"He believes there are some humans whose DNA is slightly irregular. Their telomeres, the sort of lead part to their DNA strand, doesn't degrade as fast or often as normal humans. This telomere acts as a buffer for the strand, correcting any errors in replication or damage to the actual strand itself, which helps create a longer life span. He has been studying those people who live past one hundred for nearly a decade and believes it is a mutation of their body composition. Only a few humans possess this type of telomere, less than one in ten million if his calculations are correct. He believes this human element holds the key to true immortality and health for him. He intends to find and harvest the DNA from these people. In his last missive, he told me he has discovered how to identify them." Her eyes met his again. "McCallister, Sheridan Aames possesses this gene."

† † †

"This better not be a freaking wild goose chase, Brian," Sheridan muttered to herself as she pulled Tess into a public parking lot on the outskirts of Boston. The strip of nightclubs, restaurants, and eclectic shops was brightly lit and filled with people, even in the middle of the afternoon.

She clambered from the car, checked her purse for the digital voice recorder, then hot-footed it across the street and down to The Dizzy Devil. Through the throngs of people, she caught sight of Brian pacing near the front door. Sunshine glinted off the gel in his auburn hair making it look like he had icicles nestled in his dark locks.

She smothered a grin and whacked him on the arm. He yelped and whirled around. "Sheridan. You came."

He seemed dumbfounded. And a little skittish.

She cocked her head. "Well, yeah. You said you had a confirmed buyer of Dust who wasn't dead or crazy. Can I still talk to them?"

He wiped a shaking palm over his lips. "Uh, yeah. Of course." His brown gaze darted around the flow of people before he straightened and waved toward the building. "Let's go."

He pulled open the door and waited for her to step inside. The outside noise of the crowd immediately ceased. It took several moments for her eyes to adjust to the darkened shadows of the dim interior. Some sort of black sound-dampening fabric covered the walls and was dotted with bits of paint in odd symbols. A low wall with a cut-out window looked onto a standard, wooden dance floor. Tables, chairs, and plush bench seats lined three sides of the floor while a fully stocked bar framed out the far side.

The place was empty.

"Are we even supposed to be in here?" she whispered.

"Yeah, let's cut across the floor." Brian placed a hand on her back and lightly pushed.

She stumbled forward and threw a glare over her shoulder. "Hands off, Perkins. I can walk on my own two feet."

"Sorry," he said. A sheen of perspiration dotted his upper lip again.

She wondered if he was hot, nervous, or hopped up on something. He didn't seem the druggie type, though. The guy ate clean and exercised as often as most people blinked.

Their feet echoed loudly in the silence of the club. Sheridan looked around, wondering where the music came from. Movement from her left made her look up. Above the bar was a wide open, mirrored space that held a plethora of speakers and black boom boxes. A shadow melted back into the darkness.

Sheridan shivered.

"I think we should leave," she said.

"No, my contact is just upstairs."

That's what I'm afraid of.

But, like the idiot she was, Sheridan followed him up the stairs. The allure of finally getting solid evidence for her story was much too great for her common sense to overcome.

At the top of the narrow steps, a red door stood partially ajar. Brian reached over her shoulder and pushed it open.

"Hello? It's Brian Perkins. I brought Sheridan like you asked."

Sheridan froze at the doorway and looked back at him. "They asked for me?"

"Please, come in."

The low, sultry voice slid over Sheridan's skin like sumptuous silk. She shivered but found herself compelled to move forward.

She stepped into the sound room aware of Brian moving quickly behind her. The door shut with an almost ominous snick. A low whistle started in her ears and she instinctively lifted the mental tower shield she'd constructed even as she turned to leave.

Brian blocked her way.

The noise stopped.

"I mean you no harm, Miss Aames."

Again the voice wrapped through her, turned her around. She stared, captivated by the beautiful woman in front of her. Long, dark hair. Beautifully white skin and a body designed to make men drool themselves silly.

But her eyes were flat and cold. Completely lifeless.

Sheridan couldn't suppress a shudder.

"Who are you?" she asked.

The woman glided forward, stopping a few feet away. "My name is not important. My information is. You are involved with Logan McCallister?"

Another blast of noise receded as soon as the shield re-formed. Sheridan was rather proud of how fast she was learning to raise that thing.

"You're a vampire."

Behind her, Brian cursed.

The woman inclined her head. "Guilty. Please answer the question."

"Why should I? Are you one of his exes?" Sheridan crossed her arms and shifted to the right. If she needed to bolt from the room, she wanted to make sure she could get past Brian. She decided his ass was grass as soon they got out of there, too. *If we get out of here.*

"Because the answer could save your life, Miss Aames."

Well, that was straight to the point. She debated for all of five seconds before shrugging. Besides, it wasn't like she could lie. She had no desire to re-enact the pain of earlier that morning when she'd told McCallister their brief, hot tryst was *finito*. "Yes."

"Good, that will make this easier." The woman lifted a long, elegant hand and casually swept back her hair. "I am Desdemona." She paused, tilted her head, and offered the smile of a woman who knew the information she'd just imparted was sure to shock and surprise.

It took every ounce of willpower Sheridan possessed, and then some, not to react. She pasted a frown on her face. "Sorry. Who?"

Violent annoyance flashed in the vampire's eyes. "Desdemona. Surely he's told you of me?"

"Nope," she said cheerfully. This lie was easier. While she wanted to claw the woman's eyes out because she'd hurt McCallister, Sheridan decided tweaking her would have to suffice for the moment.

A muscle pulsed in the woman's jaw and her lips pulled back revealing fangs more lethal than Sheridan had yet seen. A look of disgust turned Desdemona's pretty, patrician features ugly. "You lie. I am with him always. He is mine."

Anger surged in Sheridan. "Last time I looked, he was sleeping in my bed."

Great, I'm in a pissing match with a vicious bitch vampire. Smart move, Sheridan.

Desdemona rose in the air, her black head brushing the equally dark ceiling. She glared down at Sheridan, eyes flashing and fingers curled into sharp red-tipped talons.

Then, as suddenly as the anger flared, it subsided and she floated back to the floor. "My apologies, Miss Aames."

The words actually sounded sincere but Sheridan wasn't buying it.

"Suffice it to say I turned McCallister many years ago and I still feel a sense of...ownership. When he fled, I was devastated but I understood."

Big fricking deal. You want champagne and a ticker tape parade for that?

Desdemona tipped her head again and her eyes narrowed slightly before she sighed softly. "How well do you know him, Miss Aames?"

"Well enough," Sheridan replied. "I trust him."

Which is more than I can say about you.

Sheridan shifted back a few more inches. Brian stepped closer. She shot him a glare. He shrugged.

"Please don't blame Mr. Perkins for his deception. He had no choice. His is under my command." She wiggled her fingers at him.

Sheridan stared at him with new eyes, her gaze zeroing in on his neck. She couldn't see the telltale dots marking him as a Consort but maybe that was due to the perma-tan he wore.

"Sorry, Sheridan," he muttered.

"Apology not accepted."

Sheridan looked at Desdemona again. The woman was unnaturally beautiful but her eyes held all the warmth and life of a dead squid. But something in them seemed haunted as if she struggled with a weighty issue. "Why am I here?" She made a production of looking at her watch. "I have to be back in the office within the hour or Steve, our boss, will be on the horn to McCallister and every other cop in this city. He knows exactly where I am." She tossed another poisoned glare at Brian. "And who I'm with."

Brian shifted and slunk backward, moving to the far side of the door. He slumped against a giant speaker and stared down at the tip of his too-damn-pointy-for-a-man dress shoes.

Desdemona pulled two chairs out from the stainless steel desk that held a plethora of turntables, CD holders, and headphones. The computer equipment on the desk was valuable enough to feed a small third world nation for a year at least.

"Sit down, Miss Aames. We have a lot to discuss and, as you've pointed out, we don't have much time."

Tea and crumpets coming next?

Sheridan hooked the proffered chair with her foot and pulled it away from the vampire. She shoved it against the DJ set-up in front of the wide-open space looking down onto the dance floor and carefully sat. Both Desdemona and Brian were in her sights. Made her feel better. Less likely she was going to get jumped.

She hoped.

"Comfortable?" Desdemona asked with just a hint of sarcasm.

"Hell, no. But I'm sitting and I'm listening, though God only knows why. Spill what you've got on your mind and let me the hell out of here."

Desdemona's full, red lips lifted though no humor touched her dead eyes. "Heaven, hell, and arrogance all in one sentence. I can see why McCallister likes you, Miss Aames." She tipped her head and the velvet curtain of her black hair tumbled artfully around her shoulders.

She looked so damned seductive that Sheridan was having trouble concentrating. She blinked and dug her fingernails into her thighs to distract herself. The tiny dart of discomfort worked well enough. "Go on."

A small tic developed at the corner of Desdemona's right eye.

Sheridan tamped a bloom of satisfaction at getting the witch's goat. Vampire's. Whatever.

"I'm sure it's all fantastic sex— McCallister is *very* good in bed—and such but I'm also certain it hasn't gone any deeper than that, has it? He hasn't shared much of his past with you."

Sheridan shifted uneasily. "I know enough."

"Such as?"

She snorted. "No way, lady. I'm listening to you, not the other way around. You got something to say, freaking spill it."

Ire flashed in Desdemona's eyes and her butt floated off the chair again but she quickly regained control. She smoothed a hand over her hair. "Very well. I can see you're as stubborn and prickly as Brian mentioned."

Sheridan rolled her eyes. "I'm guessing he said that because I constantly turn him down for dates."

Desdemona flicked a glance at the still slumped man before meeting her eyes again. "Good call. It's all very complicated, Miss Aames."

"These things usually are."

The vampire flicked at her red fingernail for several seconds. The constant *click, click, click* was as annoying as a third-grader noisily chomping gum. Finally, blessedly, she stilled. "You are in danger."

Sheridan snorted again. "Duh. I'm locked in a room with a vengeful vampire and a dipshit errand boy. Okay, he's no problem, but you...you could do serious damage to me."

A pleased expression lit up Desdemona's face, taking her from beautiful to breathtakingly alluring.

"What a sweet thing to say. Thank you."

"Ohmigod, really?" Sheridan wondered if all the years of death, destruction, and evil had turned the vampire's brain to absolute dog shit.

Desdemona cleared her throat. "My apologies. In this day and age, creating fear is such a rare thing. Today's society is much less superstitious. They lack the proper respect for vampires. I blame Hollywood."

"Don't we all? Can we get on with this?" Sheridan spread her hands. "Me, danger, yada, yada, yada?"

The vampire nodded. "Despite what you think, I am not going to harm you. Today. You're in danger from Paxton Barrett."

Sheridan decided to ignore the other woman's 'today' qualifier. "Yeah, he made that pretty clear."

"He's approached you?" She looked so shocked that Sheridan couldn't help the small grin from creeping out.

"Yeah. We had drinks and conversation at Vesper's Bite the other night. That was before he blew his wig and killed Ernest the bartender, though."

Desdemona's fists curled. Even in the gloom of the black sound booth, Sheridan could see the white stress marks on her knuckles. The tendon throbbing unappealingly on the vampire's forehead also clued her in to the fact she was pissed.

"That man is an abomination, Miss Aames." Her voice lost all sultry attraction. Deep-timbered and as rough as a hangnail, she spoke with real hatred. "He is dangerous, maniacal, and not to be trusted. No matter what he's promised you, it's a lie. He must be destroyed." Desdemona sucked in a deep breath and bowed her head.

Sheridan inched her chair toward the door.

Desdemona's head snapped back up. "Do you know why he approached you?"

"Yeah, he wants McCallister. He expects me to deliver him." She crossed her arms and lifted her chin. "I'm not doing it, either. Not to him, not to you."

"I'm not asking you to. But you're mistaken if you believe his real goal is McCallister." She shook her head, dislodging more of her beautiful ebony hair which she shoved back over her shoulder. "He wants you both."

All the air left the room. Sheridan felt as though she were trying to breathe through a vacuum cleaner hose. "No, I'm just a tool to get to McCallister."

"You're wrong, Sheridan."

Hearing her first name on the vampire's lips jolted Sheridan, threw her off-kilter, and made a scrambled mess of her brain. She clutched at her temples, closed her eyes, and focused on the image McCallister told her to, even though no noise infiltrated her mind.

Calm returned almost immediately. She dropped her hands and stared at the watchful vampire.

"McCallister won't let him have me."

"You're right. He's very protective of his Consorts. And you, he will guard especially well."

"Why do you say it like that?" she asked warily.

The vampire smiled. "You are special, Miss Aames. McCallister knows it as does Barrett. But they discovered you in vastly different ways." Desdemona's eyes actually took on a gleam of interest for half a second. "Did McCallister tell you about Sine Qua Non? The Life Legend?"

Sheridan nodded. "He said it's crap."

"No, it's very real. I knew a Joined pair once who had it. Do you believe?"

"That I'm the missing part of his soul?" Sheridan asked the question with intentional flippancy because she was scared as hell that her answer was a resounding yes. Despite her protestations, her anger, and her unwillingness to submit to him, McCallister had become as necessary and integral to her as breathing. "Maybe. But then, I've been accused of being a romantic." She frowned and sat up a bit straighter. "Wait a minute. You don't think that's why Barrett wants me, do you? I can tell you right now there's no way in hell I'm connected to that bastard. Uh-huh. Not happening."

"Rest assured, you are not Barrett's Sine Qua Non. No, he wants you for a vastly different reason." Desdemona lifted her patrician nose and sniffed delicately. Arousal, hunger, and curiosity flitted across her face with the speed of a lightning strike. "I can barely tell but I don't have Barrett's unnaturally enhanced senses."

Sheridan sniffed at her armpit. Fresh as the proverbial daisy. "What are you talking about? Tell what? What senses?"

"Barrett has been experimenting on himself for the last hundred years, Miss Aames. His body was riddled with filth and disease when I turned him." Desdemona shuddered. Her lips curled and her tongue swiped quickly across her beautiful mouth. "He is the only one I have turned and regretted. I still taste his foulness. The ailment seized when he became a vampire but did not leave his body, and he has sought a cure all these years. He was too frail at the turning to take on the traditional powers of our kind. One more reason I should have killed him when I had the chance." A dark smile replaced the disgust. "I had plans for him. Each night I'd go to the cellar where he sat chained and drain him until a heartbeat before death before replenishing him. I planned on keeping him as a pet for a week, no more." Her gaze turned inward and annoyance flicked quickly over her face. "I never expected his stupid daughter to rescue him. He sacrificed her! She should have hated him and revered me for saving her."

Though disturbed by the relish Desdemona displayed during the re-telling of Barrett's torture, Sheridan scoffed. "Yeah, hey thanks for turning me into a vampire. Let's party. Lady, you are cracked."

Desdemona shook her head. "You have a pert tongue, Miss Aames. The next time we meet I fear I will not have as much control as today."

The blunt danger in her tone made Sheridan swallow hard. She stayed silent.

"Ah, you are trainable. Good."

Sheridan bit her tongue nearly bloody keeping her smart ass retort to herself.

"Suffice it to say, some of the things Barrett has done over the years to himself have worked and some have not. I've learned he's recently had excellent success with increasing himself physically and in ways that are very dangerous. I have waited too long to kill him and now, I fear, he is too strong."

"What does this have to do with me or McCallister?"

"He loathes McCallister, even now after all these years. Revenge is the blood that fuels him. As for you...it seems you are very valuable to Paxton Barrett, Miss Aames." Her face took on a superior, knowing smile. "Tell me, how many times have you been ill? In your entire life?"

Thrown for a loop by the odd question, Sheridan frowned. "I had colds like anyone else," she said.

"I dare say, your colds lasted less than a day, no more than two and you rarely took any medication for them. Nothing more serious than that, correct?"

"What does this have to do with anything?" Sheridan stood. "Look, I'd like to say this has been fun but my mother taught me not to lie, so whatever. I'm out." She stomped toward the door, glowering at a now-erect Brian.

Go ahead and try to stop me, you slimy bastard.

"Miss Aames," Desdemona's voice cut through Sheridan's determination.

She stopped, turned, propped her hands on her hips, and stared. "What?"

"I ask about your health because it's apparently what draws you to Barrett. For whatever reason, he believes you are the key to all he's sought these hundred years. He knows you are McCallister's by now." Her lip curled. "You reek of his scent." She frowned and moved so quickly, Sheridan didn't have time to dodge.

One second the vampire sat in her chair, the next she stood directly in front of Sheridan. "Perhaps now McCallister will deign to turn someone. Yes, I like that. He has fought the urge for so long and to turn you, his soul mate, will be both joyous and painful. Fitting."

"No way," Sheridan muttered, stepping back. "I already agreed to this Joining thing but no way will I let him turn me into a vampire."

Desdemona studied her even more intently. "When will you complete the Joining?"

"We did," Sheridan said then wished she could slap a gag over her own mouth. *No need to spill any more secrets, idiot.*

"No, Miss Aames, you have not. Oh, McCallister might have taken you, but he has not *given* to you. He has not fulfilled this particular Joining."

Dread pushed the annoyance from Sheridan. She shoved at her hair, tucking it behind one ear. "What are you talking about? We did it, he bit me, done."

Desdemona drifted closer and this time Sheridan stood her ground. "This makes sense," she said on a long breath. Her eyes closed briefly.

"None of this makes sense."

Desdemona grabbed her shoulders, holding her with a grip that Sheridan was sure she could break if she wanted to. The knowledge kept her still.

"Yes, you are his Consort now, Joined to him in the ways of old. But the true Joining of Sine Qua Non has not been completed. He trusts no woman and he does not trust you."

"Bullshit."

"Really?" Desdemona lifted a perfectly plucked, arched brow. "Have you seen his face as he enters you? Does he allow you to hold him during the act of love? Or are you bound, helpless, and totally at his command?"

Each truth-filled word punched Sheridan with the force of a prize fighter's blows. Tears stung her eyes, filled her nose, and made her cough. She dug her face into her sleeve, wiping away the success of Desdemona's taunts.

The vampire shook Sheridan lightly. "Don't you understand? This is my fault. All of it. I turned McCallister into a vampire but then did so much worse. I turned Barrett and created a scourge that now threatens us all. He seeks domination and immortality and he won't stop until he gets it. You are his chosen weapon and he must destroy McCallister to get you. Barrett has realized the control McCallister so desperately prizes is now his greatest weakness. It makes him vulnerable. *You* make him vulnerable."

Panic flooded Sheridan. "You're mistaken. Even if Barrett somehow got hold of McCallister, we're protected. We have been Joined." She repeated McCallister's words with desperation.

"You have his body, his honor, and his vow of protection. But you do not have his trust. That one element is enough to keep the Joining from fully succeeding." Desdemona released Sheridan and pushed her toward the door. The motion was almost violent, as if the vampire needed space between them immediately. "Go now, Miss Aames. You must find a way to gain his trust or I fear we are all lost. Human and vampires alike."

Sheridan didn't hesitate. She bolted for the door and down the stairs. She heard Brian's lumbering footsteps behind her. She sped up, nearly skidding along the slick wooden dance floor. Bolting from the dark night club, she ran into a gaggle of people standing near a hot dog cart.

She didn't want to trust the woman but the truth of her words echoed in her heart. Trusting the poisonous viper who'd nearly destroyed McCallister seemed like the most foolish thing on earth and still,...

Having her on our side might not be such a bad thing.

Sheridan saw Tess's gleaming fender across the street, started forward, and then came to a full stop when she ran into the VW's door. "Oomph," she muttered as she rubbed her smarting elbow. Super speed was good but only if one knew how to properly use it.

Wrenching open the door, she plopped inside, pulled the door closed, and locked the door. Her fingers trembled so badly, she dropped the keys twice before finally stabbing it into the ignition. She looked at The Dizzy Devil and watched as Brian frantically sped up and down the sidewalk, presumably looking for her.

"Too damn bad," she muttered. Without a backward glance, she put the car into gear and sped from the lot.

She couldn't outrace Desdemona's words though. *He doesn't trust you. You're vulnerable. He won't give up control.*

He doesn't trust you.

Hot tears blinded her and she ran onto a curb taking a corner too fast.

"Son of a bitch," she yelled as she righted the car. Slowing down, she forced calm, deep breaths in and out. "What the hell do I do now?"

Her first instinct was to find McCallister and confront him. Her second was to find Bert and get his input.

Instead, she made her way back to her desk at the Metro. She found Steve, told him the lead was crap and, for reasons she couldn't explain, he needed to fire Brian for being a piece of shit worm.

"I'm also going to take the rest of the day off," she said while he stared at her dumbfounded. "Tomorrow, too. Actually, I'll be working from home. Safe and sound, just like you and McCallister wanted. Call me on my cell if you need anything."

Sheridan didn't wait for a yes or no. She spun and blinked back to her desk, gathered her purse, notes, and a fresh pad then headed outside.

Tess waited in front of the building where she'd left her but now sported a parking ticket. "Just fucking great," Sheridan muttered. She crumpled the paper, tossed it to her floorboard, and headed for home.

Her home.

She was in no mood to see McCallister right now. She had a hell of a lot of thinking to do over the next few hours.

And, if Desdemona was correct, the fate of the world just might rest on her decision.

CHAPTER TWELVE

"Do you think Calliope is right about Barrett?" McCallister asked Brooks as they sat in the billionaire's opulent library.

Brooks had pulled down several books and flipped through them for the better part of the afternoon.

He looked up, his blue eyes as unfathomable as the turbulent North Sea. "I hope not, McCallister. If she is and Barrett succeeds in imbuing himself with all the powers of our kind, he will be without equal."

McCallister frowned. "Surely the Brigade can deal with him? We should talk to them."

Brooks nodded. "Calliope and I have an appointment tomorrow to report her findings." He shut the book with a snap, raked a hand through his ebony hair and grimaced.

Unease trickled over McCallister like tepid water. "What's wrong?"

"I don't know," Brooks admitted. "I've wanted to kill him from the moment I knew he existed and Calliope's objectivity was destroyed the second he sacrificed her to Desdemona. You knew him best, before the turning. Do you think he's capable of all this?"

McCallister shifted in the luxurious chair but the velvet covering scratched like sandpaper. He rose and paced in front of the fireplace, before staring into the flames. "Why do you have the fire going in the middle of summer?"

"I keep it lit for Valdór. You know how cold he gets."

McCallister smiled fondly. "I suppose that's what happens when you're encased in ice for three hundred years."

"Are you going to answer my question?"

He sighed and turned around. "The Paxton Barrett I knew was firm and ambitious. He grew his business to levels that other men marveled at but that success only made him want more. More wealth, more prestige, bigger houses, better carriages."

"More power?" Brooks asked.

"No," McCallister replied. "Oddly enough, the man was never consumed by power. He felt having wealth and prestige inherently gave him that power. He never flouted it, either. He just exuded it."

A light, high pitched whine started in his ear and he frowned.

"What's wrong?" Brooks asked.

McCallister's heart suddenly pulsed with the force of a jackhammer. He staggered back, blindly seeking a handhold. Brooks' strong arms steadied him at the shoulders.

"Sit down. You're as pale as a whiteboard."

The whine settled into a low thrum and pink dots bounced in his periphery.

"Sheridan," he said on a gasp. He pushed against Brooks' grip. "She's in trouble."

Brooks frowned and let go. "I'll call my car."

The whine ended abruptly and McCallister's heart smoothed back into a normal, even rhythm. The dots faded and he could feel the blood rushing back through his body.

Sheridan?

He sent the mental probe out, regardless of how idiotic he thought it was. Psychic connections were not a part of his genetic make-up.

Closing his eyes, he concentrated on her face, her azure eyes and lush, full lips.

Though she appeared full formed and nearly touchable in his mind, there was no response to his query.

"McCallister? Do we leave?"

He shook the odd interlude away and checked his watch. "No. It's nearly eight-thirty. She should be at my house, safe and sound." He managed a weak grin. "She's probably ticked I haven't come home yet. Dinner waiting and all that."

Brooks snorted. "Right. She seems that type."

McCallister shrugged and picked up the thread of their conversation before the odd happening distracted him. "Back then, before he turned, I think Barrett wanted only what was best for himself and Calliope. When he learned of his illness, it's possible he went a little insane. He was so desperate for a cure that he took unbelievable chances. Underground drugs, electrical experiments, mechanical transplants. This was 1898 and half the things he tried were unstable at best. He tried everything and nothing worked. He was at his last hope when he came to me." McCallister met Brooks' penetrating gaze straight on. "I could not turn him, Brooks. I couldn't."

The other man's face softened. He clasped an elegant hand on his shoulder and squeezed. "I know that, brother. None of us blames you for what happened, least of all Calliope."

Calliope's sweet, impish face poured into his mind. When she'd been a true twenty-three year old, she'd been full of life and grace and dreams. She'd viewed him as a big brother and sought his advice on everything from the latest fashions to horseflesh to marriage prospects. She'd been so much like Georgette he could never turn her away.

"I could have saved them both," he said harshly. "How can she not blame me?"

"Because it's not in her nature." Brooks dropped his hand and stepped back. "I think the Brigade will probably send a few Guardians after Barrett. I suspect he'll spend the remainder of his days cloistered in some tower."

McCallister felt sick. "They'll starve him to death."

"They will do what is necessary," Brooks said. "I feel the evidence Calliope has, coupled with your testimony, will give them the impetus they need to stop him before he hurts any more humans or vampires."

"Let's hope so."

Brooks hesitated for a second.

"What's on your mind?" McCallister asked.

"What's it like? Sine Qua Non. Joining with the other half of your soul?"

McCallister frowned deeply. He didn't want to desecrate what he'd shared with Sheridan by blabbing about it.

"I'm not asking for details," Brooks said, flashing a wry smile. "I just want to know how you feel. How is it different?"

McCallister shrugged. "Except for an interesting little light show, it really wasn't all that different from taking a regular Consort."

Brooks frowned. "That doesn't sound right." He nodded to the stack of books he'd pulled down. "According to the literature, you're supposed to be more connected than you've ever been with another. Do you feel any different? More powerful? More intuitive?"

"Nope." He rocked back on his heels and shoved his hands in his pockets. "There were some pink lights—I'm beginning to think that's her signature color—and a surge of energy, but that's about it."

"Odd," Brooks muttered. "I don't like it. You're sure you did it right?"

McCallister laughed. "For God's sake, Brooks. What kind of question is that?"

A light flush rose in the other man's cheeks and he coughed. "Right. Strike that. Okay, I'm going to sit and prepare my argument for the Brigade for the morning. You should probably get home and find out if she burned your dinner."

McCallister grinned and spun around, heading down the long marble hallway. "If she did, I'm going to tan her hide."

As soon as he settled into his Mustang, McCallister picked up his cell phone and dialed Sheridan's number.

"You've reached Sheridan Aames. Well, not really since this is my voicemail. Leave me a message with your name and number and I'll call you back. All story leads, sources, and tips are welcome. Confidentiality guaranteed."

He cursed and set the phone in the cup holder then hit the gas. A few minutes later, he called again.

"You've reached Sheridan—"

Sweat broke out across his brow and he dropped the phone to his lap as he increased his speed. His radar beeped just in the nick of time and he slowed down as he passed a BPD black and white. As soon as the Other Side cop was out of range, McCallister floored it.

Tires squealed as he turned onto his street.

Even from the far end, he could see her lunch box of a car wasn't in his driveway. He slammed on the brakes, punched the ceiling, then viciously cranked the steering wheel and headed out of the subdivision.

He dialed her one more time as he sped to her house.

"You've rea—"

Disconnecting, he gritted his teeth so hard, he thought he might bust a fang. Relaxing his jaw took massive concentrated effort which gave him enough time to calm down. *She has a perfectly reasonable explanation for not being at my house as instructed.*

He'd known she was a wild submissive. Her need to buck authority and ensure she didn't lose her sense of self was something he understood completely.

But when he gave an order, he expected it to be obeyed.

He pulled into her drive and idled behind her toy car for a long moment before killing his engine. Relief made him weak. He refused to acknowledge the tremble in his hands or the untwisting in his gut. He'd been worried about her as he would have been any of his previous Consorts.

He swallowed the lie down. Sheridan wasn't like *any* other Consort. Not only physically, but emotionally.

And that scared the hell out of him.

Love was not in his future. Ever.

He would never love a human only to watch them die while he continued on for what would amount to a painful eternity.

McCallister shoved the car door open and stepped out. He'd moved only a few feet when her front door opened.

McCallister's anger dissolved in a new burst of worry. She looked like hell. She looked beautiful, too. Her blond hair was mussed like she'd run her hands through the mane a dozen times, she didn't have a lick of make-up on, and the circles beneath her eyes were as dark as baseball black. Dressed in skimpy cut-off jean shorts, a bright pink tank top, and striped black and hot pink socks decorated with skeletons, she stood rigidly in the doorway.

"Scram, McCallister," she said. Fists propped on her lush hips, she glared at him as if he was the cause of every ill in the world. "I'm done with this baloney. You and the rest of your friends can figure out what to do because I am D-O-N-E done. Do you hear me?"

He strode up the sidewalk and crowded her, hoping to force her back into the house. "I hear you and probably everyone in a three mile radius can, too."

She didn't give an inch. Her blue eyes were wild and stark and deep with fear.

His breath caught in his throat. McCallister hauled her into his arms, stepped over the threshold, and slammed the door shut with his foot.

Sheridan's squeak was quickly muffled as she put her forehead to his shoulder and her arms around his neck.

He strode through the house, taking in the haphazard piles of paper, pens, books, magazines, and movies. His quick glance into the kitchen showed gleaming countertops filled with all manner of bake ware and accessories. Nearly every horizontal surface in her house was covered with some little something. Only the large farmer's table sitting against the far wall was devoid of clutter. Instead, a computer monitor, wireless mouse and keyboard and a tidy sheaf of papers lay upon it.

"Are you okay?" he murmured into her ear.

"Shut up," she replied with a sniffle. "I'm not talking to you. "I didn't ask you to come in, you know. You can't just bully people like this."

Her entire body quivered in his arms and he was damn positive it wasn't his sexual prowess that had her quaking.

He found the living room. The wide, spacious area held a long, navy blue couch with cushions piped in white and topped by three ridiculously over-stuffed pillows. A low, intricately carved coffee table sat in front of the sofa. Her laptop stood open and humming atop it while an e-reader, three remote controls, and a basket of butterscotch candies littered the rest of the tabletop.

A matching loveseat anchored the left side of the room and a massive flat panel television hung on the wall. A sweet electronics set up staggered below on a metal, stair-step display. Cheery, white, lacy curtains covered a sliding glass door just to the right of the television. A carved hutch that matched the coffee table stood silently on the other side. He caught a glimpse of delicate figurines made of lace, shiny crystal animals, and a plethora of Dick Tracy related memorabilia.

He settled onto the couch, grimacing as the cushions pushed at his back. He shifted into a more comfortable position and stroked her spine. He probed lightly at her mind but the only thing he found was a giant tower shield with a yellow piece of lined paper taped to it. *Keep Out* was boldly slashed across the paper in black lettering.

He chuckled.

"Didn't I tell you to hush?" she grumbled.

"Didn't I tell you I give the orders around here?"

That got her attention. She pulled her head from his shoulder and glared but didn't move from his lap. Her hands flexed at his neck.

"Trying to decide if you're going to strangle me?" he asked, hoping to lighten the mood.

"Ha. I'd need the strength of a bear for that."

He winked and pulled one hand down and kissed the back of her fingers. "You've gotten pretty strong, Sheridan. I bet you could do it. Wanna try?"

She sniffed. "Don't tempt me. I've had a very hard day. A very trying day and it's all your damn fault."

McCallister nuzzled her unkempt hair. Her heart beat strongly against his chest, her breath came and went with deep regularity. She was okay. *Safe*. McCallister tamped his shiver of fear, glad to put away the terror that rode with him to her house. Holding her helped even more. He didn't care she wasn't at his house, he was damned relieved she was all right. "Tell me what happened."

Tension spiked her fingers into talons and her breath dropped into ragged, wet gasps.

McCallister tipped her head back, wiping away the tears forming in her eyes. "Come on, sweetheart, talk to me. Let me help you. Is it the Joining? Are you feeling...weird?" He groaned inwardly at his choice of words but he really didn't know any other way to describe it.

"Yes, it's the Joining," she said. "Of course it's freaking weird and…"

Her blue gaze met his again, washing him with apprehension. "And what?"

"And I think we're in big, big trouble, McCallister." Another shudder wracked her. "I don't mean just us, either. If what she said is true, 'we' could mean the entire human and vampire races."

He frowned. "Whoa, whoa, whoa. Let's take this a step at a time. Who is she?"

Her heartbeat increased and she looked over her shoulder then all around the living room. She leaned closer to him. "Desdemona," she whispered.

A sledgehammer the size of a jumbo jet impaled him dead center in the chest. Dread encased his entire being. He held her at arm's length. "What did you just say?"

Sheridan wriggled on his lap. "It's a long story."

"We've got time," he gritted out. He swept her entire body with another long, penetrating glance. Whisking his hands down her arms, along her ribs, and down the lean strength of her mostly-bare thighs. She giggled, albeit rather hysterically, when he touched her knees. He filed that away for future reference.

"You're okay? That bitch didn't hurt you? How in the hell did you meet up with her? And where, for that matter? And why the hell didn't you call me?"

Sheridan caught his roaming hand in hers. The warmth of her fingers oddly soothed him. Let him know she was alive and well. Again.

"No, she just wanted to talk."

His mind whirled and he found himself gnashing his back teeth again. "Start from the beginning and talk fast."

Sheridan frowned. "Hey, this damn meeting wasn't my idea, so don't get all pissy with me."

"Sheridan," he said on a long drawl. "Start talking."

"God, you're bossy."

McCallister couldn't help his strangled laugh. It was either that or go absolutely bat-shit crazy and wreck everything in the house to vent his anger. Somehow, he didn't think she would appreciate her little figurines in a zillion pieces on the floor. *Not enough super glue in the world to put them back together.*

"I told you so seems appropriate right now," he said with as light a tone as he could manage.

She gifted him with an impish smile and quick hug. He felt like he won the damn lottery. Except millions of dollars could never make him feel as good as a single, sweet glance from Sheridan Aames.

Hooboy, you've got it bad, bucko.

"Tell me what happened, sweetheart," he said in a desperate attempt to outrun the truth in his thoughts. He stroked her cheek. "Talk to me."

"All right. It was the weirdest thing."

As Sheridan detailed everything that happened, McCallister forced himself to remain calm and not put out an immediate APB for Brian the Bastard. He'd make sure the Other Side dealt with that little weasel properly. Losing his job was not enough for the danger he'd put Sheridan in.

"I left the club, went back to the office to gather my stuff, and came home. Been here ever since."

"You would have been safer at my place," he said.

She shook her head and wiggled off his lap. "You don't get it, do you, McCallister? I just got a bomb dropped on me. I needed space, familiarity, and my own damn shower."

He held up a consoling hand. "I'm sorry, I *do* get it. I can imagine how terrified you were. Desdemona is very, uh, forceful."

She dropped back down to the sofa. "And by forceful, you mean a raging beyotch?"

"Yeah, something like that. You're sure she didn't hurt you?"

"For the hundredth time, yes. I'm positive. She never physically hurt me. Didn't try to bite me or anything."

"Hm, too bad."

She shoved his shoulder. McCallister rocked backward and stared at her in surprise. The Texas girl had a little bit of strength to her.

"I told you, I'm not a weakling. Why is it too bad?"

He smiled. "Couldn't resist, huh?"

She lifted her fist again. He caught it, tugged her forward so she sprawled face down on his lap, and smacked her ass a couple times. She gasped and jerked, raising his dick and his lust, despite the discussion topic.

He smoothed his hand over her butt, fingering the silken curve of her bottom beneath the frayed fringe of her shorts.

"It's too bad she didn't try because I'm fairly certain something unpleasant would have happened to her."

She twisted around and peered up at him through a curtain of honey blond hair. "Yeah? Why?"

"We're Joined, Sheridan. You're not as susceptible to the allure and commands of other vampires regularly. But you and I are Joined by Sine Qua Non. We have the unbreakable bond. She cannot destroy it and should she try, she herself could be destroyed." He lifted a shoulder. "At least, that's how the legend goes. And I'm coming to realize these legends hold a lot of truth."

Sheridan's expression went dark and her heart rate increased to the speed of jack rabbit. She nibbled her bottom lip and slowly sat up. "Uh, yeah. We might have a problem there."

He frowned. "What are you talking about?"

"Set aside your prejudice involving her for a minute, okay?"

"Uh-huh."

"Come on, McCallister. I've had to deal with a lot of whacked out stuff the last couple of days, the least you can do is try this one thing."

"Fine, fine, fine. I'll listen."

Her pulse hitched upward another notch. "She said I reek of your smell."

He nodded sharply. "Good."

"Spare me the machismo. She also said our Joining was *not* complete in the way you think it is."

"Bullshit. You were there." He cupped her tit and squeezed. "Do you need a repeat performance?"

Sheridan wrenched away and stood. She stalked to the television and faced him, arms crossed. "Do you trust me?"

The question hit him like a two ton semi. The way she phrased the query, the intensity in her eyes, and the fear in her voice made him choose his words carefully. "If I didn't, do you think I'd have let you leave the house this morning? I know you're not going to shout the news of our existence to the masses, Sheridan."

Her head started shaking after his first few words. "That's not what I'm talking about," she said hoarsely. "I mean—do you trust me? Trust me in every aspect of our relationship, such as it is."

Sweat pooled between his shoulder blades, dripping down his spine leaving a trail of icy fear. "Why?"

She inhaled deeply, fingers knitting wild, random patterns. "Both times we've had sex, you've been behind me. You've been in control. I'm nothing more than an object for you."

He shot to his feet, the fear morphing into a solid lead weight in his gut. "Sheridan—"

She held up a hand and shuffled backward. "She said because you don't trust me, our Joining is not complete. It will never be complete." Her gaze lifted to his and he was sucker-punched by the depth of pain she showed him. "Don't you understand? I'm *not* fully protected. And you...well, you've *never* been truly Joined with a Consort. Not in the way you told me about. Not in the way we need to stay alive."

McCallister's knees weakened and he dropped down to the sofa, cradling his head in his hands. *Could this be true? Could this be why I never felt anything beyond affection for my previous Consorts? Why it was so easy to let them go into the Heavens when it was their time?*

But he felt deeply for Sheridan. He'd never been as attuned to another woman as he was her. Had never felt as much passion and need for anyone before her. *No, Desdemona is wrong. It's some kind of trick.*

"McCallister?"

He looked up. Sheridan stood across the room, honeyed hair in a wild tangle around her shoulders, wary sadness in her light blue eyes. His gaze drifted down to the two small puncture wounds at her neck.

His mark.

His woman.

His Consort.

But what if she wasn't?

"McCallister," Sheridan's soft voice called to him again.

He met her gaze.

"Tell me what happened after she turned you."

His entire body bucked and his eyelids slammed shut, trying to keep the pain and terror at bay. Much as Sheridan had trembled when he first arrived, soul-deep tremors now shook his body. The chill of memory seeped from his veins, winding insidiously through every part of his being.

Then Sheridan was there. She wrapped her delicate but strong arms around him and hugged him close. Soft, sweet kisses dotted his head and cheek and jaw before settling against his lips.

"It's all right," she whispered on a ragged breath. "It's all right."

He shuddered again. "I wish I'd died that night."

"You don't have to," she started.

McCallister laid a finger against her lips. "No, I do. For you. For us."

She eased back to the couch cushions and held her arms to him. He sank gratefully against her bosom, inhaling the now-familiar aroma of roses, hydrangea, and lavender that was uniquely Sheridan.

"I stayed in the dungeon for two weeks. Chained to the wall like an animal."

Her fingers slipped through his hair and scored lightly on his scalp. He felt himself relaxing at her soft touch.

"Leopold was there, too. And Brooks' brother, James." He sighed heavily. "He didn't make it through the two weeks.

Desdemona killed him in a fit of rage one night."

"My God," Sheridan whispered. Her fingernails bit at his head for a second before relaxing. "He must hate her."

McCallister nodded. "Yeah. It's kind of a toss-up between all of us who gets her first. Well, except Valdór."

"He's an interesting guy."

"And then some." McCallister shifted on the couch, stretching out his legs until his feet hung over the stuffed arm. He toed off his shoes and nestled his head into the warm crook of her lap. She stared down at him, a soft, gentle smile on her lips. Empathy and concern filled the depths of her eyes like sapphire sunshine.

McCallister's heart spasmed with shame and he closed his eyes. He didn't want to see her compassion turn to revulsion when she heard the rest of his story.

"Every day in that dungeon, Desdemona would come to us. She would drink from our bodies then force us to drink her blood. If we didn't, she would torture us. That's how James died. She pushed him too far, believed in the fabled power of a vampire's body a little too much. We are not immortal, garlic is our friend, but we *can* be killed. She drained him down to nearly his last pint of blood then waited too long to offer him the blood maidens she kept."

Her fingers stilled and he felt the shudder rush through her frame. "What are blood maidens?"

"Exactly what they sound like. Poor souls Desdemona kept enslaved for the express purpose of supplying herself and her legion of vampires with a ready source of blood. Back then, it was perfectly legal. Now, the Brigade has outlawed it but you can bet she still does it. I suspect quite a few of the old school vampires do." He shifted again and stroked her naked calf, smiling a bit as he felt goose bumps rise in the wake of his touch. He liked making her react to him in unexpected ways.

"What happened after the two weeks?"

The soft question shoved any relaxation he may have felt straight to hell. "I was moved upstairs. The third floor." He closed his eyes, hoping to stave off the bitter memories and the accompanying, lingering effects but he couldn't. The stench of heavy perfume and blood mixed in his nose and he clamped his teeth against nausea. "The second floor was where her whores, human and vampire alike, entertained gentlemen. The third floor was something entirely different. Six rooms. All male vampires."

Sheridan's fingers stilled. He licked his lips then slowly opened his eyes to stare up at her. She looked stunned and disgusted. He started to move away but she held him down with a soft hand and gentle plea. "Don't go," she said, voice as soft and appealing as a summer breeze.

McCallister allowed himself to re-settle on her lap.

"Tell me the rest."

"I was put in a room, though my chains were not removed. Strange but I remember just how it was decorated. Heavy French furniture. Frilly curtains in a hideous shade of red, a thick, expensive carpet on the floor, a wash basin, and soft, fluffy towels. The bed was a giant four-poster with a heavy brocade canopy over it. There was a matching desk and chair with papers, ink, and quills for writing. Current newspapers and magazines were in a holding box on the floor." He fisted his hands. "I wish to God I could rid myself of the memories."

Sheridan's fingers smoothed over his scalp again and once more he found himself relaxing.

"The first night was the worst." He swallowed hard, trying to clear his suddenly tight throat. "I was stripped, held by two huge men I now believe to be corrupt Guardians, and forcibly washed by the blood maidens. When they were done, the doused me in some horrid cologne that stank to high heaven then clothed me—if you can call it that—in a pair of white half-pantaloons and nothing else. Desdemona appeared and told me what my role in the house would be." The lump in his throat slipped to his chest. Pain radiated from the center of his sternum. He shifted again. Suddenly, Sheridan's palm dropped down, covering the ache and driving it away.

"I'm right here, McCallister," she whispered. "This is just a story, nothing else."

"No," he said on a rasp. "It's what defines me. What happened made me the man I am today. It colors everything I do."

She rubbed his chest lightly. "You can change that."

He nodded even though he wasn't sure such a thing was possible. Her optimism washed through him, buoying him. "Desdemona is twisted. Back then she provided the services of her girls in ways that were familiar to men the world over. But she wanted more. She knew women were just as sexually needy as men and found a way to create a supply chain for that demand."

Sheridan's hand flattened against him. "What did she do?"

He drew a hand over his face, turned his head toward the couch back, and closed his eyes. He couldn't bear to see her compassion turn to revulsion. "She turned me into a sex slave."

Sheridan gasped. "My God."

"There was no God involved, believe me. I prayed hard enough for an intervention that never came." He continued his tale, determined to be done with the damn topic once and for all. "Each night, the two men would bind my hands and feet to the bed. Desdemona's blood maidens would come into my room and torment me sexually until I was aroused and ready to 'perform.' Then a female customer would enter my room. She would take her leisure of my body, playing with me however she chose." He shuddered in distaste. "I cannot tell you how many times some filthy beast clambered onto my face and demanded I satisfy her."

"Oh, McCallister," Sheridan whispered. She leaned down to hug him and her warm, soft breasts enveloped his head.

Pleased shock held him immobile for a long moment. Sheridan had not pulled away or expressed any abhorrence at his revelations. He smiled against her flesh, the memories a little more distant and a little less acrid. "The first time I refused, Desdemona had me strung up naked in the middle of the house. She whipped me until my entire body was a mass of bleeding welts then she let the vampires drink from my body. She left me there for three days then hauled me back upstairs, cleaned me up, and bound me once more." He closed his eyes as hot shame poured through him. "The next time...the next time I did what she wanted. And from that night on, I continued to do so." He covered Sheridan's hand with his and pressed down on his chest. "You'd think a man could control his own cock, wouldn't you? But I was just a boy. My virginity was taken from me without my consent and all I learned about sex came from those women. Each night they'd taunt me, lick me, touch me when I wanted nothing more than to die. But they always managed to rouse my cock hard enough to climb on board and ride me. I felt helpless, powerless. The women—and Desdemona—were always in control. I could do nothing."

His eyes snapped open and he looked up at her with a grin. Sheridan's eyes narrowed with suspicion. "That's an awfully devious smile."

"I could do nothing until I learned how to control my orgasms. After I figured that out, I never came inside one of those bitches again. It was my only means of defiance and half the time they didn't even care. They just wanted to fuck themselves to climax then totter away, leaving me a disgusting mess in their wake. But I cared. It was my way of rebelling."

Sheridan laughed and smoothed her hand over his forehead before tracing his lips. "Very smart, McCallister."

Her praise warmed him from the inside, pushing aside the unease, the shame, the horrid stench of the past he'd been unable to escape for so long. "I was so damn young when it happened. I didn't know what the hell I was doing in or out of the bedroom. Desdemona also held us as thralls to her. She had us believing we would die without a daily dose of her blood. Each night, after the women left, she would visit the six of us and force us to drink from her. I fantasized about draining her into a husk but those damn Guardians were always too close. Day after day, year after year, I could feel myself becoming less human and more monster."

He sat up from her lap and spun to look at her, studying her face with an intensity he knew bordered on insanity. "Being a vampire is a living hell, Sheridan. The hunger is always there, the need to drink nearly unquenchable. There are changes in your body and mind that take you to dark places filled with the most wretched kind of thoughts you could ever conjure. It's like being a druggie or alcoholic and battling the urge for one more score. The constant battle is hard and tiring and yet, it never ends. The hunger instinct begins to take over and what semblance of humanity and ethics you have slowly disappears. I felt it happening. I *knew* it was happening. I couldn't live like that, Sheridan. I watched the man I thought was my best friend, the one who took me to her, destroy himself because of this curse. I knew I was heading for the same fate." He rose and paced the living room to stand in front of her hutch. He picked up one of the lace figurines. A ballet dancer poised on one pointed toe, the other slender leg jutting out with delicate precision. He could crush the porcelain with one touch. Destroy the beautiful object in his hand with quick, easy strength, and not look back. Just as he was afraid he could destroy her if he weren't careful.

He replaced the dancer and turned back to her. "I lost my life once and I was becoming a ravenous beast. I felt the only thing I could do was find a way to kill myself."

"No!" She leapt to her feet and rushed forward.

He held up a hand to forestall her touch. He needed to finish the tale. "It was the only way. I could no longer live with what I had become. Even the nightly visits from the women were becoming tolerable. I was losing myself, Sheridan. I decided I would attack Desdemona when she came into my room that night. Over the five years I'd been her slave, she'd become lax with security. Some of the other men on the floor were allowed to roam freely. Leopold was one of them. She only brought one guard with her that night. He stood outside my room with the door open, as he sometimes did when she sought to satisfy her own sexual desires." His throat convulsed. "She approached me and ordered me to kneel. I sank down and she held out her wrist then told me to drink. I knew I would need sustenance and strength. I also knew she was always momentarily weakened after a feeding. I took my fill, careful not to go over my allotment. Then, instead of releasing her, I grabbed her hand and twisted so hard, I broke bone. She cried out and struggled to free herself but I had the upper hand."

Sheridan's eyes were wide and both hands covered her mouth. He couldn't really tell if she was disgusted or terrified but he could hear her heartbeat pounding as hard and fast as any train could ever run.

"I had only moments to finish the job. I knew I couldn't kill her, but I could temporarily incapacitate her. That would leave only the Guardian at the door. I managed to get her to the ground where I put my hands around her neck." He looked down at his fingers, still able to feel her soft, smooth flesh trapped between them. McCallister returned his gaze to Sheridan. "Vampires have to breathe, you know. If she'd been a little weaker, I could have killed her. But I knew I didn't have that kind of time. I choked harder until she gurgled and passed out. Her mad heartbeat rang in my ears as I ran to the door, expecting to fight the Guardian. Instead, Leopold and four other stood in the hallway, the Guardian dead on the floor between them. We all escaped that night. Tore off into the darkness and never looked back.

"I didn't know where to go, where to turn. I feared Desdemona's retribution but I knew she was no idiot and wouldn't ever attack me unless she could get me alone. I made sure that never happened. I returned to my family home and tried to live a normal life." He scoffed at his own stupidity. "That worked out well. My family was shocked as hell to see me and why not? I had been missing for five years then returned looking exactly as I had as an eighteen year old."

Sheridan crossed the room and took him into her arms. Her scent, her heat, her compassion flowed around him like warm sea water. He cuddled her close, laying his cheek to her soft golden hair.

"My God, McCallister. You've been through enough to turn anyone bitter and distrustful."

He eased back. "Do I seem that way to you?"

She gave him a soft, sad smile and caressed his cheek. "You have barriers no woman could ever breach. With good reason, I admit. If I had been raped—" She faltered on a sharp inhalation and he winced at the harsh but accurate word.

"If I had been raped as you were, used as you'd been, I would make damn sure only I controlled every aspect of my body until the end of time. I understand. Our Joining, such as it is, will have to be enough. We'll make certain it is. No matter what comes our way, McCallister, we'll face it together."

His nose tingled and his throat swelled, rendering him speechless. Afraid he would start bawling like a baby at any second, he hauled her back into his arms and shoved her face into his chest.

"Mcfffstrr..."

He eased his grip so she could breathe.

His mind was a dizzying, light-speed-fast whirl of thoughts and impressions. Despite her mental *Keep Out* sign, he could feel the tenderness for him radiating from her. Sheridan's genuine depth of caring filled him to the brim before overflowing his heart.

She'd heard every word he'd said and it didn't matter to her. Not that he'd been a sex slave, not that he'd drank blood every day for years, not that he'd nearly, purposefully killed Desdemona.

She understood.

He was humbled by her empathy.

"Sheridan," he said hoarsely.

She looked up. "Yes?"

McCallister stepped back, freeing their bodies of any contact then slowly sank to the floor in front of her, knees cushioned by the soft rug. He took her hands, kissed her fingers, and met her startled gaze.

"Sheridan Aames, I do trust you."

Her inhalation was fast and sharp. She swayed lightly and tears turned her eyes an indigo pool of cautious hope.

"I trust you and I offer myself—my whole body—to you to do with as you please. Sheridan, tonight I give you all the control."

CHAPTER THIRTEEN

Sheridan stared down at McCallister. Tender emotion swamped her. This strong, confident man was on his knees, offering her his greatest fear. She tried to imagine how it would feel to be the one in charge. To have this wild, rugged man obey her every whim, ordering him about and denying or granting him his pleasure as he'd done with her.

A wellspring of affection filled her. Bending, she tugged at his shoulders. "Stand up, McCallister," she said.

He frowned then slowly rose, towering over her.

Yes, this is how it should be.

One step closed the distance between them. Sheridan cupped his cheek, stroking skin darkened and bristled by his five o'clock shadow. He remained still and neutral under her touch. Rising on tiptoe, she pressed a soft kiss to his lips.

"Thank you."

"For what?" he asked, wariness in the words.

"For trusting me enough to tell me your story. For trusting me enough to offer your body. For trusting me enough to know I would never hurt you." All the pieces fell into place and she smiled softly before stripping off her pink tank and pushing down her jean shorts and underwear. Still smiling up at him, she sank to her knees, spread her thighs apart, and laced her fingers behind her head. "Thank you for your offer, but I know this is where I belong. At your feet and at *your* command."

McCallister's eyes flashed a brilliant green. "Are you certain, my sweet?"

The soft warmth of certainty covered her again. "Yes, Sir."

He visibly jerked with those two simple words. Sheridan realized she had just as much power over him as he did her.

The knowledge was both comforting and exhilarating. She bowed her head. "I am yours."

As she waited for his first order, her entire body tingled with anticipation. Her naked pussy, spread open and gaping, pulsed hotly. Her clit swelled and her nipples hardened.

Will he flog me again? Spank me? Lightning fast memories of their last encounter zipped through her, making her lust grow even greater. She'd really liked the feeling of those nipple clamps.

"Rise, little one."

Startled, she jerked her head upward. He stared down at her, arms crossed, legs spread, expression unreadable.

Her heart skipped several beats before speeding up uncomfortably. "Did I displease you, Sir?"

His face softened. "No. You please me greatly. Stand, Sheridan, so that I may take my pleasure of you."

The formal words seemed exactly right and she slid her legs together. He reached down and lifted her upward. He threaded his fingers in her hair and tugged her head backward.

"You are more beautiful and special than you will ever know, Sheridan."

"Thank you," she whispered.

He bent to nuzzle her neck. A rash of goose bumps erupted when he nipped at her with his fangs. "Take me to your bedroom," he said with soft, firm command.

She laced their fingers, turned, and led him down the hallway to her spacious master bedroom.

Like every other room in her house, this one was cluttered to the rafters with knick-knacks, furniture, clothes, purses, and shoes. Most of the items were thrift store finds, but she was proud of the few real antiques she had. Like her bed.

She released his hand and walked to the large, four-poster bed. She grabbed on to a wooden post and grinned at him, battling a sudden bout of shyness. "Guess this was meant to be, huh? I never cared for four-poster beds until I saw this one and had to have it. That was about two years ago when I moved to Boston."

McCallister didn't so much as glance around the room. His steady emerald gaze remained focused on her. "It's nice," he said.

"Yeah." She hung on to the bed, wondering what the hell to do next. She didn't want to be in charge, wanted him to be the one making the decisions while she got to enjoy the hell out of herself.

She'd never realized just how freeing *voluntarily* giving up control could be.

She tipped her head and winked at him. "Coming to bed, McCallister?"

Between one blink and the next, he stood in front of her, disrobing with haste.

Sheridan watched avidly as he stripped his shirt off, revealing once more the ripped, toned muscles of his chest and abdomen. Her fingers curled with the itch to caress him. When his hands dropped to his waistband, her gaze eagerly followed.

He flicked open the button, then slowly slid the zipper down.

And stopped.

She continued to stare, breath held, waiting for him to reveal himself again.

Except he didn't.

She looked up at him, finding him smiling widely with a devilish twinkle in his eye. Quite a change from a few moments ago. Her heart swelled with happiness.

"Waiting for something, little one?" he asked with velvet smoothness.

Her lips twitched and she shifted. "Duh. I'm waiting for you to take your pants off."

He half laughed, half sighed and pulled his hands free. "I'm beginning to despair you'll never learn just what a submissive is, Sheridan."

She shrugged. "Be positive, McCallister. Don't view training me as a challenge." She reached out and tugged open his fly before shoving the pants downward. "Think of all the opportunities you're going to have to correct me with fun things like spankings, floggings, and whatever else your devious mind will conjure."

She dropped to her knees as his pants pooled. Gently, reverently, she pulled them off when he lifted first one foot, then the other.

He chuckled. "You're not supposed to find spankings all that fun if they're for punishment or correction."

It took her only a second to realize she'd slid down into submissive position automatically and wondered if he'd noticed. When she tipped her head back and met his hooded eyes, she knew he had.

And he approved.

Her pussy tingled at the silent praise.

Sliding her palms up his legs, she squeezed his taut thigh muscles before circling his hard, thick cock.

McCallister's hand landed on her head and urged her forward.

She didn't need to be told twice. Her mouth ached for the taste of his cock. Fingers wrapped around the base of his shaft, she opened her lips and took him inside.

"Christ, Sheridan, I love your mouth."

"Mff," she replied. She jerked the base with light pressure as she laved her tongue up and down the length of his cock.

His fingers tightened on her head.

Sheridan closed her eyes and gave all she had to sucking his beautiful cock. He was hot and rigid and heavy against her tongue. Each downward stroke filled her nostrils with his masculine sandalwood scent, further spiking her arousal.

His cock jerked and bobbed as she moved up and down, seeking to draw out his pleasure. Pursing her lips, she popped his head between in and out with tight compression.

"Fuck, you're going to make me come if you keep that up."

She grinned around his dick.

"Is that what you want, minx?" he asked. "Do you want me to spray your mouth and throat with my cum?"

"Mm-hmmm," she moaned around him. Then she pulled away and rocked back on her heels. "That would be lovely but I think I want you inside me, more. I want to feel your hands on my hips as you drive this lovely hard dick deep into my pussy."

His cock jerked with her words and she knew he liked them.

But he shook his head and helped her to her feet. "Sorry, minx. That won't be happening today."

"Um, it won't? I'm confused."

His smile was wickedly sweet. "Get on the bed, Sheridan, and I'll show you exactly what I mean."

She crawled onto her queen bed, settling her hands and knees on the burgundy comforter.

McCallister's big hand smacked her butt and she jerked forward, staring back at him.

"On your back."

She blinked a couple of times, frowned, then slowly turned and plopped her butt inelegantly down. McCallister stood at the end of the bed. He grabbed her ankles and gave a light jerk, pulling her flat, head on the pillows and body prone. He spread her legs, nearly to the point of discomfort.

"Don't move," he ordered. The bed dipped as he joined her, settling himself between her wide-spread thighs.

She lifted her head and stared at him. "What are you going to do?"

He slapped her sensitive inner thigh. "Didn't I tell you not to move? Proper submissives do as they're told."

She bit her lip and dropped her head back to the pillow. "I'm sorry, Sir."

"You'll pay for it later," he told her, voice sensually hard.

She grinned. "I'll hold you to that."

McCallister's chuckle reverberated against her pussy and she gasped, hips jerking. She lifted her head enough to see what he was doing. *What the hell, I'm already in trouble.*

She grabbed a second pillow, shoved it beneath her head and watched in wide-eyed fascination as his handsome, stubbled face descended to her pussy.

An involuntary clench made her lower lips gape.

"I'm aching to taste you," he said. "Since the second I smelled you, I wanted to delve into your sweetness."

Before she could even respond, his hot, wet tongue laid flat to her pussy. He licked upward, spreading her lips and ending at her clit.

Sheridan squeezed her eyes shut. "Again," she whispered.

She felt his smile at her sensitive skin. His wide shoulders rubbed against her legs, pushing them even further apart. His big fingers peeled open her pussy lips, exposing her to the warm heat of his breath.

Sheridan shuddered again. Her hands slid to his head, caressing the soft, silkiness of his hair. She bumped her hips upward, hoping he'd continue this hot torment.

McCallister didn't disappoint. He speared one finger into her hole, easily sliding in because she was so wet. His tongue lapped and tapped up and down her channel, lingering at her clit for a few maddening beats before descending again. He drove his finger in and out, pausing every few strokes to withdraw and suckle at the juices which ran down from her pussy to the crack of her ass.

Each pass of his tongue made her more excited, ratcheted her excitement upward.

She swallowed hard and tugged at his head.

He looked up at her but didn't pause his talented mouth. One black brow lifted in silent, amused question.

"If you don't stop, I might come," she told him.

His smile grew wider as his amusement increased. Still holding her eyes, he clamped his lips around her clit and suckled hard.

The sensual explosion hit her body with the force of a two-ton bomb. Heat poured through her as each part of her body clenched, released and clenched again trying to hold on to the euphoria cascading through her. The world turned fuzzy pink and green. She heard McCallister's voice in her head, coaching her, encouraging her, even as his finger and mouth continued their onslaught.

Her clit became ultra-sensitized and she moaned, bucking against his warm mouth then pulling backward, trying to ease the rapidly expanding sensation.

"Come again, Sheridan," he ordered.

And she did.

Her body bowed upward, she dug her fingers deep into the luxurious silk of his hair and squeezed her eyes shut as the pleasure rolled over and over and over.

When he finally lifted his mouth, she collapsed to the bed and trembled, breath coming in short, hard gasps.

"Ohmigod, ohmigod, ohmigod," she muttered. She raised a shaky arm and laid it over her eyes, blocking out the still swirling green lights.

The bed swayed as he moved up beside her. His hot body molded to hers and just like that, her desire returned full force.

"More," she rasped.

He tugged her arm away and turned her face to his. He kissed her lightly and Sheridan recoiled at the taste of her own juices but he wouldn't let her escape.

"No," he said. "Taste yourself. Sweet, like honey with a bite that promises pleasure time and again."

Tentatively she pursed her lips then gasped as the slickness of her juice hit her tongue. Another tremor rolled through her.

"It *is* sweet," she murmured.

"You sound surprised."

"It's not like I've ever tasted myself before."

He stroked her cheek. "A pity, as you can tell. You are exquisite."

Sheridan rolled to her side, propping her head on one hand and touching his lightly matted chest with the other. "That was a nice trick at the end."

He lifted a brow. "Which was?"

"You know, telling me to come and I did. I'm thinking you totally fed me a load of bullshit with that whole 'we can't compel anyone' line."

His lips twitched and she knew she'd caught him red-handed. Or red-tongued, as the case might be.

"Well, maybe I fibbed a little bit. It just depends on the person." His face grew serious. "But I wasn't kidding with you, Sheridan. You're strength of will is as great as any I've come across. Getting you to do something you don't want to do is impossible, whether someone has vampire powers or not."

"Are you saying I'm stubborn?" she asked with a mock gasp.

"Holy hell, yes." McCallister inched closer and his hard cock grazed the inside of her thigh, leaving a heated trail of need in its wake.

She reached down and gripped him, lightly jerking his thick shaft.

He hissed and his jaw clenched but he shook his head and rolled to his back.

Her hand fell away only to be replaced by his. McCallister tucked his other arm behind his head and watched her through half-lowered lids as he pleasured himself.

She sat up slowly, her own hand dipping between her legs as she watched. She'd never seen a man so unabashedly enjoying his own touch so much and it turned her on unbelievably.

His cock swelled and grew and lengthened with each sensuous slide. She could feel his gaze on her, but she couldn't tear hers away from his dick. Her mouth watered and her body constricted.

She wanted him so much.

"McCallister," she said, reaching out for him.

He let go of his cock and caught her hand. She met his clear green gaze, struck by the depth of passion and need in his eyes. He tugged her closer. "Straddle me, Sheridan."

Her heart leapt at the raw request. "Are you sure?"

His expression never shuttered. He stared at her with equal parts arrogant assurance and intense need. "Get on my cock. Now."

She grinned and crawled over him, laughing as she threw her right leg up and over his hips, careful not to graze his straining dick. Slowly she settled her wet pussy against his hard cock, sliding back and forth along the shaft, tormenting them both.

He groaned and gripped her hips. "Teasing a wild man is dangerous."

She settled her knees and leaned down, pressing her palms on his chest and grinding hard with her pussy. "I know. I like danger, haven't I told you that?"

He hissed and his fangs dropped. His face took on a dark, sexually-charged expression that chased every particle of lust she owned straight to her clit. She shuddered and nearly came just from that look, from the glint of his fangs, from the idea of being bitten by him again.

Sheridan lifted her pelvis, reached down and grasped his hot dick, then fitted him to the wet entrance of her pussy.

She kept her eyes locked with his as she sank lower, stopping only when he was fully embedded and stretching her open. Leaning forward, she licked the hollow of his neck, flicking lightly at the rapid beat of his pulse. His hands dug into her hips and yanked up.

She obliged his demand and started a slow, long rhythm that threatened to drive her insane in short order.

"Damn, McCallister."

He grunted, lifting his hips as she moved upward. "What?"

"You're big," she said. "I can feel every inch of your skin rippling inside of me."

His smile was smug. "Tit for tat, minx. Your sweet little pussy is clamping me so tight, it's like I'm caught in a vise."

"Good," she whispered and concentrated on the feel of him pushing into her, spreading her open, filling every bit of her. His flesh was molten and as hard as steel but very much alive. His eyes glittered with desire as he moved inside of her, and she couldn't tear her gaze from his. She wanted to watch him explode with the pleasure they were giving to each other.

She wanted *him* to enjoy the love-making for the beauty it contained.

His hands roved over her body as she rode him, long fingers molding her breasts, circling her nipples and tugging with alternating bouts of tantalizing gentleness and abrupt brute strength. Sheridan realized that even though she was on top, that she was in charge of the pace, McCallister was the one truly driving her. His hands commanded the speed and played over her body at will. He pinched her breasts, caressed her tummy and back, slid wetly between her legs and dallied at the tight hole of her sphincter, even when she protested.

Especially when she protested.

"Remember, my sweet slut, every part of you is mine to do with as I please." McCallister clenched his teeth and surged deep inside her pussy as his finger delved ever so slightly into her rosebud, effectively freezing her. "One day I will have your ass and you will beg me to fuck you there."

She didn't doubt it and his absolute certainty upped her lust by yet another level. She would fight him but he would persevere and they'd both come out on top. She curled her fingers into his chest, scoring his taut muscles, the need to mark him suddenly strong.

He groaned and pulled her down. "Kiss me," he demanded.

She adjusted her hips, gasping at the deeper plunge of his cock before pressing her mouth to his. The kiss started sweet and gentle but as her hips rose and fell, the rise of lust increased and she battered his lips with her tongue, demanding entrance.

He complied but his hand snaked into her hair, preventing her from moving forward. He suckled her tongue, flicked it with his own then rimmed her lips before pulling her head backward.

His cock pulsed and throbbed inside of her and Sheridan jerked her hips up and down faster. From the corner of her eye, she saw a soft green glow rise from the floor then lower from the ceiling, mingling with a wild cacophony of pink and white light. Motes of colors danced and bounded through the room.

Her pussy ached and heat burned upward from her clit, snaking through her belly and spreading to her tits before surging upward and exploding in her head.

"Sheridan," McCallister said. "Keep riding me, Sheridan. Do you understand?"

His hand fell away from her hair and she snapped upright, landing against his bent knees. Using them as a brace, she increased the rapid tempo of her wild thrusts. "Yes, Sir," she said between gasps. "I understand."

The room was enveloped by a mix of floral scents that nearly overwhelmed her. Roses, lavender, hydrangea all burst through her senses mingling with sandalwood, leather, and oak.

McCallister bucked up, grabbed her around the hips and rolled to his right, tucking her beneath him as they moved. His cock never left her pussy, nor did he stop his bruising, feverish thrusts.

She wrapped her arms around his shoulders and held him tight. His mouth found hers, her name a gasp of pleasure on his lips as he drove into her again and again.

A turbulent crescendo of light, scents and the wet slap of flesh on flesh built as he continued fucking her.

"God yes, McCallister," she muttered. "Please, please, please."

His hips moved with lightning speed, pushing into her pussy with urgent demand. She felt his dick swell and pulse. Her clit responded in kind.

"Hurry, McCallister," she pleaded. "Please, I want to feel you come inside of me."

He stared down at her, his green eyes bright as a mid-day sun, a feverish need pulsating in their depths.

She dropped her gaze to his mouth and suddenly she *knew*. Tipping her head back, she offered him her neck. "McCallister, I want to feel your fangs in me as you come. I want to give you life as you give me pleasure."

He stiffened and his expression grew savage. She should have been afraid.

Instead, she clenched him tighter with her pussy and tipped her head even further.

"Claim me, McCallister. Bite me."

He growled, then fastened his mouth to her neck. She thrust her hips at his just as his fangs pierced her skin. He stiffened and slammed into her body. The entire world exploded around them, raining down warm bits of light and scents. Sheridan felt her blood filling him even as his seed filled her, triggering her own orgasm.

She groaned, cupping his shoulders, his neck, his head as he took what he wanted and gave what she needed. She trembled and shook and held on to him as her only security. Her world narrowed down to

Logan McCallister and it made her heart surge with joy.

At last, the feral intensity faded and she drifted back to earth. McCallister lay atop her, his lips gently caressing her throat even as his hands feathered along her sides.

She shuddered and closed her eyes, smiling at the sheer impossibility of how damn good she felt.

"You okay?" he murmured.

She nodded, wincing only a little at the tenderness from his bite. "I'm great. You?"

He lifted his head, met her eyes, and slowly pulled free of her still grasping body. They both groaned. "Fucking fantastic."

She grinned up at him. "I agree. That was a fantastic fuck."

He rolled to the side and gathered her into his arms. He rained kisses along her cheek and chin before settling lightly on her lips. "No," he whispered. "That was us making love, not just fucking."

"Oh, McCallister." Sheridan sniffled. "That's very sweet."

His expression turned serious. "Thank you," he said.

She cupped his jaw, stroking his now familiar and beloved face. A surge of strength hit her, followed quickly by what seemed to be a movie featuring a young

McCallister. Instead of the brief glimpses she'd had the first time, now she saw everything that happened to him from the moment he'd been born until he died and was re-born. It all collided so quickly, she grew dizzy from the mental assault.

Tears formed in her eyes as she watched him triumph over his past and carve out a niche in the world under his own terms.

When she blinked the tears away, she found him staring at her with a stunned expression. She figured it matched her own.

He held her close and stroked her hair. "You'll never have to worry again, Sheridan."

She realized he must have had the same experience and that he now knew all *her* memories, too. Oddly, the knowledge didn't bother her one bit.

"Neither will you," she whispered and kissed him softly. "Now, McCallister. Now, we are Joined."

CHAPTER FOURTEEN

"I have a question."

McCallister shifted on the pillow so he could see Sheridan's face. Her skin still glowed with after-sex bliss which made him want to crow like a rooster from the rooftops. He put that look on her face. That sort of hazy, "where the hell am I?" look. Yep, he did that.

"Okay, shoot."

Her pink tongue swiped slowly across her bottom lip and he was immediately distracted by thoughts of just how good and soft and wet her tongue felt sliding up, down, and all over his cock.

"So?"

He re-focused on her face. Wariness replaced the sensual haze. He glimpsed a bit of defensiveness in the depths of her blue eyes, too. McCallister pulled her closer, draping her over his chest. He slid one leg between hers and cradled one of her hands in his. "Sorry, sweetheart, you lost me as soon as that sweet tongue peeked out. You had me remembering all the wicked things you can do so well with your mouth. Would you mind repeating your question?"

She jerked then giggled and scratched at his chest. But he noticed the wariness dissolved with her smile. "You're incorrigible."

"I am at that. So, what did you want to know? Nothing is off limits, Sheridan," he said on a husky tone. "I'm an open book for you now."

"I know. I read that book start to finish, remember?"

"Yeah." He tweaked her nose. "Kudos for not completely freaking out."

She snorted. "Dude, if I were going to freak out, it would have happened a long time ago. Oh, pretty much when I realized you were a for real vampire."

He laughed.

She winked then her face settled back into serious. "When I had the dubious pleasure of meeting with Desdemona, she said you'd never turned anyone. Is that true?"

Of all the questions she could have asked, that was not the one he'd expected. He forced the lump of surprise and automatic revulsion back down his throat. "Yeah," he said on a ragged rasp. "I wasn't kidding when I told Barrett this world is a horror. I wouldn't wish it on anyone."

Sheridan plastered herself even closer. Her body warmed him, battling away the icy fingers of fear that tried to creep up on him. "Even after all these years? You haven't gotten used to it?"

"I guess I have but it doesn't mean I like it any better. The hunger is constantly there and I think that's the worst for me. I don't want to feed but I know I have to because I want to live."

"What's the hunger like?"

Her soft question hit him with the impact of a bullet and he couldn't repress a shudder. "It's like being outside on the hottest, most sweltering and miserable day. Baking underneath a two o'clock sun and feeling every bit of moisture wrung from your body. All you want is a drink of water. Just a sip. Just enough to wet your palate and let you swallow. Your tongue is thick and your throat aches from being denied. It plays with your mind and soon all you can think of is getting that one drop of water until it consumes you. You will do anything for that single, sustaining sip."

He looked down. Her eyes were wide and tear-stained. She worried her bottom lip between her teeth and a deep anguish showed in the azure depths of her gaze. He could see all the way to her tender heart and the way she hurt *for him* left him stunned and elated and humbled all at the same time. McCallister wiped away a lone tear that escaped the corner of her eye. "The worst part is that drinking never really satisfies the thirst. But like a nagging, constant back ache, you learn to live with it."

"Oh, McCallister," Sheridan murmured. She scooted higher on the bed and kissed him lightly. "That fucking sucks."

He smiled at the fervent and soft-spoken observation. "Yeah, it does. There are other reasons, too. Insomnia, paranoia, a general feeling of being unwell, amplified senses, rashes."

"Rashes?"

He winked. "Just seeing if you were paying attention. It's funny, I've met several vampires who have never experienced any of the things I've just mentioned and others who've had those and scores more. I guess everyone is unique. But I know how *I* felt. It lingers in my mind like bad foot odor."

"Ew."

"Exactly."

She stretched and her breasts slid languidly along his chest. Her nipples tightened to hard little points and he growled as he caught one between his fingers. "I want you again," he said.

Sheridan settled her breast deeper into his palm even as her fingers stroked up his thigh and cupped his balls. "Good, 'cause I want you, too."

He grabbed her nape and pulled her down for a long, satisfying, and very wet kiss. When he broke off, they were both panting like they'd run a marathon.

"Damn," she whispered and wiggled fully on top of him. She stroked his brow, his cheeks, his lips and stared raptly down at him.

"What?" he asked, feeling a bit self-conscious at her blatant admiration.

"I noticed from the moment I saw you what a sexy guy you were."

He grinned. "You did, huh?"

"Yep." She peppered his lips with soft, tender kisses. "But there's much more to you, McCallister. I've seen your horrors and I've seen the beauty that lies within you."

Another sheen of moisture clouded her eyes and she ducked her head to rest against his shoulder. He caught her slight sniffle and caressed her hair. For the first time in decades, McCallister was struck speechless. Sheridan's emotions buffeted him with the force of hurricane strength winds, knocking down the walls he'd spent so many years erecting.

Holding her close, he nuzzled her neck. "You make me that way, Sheridan." His voice dipped gruffly and he cleared his throat. "Before you teetered into my life on those ridiculous high heels, I merely existed. Now..." He inhaled a shaky breath, afraid of admitting to the riot of tender feelings swirling in him but more afraid not to give voice to the miracle she created.

"Now what?" she mumbled against his shoulder.

"Now, I can't imagine my life without you." A sudden, dark pang ripped through his heart and he gasped then trembled.

There would come a time, he knew, when he'd *have* to say goodbye to Sheridan. He would not turn her, even if she asked him to do so. That would be the ultimate horror for them both.

He pulled her head up and kissed her with a wild, frantic hunger, anxious to claim her once more. The future would wait. Right now, she was his.

His soul mate.

† † †

McCallister buckled his belt and stared down at Sheridan. She lay sprawled in the bed, a tangle of sheets and tousled blond hair. Her blue eyes were once more sleepy and sated.

"You going to stay in bed all day?"

She rolled onto her back and arched in a stretch meant to entice. His cock banged against his zipper. Taking a half step forward, he barely jerked himself to a stop.

God, how I want her again.

His need for Sheridan bordered on obsession. He wasn't sure how he felt about it.

She dropped her shoulders and grinned. "Maybe. I have my laptop and food, so I don't have to go anywhere. I can work on my story and be safe and sound in my own place, just like you want me to be."

McCallister waggled his brows at her. "Don't tell me you're choosing *now* to start obeying me?"

She sat up and reached for her discarded T-shirt. The soft cotton shimmied over her head, covering her delectable breasts from view, and he sighed with disappointment.

"Just trying to keep you on your toes, copper. I wouldn't want you to get bored." She scrambled from the bed and threw her arms around him.

He laughed and hugged her close, inhaling the soul-deep familiar scent of lavender and roses. "Don't worry, sweetheart, I don't think that will ever happen."

She kissed him then danced from his arms and out the door. "I don't want to take any chances," she yelled down the hallway.

He followed her to the living room, watching as she perched on the sofa, her supple legs curled under her. She grabbed the remote and flipped the television on then hauled her laptop bag onto the coffee table. "See, I'll be good. I'll sit right here, watch a ton of home decorating shows, dig a little more into Vampire Dust, and be in this spot when you get home."

"Uh-huh."

"Honest," she replied. As her computer booted up, she leaned against the sofa and frowned up at him. "Are you sure this Dust stuff is really something Barrett created?"

"Yeah," he said. "It fits. Barrett has always been interested in experimenting. If he can heal himself *and* become a super vampire, then he'll do whatever it takes. You are the only unknown in all of this. Why is he targeting you? Surely there's someone else out there with the same kind of DNA you possess."

Her throat worked a few times as she outwardly struggled with panic. Her nostrils flared and her head bobbed a little bit before she straightened her spine and squared her shoulders. "I think it's a good thing."

He glared. "What the hell are you talking about?"

She lifted her palm. "Think about it. If Barrett is focused on me, then we know he's not going to go out and find someone else to pick on. Some innocent soul who won't have a clue he's in danger until it's way too late."

His jaw went mulish. "I don't want you in danger, either, Sheridan. Unacceptable."

She rolled her eyes, leaned forward and typed in her password. "I'm not going to put myself in danger, McCallister. I don't have a death wish. I just think knowing his plan gives us the advantage. He doesn't know we know, right? So, he'll be less likely to suspect anything in the way of capture you guys can come up with."

"You're making my head hurt," he said.

"Take an aspirin," she replied. Her computer beeped and several windows flowed onto the screen. Sheridan stood and stretched again. He heard the pop of each vertebrae but his gaze was focused on the just-visible crack of her butt peeking from her tiny red panties. She lowered her arms and the T-shirt covered her butt again.

Damn.

"I'll walk you to the door," she said, a smile as wide as a football field on her full lips. "That is, if you're done staring?"

He kissed her then patted her panty-clad ass. "Sweetheart, I have a feeling I'll never get tired of staring at you."

Her cheeks bloomed with pink pleasure. "Awww, that's sweet."

"God, don't say that where any of the guys can hear you. I'll never live it down."

He headed for the door, aware of her trailing him. "Ooh, blackmail. I like it."

McCallister turned and pulled her close, this time smacking her butt with more force. Enough to leave his handprint, he was sure.

She gasped and bucked beneath him. "McCallister!"

He winked, kissed her hard and eased away. "Lock the door, don't open it for anyone, and don't go anywhere."

"Yeah, yeah, yeah. I'm a big girl, McCallister. I know how to stay safe."

He opened the door and stepped outside, turned and lifted a brow. "Close the door, Sheridan."

Her sigh was long and exasperated but she did as ordered. He waited until the tumblers rolled over and the chain rattled as she slid it home. "Go away, McCallister," her voice filtered through the door. "I'll see you when you get home."

He nodded at the peephole, turned and sauntered down the drive to his car.

When you get home. Damn, I like the sound of that.

McCallister realized he had to put a stop to Barrett and quickly. The man was a threat to Sheridan and that was absolutely unacceptable.

† † †

Having finished her assignments for the next day, and mind drained of any additional creative word wrangling, Sheridan plopped onto the couch and grabbed her remote control. She flipped through the channels a few minutes, settled on the latest baking challenge show, and scanned her emails. She'd deleted a good thirty messages before her computer beeped loudly.

Video call from Bert.

She grinned as she muted the TV, picked up the laptop, and settled back to the couch to answer. She pressed the answer button and waited for the image to focus.

All she saw was a hazy dark screen. "Bert?"

A slight noise sounded off-screen then Bert shuffled into view. His normally spit-shine appearance had given way to frazzled hair, a black eye and a blood-spattered white shirt. The normally rosy hue of his face morphed into wan, drawn lines. She bolted upright, jostling the computer.

"Bert! What's going on?"

He shook his head, mouth working but she couldn't hear anything. She checked her volume and found it up to normal.

A large hand settled on Bert's thin shoulder and the older man suddenly slumped forward. Sheridan gasped and grabbed at the monitor with both hands. "Bert. What's going on? Where are you?" He was slumped down. She saw the pink crown of his head and the slats of a chair behind him. Squinting into the murkiness of the room beyond him, all she could see were some kind of long tables.

Bert's head slowly lifted and she heard his soft exhalation. "Sheridan, I'm in a bit of trouble here." He sat back, smoothed a trembling hand over his head and grimaced. "I need your help."

A sick feeling filled the pit of her stomach, rising on a tidal wave of bile to clog her throat. "Where are you?" she whispered, afraid she already knew the answer.

"Barrett's compound."

She squeezed her eyes shut. "Shit."

"Yeah, thought the same thing myself."

A voice too low to hear snapped a command at the old man. He sniffed and stared into the camera. She could tell he didn't want to tell her anything, didn't want to ask her for help, didn't want to endanger her. But she also knew he would because Bert wanted to live.

"Tell me," she said. "It's okay."

He hesitated then his shoulders slumped. "Barrett says he'll let me go if you come here. I don't know what he wants with you but it's not good."

A fist shot in-frame and clipped the old man on the jaw. He rocked sideways.

"Bert!" Sheridan yelled.

Her old friend listed to the left, shaking his head and wiggling his jaw.

"Listen to me, you fucktard," she bit out. "You hurt him again and I will end you. Got me?"

Harsh, mocking laughter filled her living room. "Not scared of you." The words were hard, guttural, and barely intelligible, but she understood.

Red rage filled her vision and she broke the shell of her mouse, she gripped it so hard. "You should be. Tell me where to come."

Bert shook his head again but she ignored him, speaking to the douche bazooka hiding in the shadows.

"Where is Barrett?"

"Ask Cly-pee Jones," the voice said. "Two hours then he die."

The video call ended.

Sheridan threw the computer to the side and leapt to her feet. Sprinting to her bedroom, she yanked on jeans, a bra, and her sneakers.

"Where's my phone? Where's my damn phone?" She tossed the covers and sheet off the bed, trying to keep hold of the panic choking her.

The phone wasn't in the bed.

She checked the bedside tables, the bathroom, the kitchen, and the cushions of the couch.

"Son of a bitch, where is it?" she shouted to the living room.

The urge to throw things grew stronger with every breath she took. That would not do. Half the stuff in her house was an heirloom of some sort.

"Calm down. Breathe. One. Two. Three." The absurdity of talking herself off the ledge actually helped her rein the wildness a little bit. She flexed her fingers, took one last, deep breath, and sat on the couch, hoping to re-trace her steps.

She'd come home from the office, stormed into her house, threw her laptop bag on the couch, and her purse into the closet.

She rose, opened the closet door, and found her cute red purse upended on the floor. Her phone lay innocuously on top of her lipstick and wallet. She snatched up the cell and frantically found McCallister's number.

Pacing the length of her living room, she counted each ring. Pain radiated between her shoulder blades as the tension once more grabbed hold of her like a sumo wrestler in a championship match.

"Sheridan?" McCallister's sharp voice held frantic suspicion.

"I need you," she blurted out. Then, without warning, wrenching sobs tore from her throat. Her knees trembled, threatening to send her to the carpet at any second. She made it back to the couch, sinking into its depths, all the while trying to control her crying.

"Sweetheart? Are you hurt? Sheridan, talk to me, damn it!" Panic rose with each word.

"Not me," she gasped out. "Bert. Barrett has Bert."

"What? How do you know? Where are you?"

Sheridan finally managed to squelch the crying but a few hiccups escaped her as she replied. "I'm at home and I know because I just got off a video call with him. He looks awful, McCallister. Those goons worked him over but good."

"Did you notice anything else? Do you know where he is?"

She heard rustling, then the light scratch of pen on paper. "What are you doing?"

"Writing a note. I'm coming to you, but I gotta let Chief Holland know."

"Oh. Okay." She sniffled and wiped her eyes with the back of her hand. Her heart settled back to a halfway normal beat and she wrestled the panic into a manageable fear. "They told me it was Barrett." She gripped the phone tight. "McCallister, they said Barrett would trade Bert for me."

"No fucking way," McCallister snarled into her ear.

She stiffened. "He's my friend. It's my fault he's in the predicament. I'm not going to abandon him."

"Neither am I," McCallister said. "But I'm not giving you to that bastard either. I'm going to call Leopold. Everyone will come to you but don't open the door to anyone except me."

Relief slowly replaced the gripping fear. "Sullivan can open the door himself."

McCallister snorted. "True. Be there in fifteen, Sheridan."

"Hurry, McCallister," she whispered. "I need you."

"Be strong, sweetheart. You have me."

The line went dead and Sheridan jumped up to pace again.

Why did Barrett snatch Bert? Just to use as a pawn against her or was there something more to it? Did the old man have some vampire power that Barrett coveted? Would he inject her friend with one of his damn Dust potions?

The questions drove her more than half crazy, though it was a state of mind to which she was rapidly becoming accustomed.

Desperate to dispel the silence, Sheridan flipped the television to a rock and roll music station.

The thumping bass, rhythmic drums, and kicking riffs of one of her favorite bands filled the air. She breathed a deep sigh of relieved appreciation. Her mind started to settle down and allow her to think more clearly, with less emotion.

She trusted McCallister. He would save Bert and take care of Barrett, one way or the other. Though she didn't have as much information about the rest of the vampires he hung out with, she was willing to put her faith in them as well.

"I should make tea," she said, checking the clock on the cable box. McCallister promised fifteen minutes and that had been nearly four minutes ago. Surely someone would arrive at any moment.

In the kitchen, she taped three huge tea bags to a large measuring cup, added water and zapped the whole thing in the microwave for five minutes.

As the tea steeped, she measured out a cup of sugar, added a quarter cup more for good measure then dumped it into a large pitcher.

Six minutes remaining. Come on, McCallister.

Sheridan removed the tea bags from the water then poured the hot liquid into the sugar-laden pitcher. She frantically stirred the mixture until the granules mostly dissolved. She held the pitcher under the tap and filled it to the top, gave it another stir then stuck it in the fridge to start chilling.

The doorbell rang as she shut the refrigerator door.

Her breath caught, she spun and flattened herself to the stainless steel fridge. "McCallister would have pounded on the door, not rang the bell."

Licking her lips, Sheridan power walked through the house and peeked out the peep hole. Sullivan Alexander stood on her stoop.

He winked. "Heard you know a chap in a spot of trouble. I'm here to help."

She gripped the doorknob but McCallister's admonition stalled her. "Where's McCallister?"

Sullivan shrugged. "Don't know. Not with you, I'm assuming?"

"No," she said loudly. "Why would I ask if he was here?"

"Women can be a bit daft, love. No offense."

"Plenty taken," she snapped back.

He rocked back and forth. "Are you going to let me in or do I have to stay out here in the burning sun? I could fry to ashes, you know."

She choked on a laugh. "McCallister said that was crap. He also said not to let anyone in until he gets here."

Surprise rippled over the vampire's face. "And you're listening? Huh, impressive."

"What's impressive?"

"Nothing," he replied. His hazel gaze drifted downward and she let go of the doorknob.

Surely he wouldn't...

"I could open it myself, if I had a mind to, you know."

She couldn't stop the giggle this time. "Exactly what I told McCallister. Are you going to?"

Though distorted by the fish-eye lens, his handsome face twisted with humor. "As I don't relish having my arse handed to me on a platter, no. Believe I'll wait right here for the chap. He can be quite unpleasant."

Sheridan leaned her head against the cool wood door. The absurd, shouted conversation was actually making her feel better. Had that been Sullivan's intention all along?

"Probably a good idea," she said softly.

Seconds later a warmth infused her and she looked out the peephole again. McCallister was stalking up her carefully edged sidewalk. She winced as his heavy foot sliced through a once-cheery row of daylilies. She didn't have much of a green thumb but he was dicing her attempt like a professional chef julienned carrots.

She gripped the handle, flipped over the deadbolt, and opened the door. Her heart banged against her rib cage. She wanted desperately to fling herself into his arms and lose herself in the security she knew he'd offer but she hesitated.

Wonder what his position on PDA is?

McCallister bulldozed past Sullivan, yanked her into his arms and held her tight. A wild tangle of emotions swamped her—relief, fear, fury, resolve. Sheridan wrapped herself around him and buried her face in the crook of his neck. Inhaling deeply, she sucked down his leather and sandalwood aroma then did it again.

Her nerves seemed to settle in proportion to the breaths.

"So, we gonna stand out here all day or what?" Sullivan's tone held equal parts mirth and snark.

Sheridan barely had time to gasp as McCallister stepped over the threshold into her hallway. He stopped, put her down, and looked back at Sullivan who hovered at the doorway. Unease had replaced the light humor.

She waited but the other vampire didn't come in. With a frown, she waved at him. "Well come on in, Sullivan. Can't have you catching a sunburn, can we?"

The expression on his face melted back into cock-sure arrogance. He sauntered inside and immediately cased the joint.

She glared at him. "Hey bub, keep those light fingers to yourself."

McCallister snorted and Sullivan held up his hands, palms out. "No worries, Sheridan. I don't lift from friends. Unless they really deserve it. Besides, I'm a legitimate businessman. Got my own company and everything. I'm the most trustworthy thief you'll ever meet."

She rolled her eyes and headed for the door to shut it but caught sight of Brooks, Calliope, and Valdór making their way up the sidewalk. She stepped back but they, too, hesitated on the stoop. With an exasperated sigh, she motioned them in. "Come on in. I'm not as rich as Brooks. Can't afford to air condition the outside, you know."

As with Sullivan, their expressions lightened. Suspicion bit at her. As soon as the group trouped inside, she closed the door then turned slowly to pin McCallister with a demanding glare. "You lied, didn't you?"

He pursed his lips. "About what?"

"You mean you lied about more than the invitation thing? What about garlic, holy water, and silver crosses?"

Sullivan laughed. "What loads have you been feeding this girl, McCallister?" He nudged the detective. "Though kudos to you on her training. I'm shocked by how fast she's progressed."

Heat burned Sheridan's cheeks. *Could they all tell? Is my growing desire for submitting really that evident? I'm going to kill McCallister.*

"No, I didn't lie. Much. The invitation thing just makes it easier. Should it come to that, don't ever invite anyone in you don't absolutely know and trust."

"Well, I'm so glad that worked out well with you," she muttered, still mortified by the idea they all knew she was becoming a submissive. That should stay private. Special.

McCallister turned to Sullivan. "What are you talking about, anyway? What training?"

The hazel-eyed thief tossed her an approving glance. "She wouldn't let me in until you got here. Said you told her not to. Got to admit, old chap, didn't think she'd bow down that quickly."

"Oh for Pete's sake," Sheridan muttered.

The doorbell rang and she jumped with a light shriek, her nerves totally shot. She looked through the peephole and found Leopold lounging against the door.

She slowly opened it, swept her arm aside and asked him to come in, teeth tightly clenched.

He frowned as he complied. "Everything okay? What'd I miss?"

"Nothing," she said, tossing a glare at McCallister. "Is this everyone? No other surprises for me? I'm getting kind of tired of them."

Calliope approached and touched her sleeve. "I'm very sorry," the woman said softly. "Since his turning, my father is not the same man."

Sorrow and sadness were embedded in every fiber of the vampire's being, eliciting instant sympathy in Sheridan. Her annoyance slid away like mud off a greased pig. She caught Calliope's shoulders and pulled her into a hug. The other woman remained stiff but after a long moment, her hands did reach up and return the embrace, however tentatively.

Sheridan pulled away and stared at her, still holding her shoulders. "You are not responsible for anything he's done. His choices are his own."

Calliope nodded but tears pooled in her ebony eyes. "He's quite brilliant. That's the scary part. He's set his mind to harvesting all the best aspects of vampiric power as well as taking the DNA from those humans he deems worthy. Unfortunately his quest for perfection has led him to an even deeper level of madness." She looked at McCallister and the Sheridan saw the sadness deepen to absolute agony. Her heart pinched with empathy. "You're going to have to kill him, aren't you?"

Brooks was at her side immediately. He eased her away from Sheridan with one arm wrapped around her shoulder. "You don't have to come, Callie. We can do this without you."

"No," she said, shaking her head. "He's my father, despite the monster he's become. I must be there. Maybe I can reason with him."

Sullivan snorted. "Sweetums, the time for reasoning has long since passed."

Sheridan glared at him and Valdór elbowed him in the side. She gave the

Viking a wide smile and his cheeks flushed as he turned away.

Leopold cleared his throat. "Just so we're clear here, everyone knows this is a damn trap, right?"

"Yes," McCallister said. "But we have no choice. We know he has Bert but not how many other victims might be in that lab right now. He wants Sheridan and he wants me, so we're gonna give him that. The rest of you are just along as back-up."

"He'll set his beasts on us," Calliope said. "He's managed to make them semi-intelligent beings. They have primitive forms of communication and some critical thinking skills." She straightened, her expression moving from sadness to determination. "We are going to have to kill them all. They can't be allowed to grow. Nature is nature and once set in motion, the consequences of tampering with it can be more deadly than we know."

Valdór nodded. "I believe we, as vampires, have proven that very well."

Now that the moment of action was upon them, Sheridan's nerves rattled and her stomach pinged. She inched close to McCallister, worming her way into the safety of his arms again. He hugged her tight, resting his chin on the crown of her head.

"We know what we have to do. Sheridan and I will confront Barrett. Leopold, Sullivan, and Brooks will deal with the hybrids. Calliope, you and Valdór will remain as near to the background as possible. Try to rescue Bert, but stay out of sight."

"The girl I understand," Valdór said, "but why me?"

"Barrett doesn't know about you," McCallister said. His fingers tightened on Sheridan's arm and his heart started to pick up its pace. "If he did, you'd have gone missing long ago. He's a scientist at heart. Experimenting on you would make his century. I'm not willing to risk you for his insanity."

Valdór tugged on his beard, a huge frown marring the plane of his forehead. "I do not like this. I'm no coward to hide behind a woman's skirts."

McCallister sighed. "No one is saying you are. I'm just asking you to use caution. I need someone who can take care of themselves to look out for Calliope. I'm trusting you with that job, Valdór."

The big man continued to glare before his shoulders relaxed. "Your logic does not sweeten reality, McCallister." His silvery-blue glance slid toward Calliope and he smiled softly. "But this one I will guard with my life."

"Let's hope it doesn't come to that," McCallister said.

CHAPTER FIFTEEN

"He's definitely expecting us," Sullivan murmured from the back seat of Brooks' long town car.

McCallister studied the brightly lit house as they pulled through the open gates. The square house appeared compact and minimal. Floodlights hung from each corner and spread near-daylight illumination on the gravel driveway. The bright glare exposed the peeling, blue paint and weathered boards underneath. All the windows were covered by dark curtains. "Bastard isn't being shy, that's for sure." Even though they all knew Barrett was setting them up, walking right into the lion's den didn't feel right.

He looked at Sheridan, more afraid for her than his own life. He'd spent the last hundred years dodging death, it didn't bother him. But he'd just found her. He wasn't willing to give her up yet.

"His cockiness will be his downfall," Calliope murmured. "Father believes himself to be both invincible and smarter than anyone else."

The car stopped and they all piled out. McCallister grabbed Sheridan's hand. "Stay close to me. No matter what happens, stay close."

She gripped his fingers in a grip that would have snapped the bones of a lesser man. "Don't worry, copper, I'm not plan on ditching you any time soon."

He managed a smile, brought her fingers to lips and kissed lightly. "That's my girl."

Calliope and Valdór skirted the floodlights then disappeared into the meager shadows at the right side of Barrett's house where no bulbs burned. McCallister directed the rest of them to the front door.

"Bet it's not locked," Sullivan said.

"You sound disappointed," Brooks said, carefully picking his way over the gravel driveway.

"I'm always looking for ways to hone my craft," the thief replied.

The banter ceased as soon as McCallister reached for the knob. The door slid soundlessly open.

"Come in, McCallister. I have been waiting your arrival with great anticipation." Barrett's voice bounced down from an overhead speaker.

Cautiously, McCallister stepped inside, keeping Sheridan crowded close behind him. Despite the absurdity of using a gun on a vampire, he pulled his service revolver anyway. None of them had any idea what sort of back-up Barrett had and McCallister wasn't willing to take the chance of being unprepared.

They fanned out into the hallway. The house was entirely silent. Nothing moved. The lack of noise was unnatural.

"I'm down in the lab." Barrett's tinny voice came from another overhead speaker. "There's a corridor at the back of the house. I assure you, you're all perfectly safe." A low chuckle vibrated eerily from the ceiling. "For now."

Sullivan and Leopold disappeared into the rooms ahead of them, reappearing moments later and giving curt nods.

"Nothing," Sullivan said.

"It's clean," Leopold agreed. "I saw the corridor he's talking about, too. It's through the kitchen. Door is wide open. Smells funny, though."

They inched into the kitchen where a wide industrial door stood propped open. A small wire fan blew air from the hallway into the kitchen.

"Funny?" Sheridan said. "That reeks. Like sour onions sprayed with some sort of cinnamon." She tried to move past him, but McCallister yanked her back.

"Stay in the middle and be careful, Sheridan."

She didn't roll her eyes or huff, which shocked him. Instead she nodded once and took a few steps into the hallway. Leopold, Brooks, and Sullivan immediately surrounded her, which relieved McCallister. He knew his friends would watch over her. Even if something happened to him, Sheridan would be all right.

He followed them down the stark white hallway. Overhead fluorescents flickered with their steps while broken tile littered the floor. The smell lessened as they reached the end and another door.

This one was closed. Sullivan looked over his shoulder, one hand hovering on the steel handle. "Want me to try it?"

McCallister drew a deep breath. He shouldered his way to the thief's side, looked behind him and grinned to see Sheridan being shuttled all the way to the back of the pack. He returned his gaze to Sullivan and nodded sharply.

"Do it."

The handle jiggled but didn't open the door.

"Damn," McCallister muttered. "Guess he's not making it entirely easy on us."

Sullivan whipped out his lock set, knelt and fiddled for a few seconds. He surged upward, pushed the handle and shoved the door inward.

The room beyond was immense. It looked like a giant warehouse filled with various steel carts, chemicals, tables, tubes, and a huge vat that stood easily eight feet tall and six feet wide. A few gurneys were lined up at the far end of the warehouse, each with a form lying still on top of the metal.

No sign of Barrett or his hybrid creatures.

"Bert!" Sheridan said on a gasp.

Her small hand tugged at McCallister as she wiggled her way between him and Sullivan.

Bert sat in the rear left of the room, slumped on a wooden chair. His chest, waist and legs were secured with duct tape. His silvered head hung down and McCallister couldn't tell if the old man was breathing or not.

"Easy," he murmured, holding her back.

Brooks strode through them with Sullivan and Leopold close at his heels. A sudden bright light clicked on, flooding the three with a glare. "Far enough, gentlemen. McCallister, if you and Miss Aames would join your friends?"

Barrett's voice drifted through the room but McCallister still couldn't pinpoint the bastard. Too many heartbeats in the room to differentiate between anyone. Except Sheridan, of course. He'd recognize her life pattern no matter where he was.

He gripped her hand tight. "Stay close," he repeated.

"Damn straight," she muttered.

They cautiously walked toward the ring of light, stopping just beyond its boundaries. "Coming out, Barrett? Or do you prefer to ambush us?"

"If I'd wanted you dead, McCallister, you would be. For the moment I prefer you alive, even if it's not necessary." That damn eerie, half-mad chuckle filled the air again and grated on McCallister like a fork scraping a dinner plate.

"Big words for a hidden man," McCallister replied.

Leopold, Brooks, and Sullivan eased out of the light ring.

"I didn't tell you to move," Barrett snapped.

"Tough shit," Sullivan retorted and took another few steps toward Bert.

"Stop," Barrett snarled. He appeared from behind the large vat, training a long silver gun at them. Six hulking, furry beasts with glowing red eyes and teeth lethal enough to rival a great white shark followed him.

The six fanned out behind Barrett in a semi-circle. Their heartbeats were faster than anything McCallister had heard before and he wondered at their genetic make-up. They looked half like wolves mixed with some kind of human and bear.

He shuddered at the implications. Calliope was right—the unnatural creatures must be destroyed.

"A gun isn't going to stop us, Barrett," McCallister said.

Barrett waved the barrel toward them. "It might not stop you, but it will do significant damage to Miss Aames." His grin shone with ferocious insanity. "Despite your lovely DNA, you will die if I shoot you in the right spot." His gaze swung to McCallister's. "I don't need *her* alive, McCallister. I can harvest her genes as she dies on my floor. You'll do well to remember that."

McCallister's heart skipped several beats and fury rose in him like a tsunami. He struggled to remain calm. What he really wanted to do was leap forward and rip the bastard's head from shoulders.

"Ah, ah, ah. Your temper is showing," Barrett said. He tapped his temple with a finger. "I can hear you, you know."

McCallister frowned and slanted a glance at Brooks who looked equally as surprised.

"Didn't my daughter tell you?" Barrett asked. "I've been experimenting with all sorts of vampire traits." He winked at Sheridan. "I had to flood the streets with Dust in the last few weeks in order to get you to take an interest, Miss Aames. It's true I was trying to draw you out as I knew you'd be intrigued by the human deaths. But I had an ulterior motive as well."

He began to pace, the panting hybrids matching him step for step like a well-trained feral army.

"What was that?" Sheridan asked. Her heartbeat amped up a notch.

"I had to be certain the breakthrough I achieved was correct. The only way to do so was test the drug on humans and vampires alike."

"What the hell does it do?" Leopold asked.

Barrett shrugged. "In humans, it turned them into jelly for the most part. The two who survived were similar in gene structure to Miss Aames, though not as strong." He nodded toward the back where the gurneys stood. "The Dust stabilized their DNA regeneration, basically freezing the telomere to a length that never eroded. But their blood is not strong enough. So far, you're the only one I've found with a slow enough turnover to be viable. If that unfortunate situation with Ernest hadn't happened, I would have given you a bit of the Dust to verify my suspicions."

Sheridan's fingers tightened on McCallister's. He squeezed back. "What about the vampires?"

Barrett's mad smile widened. "Ah, yes. The other reason for spreading the Dust. I discovered a way to isolate and manipulate specific vampiric traits such as speed, telekinesis, and the like. Unfortunately, that method required their sacrifice and not many were willing to die for me. The Dust immobilized them and put them into a stasis that allowed me time to harvest and separate the traits I was looking for."

"Christ," Leopold muttered.

"Excellent analogy, Hunter," Barrett said. "However, unlike him, I will need no resurrection. As soon as I take what I need from Miss Aames, I will be invincible."

"Tough shit," McCallister said, anger swelling again. "You're not touching her."

"Wrong," Barrett said. He snapped a command and the hybrids leapt forward. Four headed toward Leopold, Brooks, and Sullivan while the remaining two loped their way. McCallister shoved Sheridan behind him. "Get back to the hallway. Close the door," he yelled.

A sudden loud click sounded over the whine of the approaching hybrids followed by a metallic thunk.

Shit.

Barrett cut off their only means of escape.

The hybrids were only feet away. He spared a glance for his friends and found them fully engaged in a brawl of fangs and fur with the others. He lifted his gun and shot one of the approaching animals in the knee. Or where he figured the knee would be. The impact made the creature stumble. It howled and wrapped long, claw-tipped fingers around the bleeding wound.

The other snarled loudly.

"You die."

The words were guttural, heavily accented and slurred but intelligible.

Damn, what had Barrett done?

McCallister lifted the barrel of his gun again but the hybrid wavered then reappeared on his left, one clawed hand swooping down and knocking the gun away.

The hybrid elbowed him in the stomach then grabbed his throat and squeezed slowly. McCallister grappled with the furry hand, tried to peel the fingers away but the creature was too strong. Black dots swam in his peripheral and he felt his heart slowing down. He drew his energy to mist, lost it in the continuing pressure on his airway, and gritted his teeth.

Can't pass out. Protect Sheridan.

The creature slowly lifted him off his feet. McCallister grabbed at its arms and swung his body backward, gaining enough momentum to slam his feet into its chest. The impact broke the hybrid's hold and McCallister dropped lithely to his feet.

He crouched and waited for the creature to come at him again. He focused on the thing's haunches and when he caught the ripple of muscle movement, he dodged to the right, grabbed the hybrid by its pointed ears and slammed it to the ground. He leapt on top of its back, dug his hands through the thick fur and twisted viciously.

The snap of bone was loud and sickening. The creature went limp beneath him.

McCallister rose, searching for Sheridan. She'd picked up his gun and was inching around the perimeter toward Bert. His smart girl kept to the shadows and behind as many pieces of furniture as possible but she was still a visible target. He didn't dare yell at her and risk drawing Barrett's attention which seemed focused on the fight still raging between the vampires and hybrids.

Three of the creatures lay motionless on the cement floor while the remaining two fought with loud howls and slashing swings. Barrett yelled at them from beside the vat, his silver gun waving just as madly as their claws.

McCallister moved stealthily forward toward the right side of the vat. He spied Calliope and Valdór hiding in the shadows and exhaled softly. There was another way out. If he could get Sheridan to them, she'd get out safely.

He turned to look for her again just as Leopold took down the final hybrid.

"No!" Barrett's voice echoed around the room in a hideous angry wail. "You sons of bitches, I'll kill you all." His gaze swung madly from vampire to vampire as he started to scuttle backward, toward the concealment of the vat.

He stopped suddenly and a look of absolute hatred crossed his face. He narrowed his gaze toward the far end of the room and McCallister's heart froze.

Barrett raised his gun.

"No!" McCallister roared. He turned, spotted Sheridan and misted just as the shot rang out. He felt the bullet pass through his shadow form as he re-appeared in front of her.

She jerked, her luminous blue eyes went wide, and she grabbed her abdomen. Blood oozed from between her fingers. She blinked a couple of times. Her heart sped up as panic set in.

"McCallister?"

She fell to her knees and he fell with her, cradling her shoulders. "Slow breaths, Sheridan. You need to calm your heart. The faster it pumps, the faster you'll lose blood."

"McCallister, look out!" Leopold yelled.

A moment later, strong hands sank into his shoulders and yanked upward. He flew through the air and crashed down near the vat. His head and ears rang with the force of the landing.

Barrett misted in front of him and knocked him prone to the floor then straddled him with both knees pressing against his shoulders, pinning him. McCallister bucked but Barrett didn't move a centimeter.

Sheridan's heartbeat faltered, sped up, then slowed dramatically.

"I told you," Barrett said on a snarl, "I don't need her alive. I'm going to take great pleasure in killing you, McCallister. I'd dreamed of long and slow but since you've deprived me of that pleasure, I'll have to settle for quick and vicious."

His hands flattened against McCallister's chest and immense heat enveloped him. He gasped for breath as the room spun and turned over. His flesh burned and seemed to melt beneath Barrett's continuous pressure. He felt the man's fingers slip through skin and muscle and bone as he drove down to his heart.

"Yes," Barrett muttered, eyes bright with maniacal glee. "I'm going to pull your heart right from your body while you watch, McCallister. You'll feel yourself die as I have died all these years. You could have saved me," he spat. "But you didn't. Now. You. Die."

McCallister's strength ebbed as both air and life leeched from him.

Sheridan.

"Fight McCallister. Fight." Her voice filled his head. A surge of energy buffeted him. A soft pink and white glow rose in his vision and the scent of roses, lavender, and hydrangea invaded his nostrils. The brush of her fingers against his head heated his body, further strengthening him.

Barrett stiffened and his hands froze. "Impossible," he whispered.

McCallister's eyes snapped open. He wrenched free of Barrett's knees, wrapped his hands around the man's wrists and peeled them from his body.

"No!" Barrett screeched. "I'm invincible, you can't do this."

Sheridan's strength continued to flow into McCallister. Empowered by her Sine

Qua Non, he rose to his feet, still holding Barrett captive.

The man kicked and screamed. He tried to mist but McCallister mentally blocked the attempt. He didn't feel the kick aimed at his stomach nor did Barrett's sudden assault on his mind get through.

"Damn you, McCallister," Barrett howled as he twisted and writhed.

"No," McCallister said as he dropped the man. He pulled a silver-tipped wooden stake from his pocket and plunged it through Barrett's black heart. "Damn you." He held the stake until he felt the final, whimpering beat of Barrett's heart, then threw the corpse down and vaulted across the room to Sheridan's side.

Her life force was so low he could barely detect it. The other vampires had crowded around her but parted now to give him room. He cradled her to his chest.

"Sheridan, don't leave me," he pleaded.

Her blood seeped through his shirt, going clammy when it touched his skin. Each breath she drew was slower and less than the one before.

"No choice," she whispered.

Her eyes fluttered open. A tiny frown formed on her brow and her hand twitched on the floor. She opened her mouth, closed it, then opened it again but no more sound came out.

"This sucks, McCallister," her voice echoed in his head, her tone as saucy as the day he'd met her.

"I know," he whispered. "It's all my fault."

"Nah, Barrett was crazy. You got him, right?"

"Yes. Hush, Sheridan. Don't talk." He looked up at the semi-circle of his friends. "She needs help," he pleaded to them. But he didn't need their somber expressions to tell him help would arrive too late for Sheridan. He'd been a cop long enough to recognize death when it took hold of a victim.

Tears stung his eyes.

He looked down at her again. "Sheridan, God, Sheridan."

"Bert okay?"

He nodded. "Calliope and Valdór are with him."

"Good." Her heart tripped a few beats before slowing even more. She shivered in his arms. *"Cold."* She smiled up at him. *"Sorry, McCallister."*

He just shook his head. "I love you, Sheridan."

Her eyes widened and her heart picked up its pace for a long moment. "You do?" The whispered words were tremulous, tentative.

"Yes," he rasped. "We need more time. I *want* more time!"

She coughed, the rattle too damn close to a death signal. McCallister cuddled her closer. "I will love you until the end of my days, Sheridan." He brushed a kiss to her clammy forehead. "It won't be long. I promise you that."

"Don't. Get. Emo."

Leopold snorted.

"Have. Solution."

McCallister's skin tightened. "What?" he asked.

She lifted her hand and gripped his. "I love you," she said with force then coughed again. "Love you 'til the end. I'm not ready to die. McCallister...turn me."

Every particle of breath left his body as joy and horror fought for dominance. He didn't want her to die, but could he consign her to his hell? She'd end up hating him.

"I can't," he whispered in anguish.

She squeezed his hand. "I want it, McCallister. I want to live."

"It's not living," he said desperately.

"I can do it for you," Sullivan offered.

McCallister's head snapped up and he snarled, fangs bared.

Sullivan lifted his palms. "Just a suggestion. She's dying," he said bluntly. "She *will* die unless we do something."

"McCallister."

Sheridan's voice had grown weaker. Soon, she'd have lost too much blood for even them to save her with turning.

He stared down into her sweet, beloved face. Stroked her cheek and kissed her lips. The pink and white glow ebbed like fading sunlight and the scent of flowers, usually so strong, drifted away.

He was losing her. Forever.

"I love you," he whispered. "Always remember that." He lifted her higher, tipped her head to the side and fastened his mouth to the faint pulse at her neck. Fear, jubilation, and certainty all assaulted him as his fangs pierced her skin.

She groaned, her hand slipping into his hair and clinging lightly as he drank from her.

Her heartbeat slowed even further.

She went limp beneath him as it finally stopped.

McCallister continued to feed, pulling out the human life force until nothing remained. He waited one second longer then wrenched free of her skin. She was pale and pallid. No life shone from her beautiful blue eyes.

"I went too far," he whispered harshly.

Calliope dropped beside him. "Give her your blood," she ordered. "You must do it quickly."

McCallister sliced open the skin at his wrist and pressed the wound to her lips.

His tension ratcheted higher and higher and defeat weighed down his shoulders. "Come back to me, my love. I need you," he begged softly.

"My love!"

Her sweet voice echoed in his head at the same moment the room exploded in a blinding explosion of white and pink light.

"What the hell?" Leopold bellowed.

"What is that smell?" Sullivan asked.

"Flowers," Brooks replied. "More specifically, Sine Qua Non."

Sheridan's lips clamped to his wrist and her soft suckling turned fierce. McCallister winced but let her take her fill. He could not contain the joy sweeping through him. He caressed her cheek, smoothing back the limp hanks of blond hair covering her face, and drank in the beauty of his returned love.

Finally, she released him. Her eyes opened and she smiled, her pert tongue reaching out to flick at a stray drop of blood.

Tiny fangs peeked through her full lips and McCallister thought it was the most beautiful sight he'd ever seen.

"Wow," she said, eyes going wide. "I feel good. Totally jazzed. Like I'm hopped up on some kind of crazy juice."

Her heartbeat revved back up before settling in a mostly normal pace.

"You do?" McCallister asked as he helped her to her feet. "I felt like shit when I was turned. For days afterward."

"Yeah, but you were turned by that bitch Desdemona. All she wanted was sex and blood," Brooks reminded him. He beamed at the two of them. "You turned Sheridan with love. Your souls have already found each other, there is no need for them to search endlessly. Completely different."

Sheridan laughed then danced a few steps away. She hugged Calliope, Bert, and Valdór before honing in on Leopold then Sullivan. She reached for Brooks before abruptly stopping and holding out her hand. He grinned and pulled her into his arms for a tight embrace.

He met McCallister's eyes and grinned then let her go. "No threats, McCallister?"

"Nope," he said. "I know she's mine."

Sheridan returned to his side, wrapped her arms around his neck and pulled him down for a long, lusty kiss. When they finally broke for air, the entire room was infused with the pink and green swirled glow again.

"Oops," she said. "Is that going to keep happening when we kiss? 'Cause it if it is, we're going to freak a lot of people out."

McCallister hugged her tight. "God, I love you, sweetheart."

She turned in his arms. "I love you, too, McCallister." Her expression went serious and she cupped his jaw. "Thank you," she whispered. "I know how hard that was for you to do."

He kissed her lightly. "I would rather turn a hundred vampires than lose you, Sheridan."

"Ooh, that's so sweet. I think."

Calliope cleared her throat. "It is time we left this evil place. The Brigade must be informed. They will know what to do with it."

McCallister settled his arm around Sheridan's shoulders as they walked from the laboratory. "Didn't I tell you to stay put?" he asked with a grin.

She lifted a brow. "I couldn't just sit there and do nothing!"

He slapped her butt and winked. "Well, it's a sure bet you won't be sitting down any time soon. I'm going to paddle your butt when we I get you alone."

She grinned, tugged his hand, and surged forward. "Hot damn, let's go home!"

THE END

ABOUT THE AUTHOR

Jennifer August is the author of myriad historical and contemporary romances including *Knight of the Mist, Her Dark Master, Two Cowboys in Her Crosshairs* and *Bound by His Blood,* the first book in her newest series Masters of the Night.

The idea for the vampire bondage series was conceived while watching a candy commercial about things that go perfectly together. A few frantic scribbles to capture ideas and the sudden proliferation of characters demanding fang time and she had enough material for six books. Each book will follow the vampires as they search for the other half of their souls but nothing in love is easy, even for Vampire Doms, so she threw plenty of obstacles in their way.

Jennifer refuses to confirm whether or not she actually had to sleep with the light on following several late night writing sessions during some of those obstacles.